M000158810

Secrets and Stilettos

Murder in Style, Volume 1

Gina LaManna

Published by LaManna Books, 2020.

This is a work of fiction. Similarities to real people, places, or events are entirely coincidental.

SECRETS AND STILETTOS

First edition. January 10, 2020.

Copyright © 2020 Gina LaManna.

Written by Gina LaManna.

To Stacia <3 <3

Chapter 1

"**E**xcuse me, but I think my bag is lost." I winced as I raised onto the toes of my shiny new heels. It was becoming more and more difficult to pretend they didn't kill me a little bit with every step, but fashion came at a price. "Are you the person who can help me find it? I hate to be a bother, but I have important stuff that I need to get back."

"Lady, everyone's got important stuff in their bags." The woman behind the counter had bark-brown hair and eyebrows that sat just a bit too high on her forehead. "Get in line."

"Oh, *um*, sorry." I glanced to the left, to the right, and behind me, but there were no other people in sight. "Can you please tell me where the line would be?"

The woman behind the counter heaved a sigh to end all sighs.

"My name should be on the bag, if that helps. Jenna Mc-Govern. My travel tag is fluffy and pink, and you can't miss it." I hesitated, feeling the prick of frustrated tears welling up behind my eyes. "Please, everything I own is in that bag. My favorite shoes, that new Gucci purse I got at the sample sale. I even have a pair of earrings from Renata DeRicci herself!"

"Renata De-*Whatzit*?" The woman shrugged her shoulders and made the groaning sound of someone who'd just discovered they'd stepped in a puddle up to their ankle on a Monday morning. "I can't get your bag back for you."

"But they told me to come over here and ask for help," I pleaded. "I have been standing watching that carousel for an hour, and my feet are about to pop out of their ankle sockets. It's these new shoes."

The woman leaned over from behind the desk. "Those shoes are impractical for this time of year."

I recoiled. "These shoes are never impractical. If anything, they're the most practical stilettos on the market. It's why I saved up for months to buy them as my homecoming gift to myself. Anyway, my bag?"

"Practical stilettos are an oxymoron," she drawled. "Fill out this slip and we'll do our best to get you that bag."

"Do your best?" I felt my lip wobble. "Are you saying that it might never come back to me?"

"Things happen." She blinked, and her eyebrows returned to the appropriate height for her face. "Look, you seem like a nice enough girl. I'm sorry we lost your bag. Hold tight, and I'm sure they'll drop it off the second they find it."

"T-thank you," I said, accepting the pen from her outstretched hand. I bent my head over the paper and scribbled out the information. "Here, I think that's everything."

"Moving from Hollywood, hun?" The woman read the departing destination from my form, then scanned me over from head to toe. If her badge was anything to go by, the woman's name was Roseanne. "That explains a lot."

"Yes. My mom remarried her old high school sweetheart, and he was from this place called..." I cleared my throat. "Blueberry Lake?"

Roseanne cracked a real grin for the first time. "Hey! My grandpa grew up on a farm there. Don't tell me you're planning on settling down in those parts." She peered closer at me. "*Are* you?"

"Well, yes. Until further notice." I forced my chin up higher, mostly to convince myself this was a good idea. "I'm helping my mom get her thrift shop up and running."

"Well, you're in for a change, movie star. Nothing but cows and huntin' to keep you busy in the boonies."

I laughed.

When she didn't laugh, I panicked. Little beads of sweat popped onto my forehead, under my armpits, in between my toes. "You don't mean that. How close is the nearest mall? Surely they have a Target? You know, Target is not as overrated as people think when it comes to finding steals. Just cut out the tag and *voila*—red carpet ready for under twenty bucks!"

"Aren't you funny." Roseanne gave a sympathetic cluck to accompany the little shake of her head. "Welcome to Minnesota, Miss McGovern."

"*Squeeee!*"

Only one person in the world has ever said the word *squee* as it's pronounced, and that woman needs no introduction. Then again, maybe she could use a little introduction, so here we go: May French is my best friend, pen pal, and cousin—sometimes in that order. She's a curvy, half-Puerto Rican firecracker who believes in hugging and kissing her greetings without regard to whether it stalls traffic right in the middle of the Minneapolis Airport.

"You're here! You made it!" May backed away and held me by the shoulders in the way that grandmothers do—except her eyes were drawn to my new stilettos, and when she recognized them, her eyes widened. "Do *not* tell me those are Melissa Moore shoes."

"They *are*!"

"They're amazing!" She properly fangirled over the gorgeous heels as she bent nearer for a look, but when she rose, she wrinkled her nose and lost the twinkle-eyed gaze. "I'm afraid you won't like them so much once we get outside. You do know those shoes aren't gonna cut it here, right? It's winter, Jenna."

I rolled my eyes. "They cut it anywhere."

"There's ice on the ground."

"But look at them," I insisted. "Maybe the heels will just cut right through. It'll be like wearing little ice picks on my feet as I walk. Really, everyone should get a pair of stilettos for winter."

It was May's turn to suppress an eyeroll. "Grab my arm so I don't have to take you to the hospital."

"Speaking of the hospital, are we close to the Mall of America?" I asked. "I've been doing a ton of research, and I think we have time for a quickie shopping trip before we go. Look here, I drew us a map. Thank goodness I didn't have it in my checked bag, or we'd be flying blind."

"The airline lost your bags?! I'm sorry, sweetie."

"I know," I grumbled. "But I think Roseanne and I had a real heart-to-heart chat. Everything will be okay."

"Who's Roseanne?"

I thumbed over my shoulder where Roseanne and her peaked eyebrows were wildly busy ignoring me. "Never mind then," I said quickly. "Here's the route I was thinking we take. If we start at Macy's, we could walk past the food court, grab a doughnut for energy, and then swing into... Why are you frowning?"

To my grave disappointment, May didn't bother to study my carefully construed Mall of America mapwork. Instead, she rested her hand over mine and gently folded the paper back along the creases. "Honey, the mall is closed this early in the morning, and we have to get you home. Your mother's already awake and bursting with excitement to let you into your grandmother's house. She also arranged an appointment for you, so we have to hurry."

"An appointment?" I shook my head. "What do you mean an appointment?"

"Do you remember Lana Duvet?"

"Ew. The girl who pulled my pants down during summer camp assembly? Yes."

"She's getting married," May said, "and your mother promised she'd have a stylist around the store to help pick out some outfits for her groomsmen and bridesmaids."

"I'm barely in town a minute, and my schedule is booked already." I heaved a sigh. "I guess we can do the mall another time."

"That's the spirit." May gave me a slap on the rump. "Saddle up, partner—we're going to Blueberry Lake."

Chapter 2

"Oh, honey." Upon laying eyes on me for the first time in a year and a half, my mother's eyes teared up as she opened her front door and surveyed her first and only daughter with fondness. "Those shoes are ridiculous."

I glanced down at the four-inch stilettos that propped me up with a false sense of confidence as I arrived in my cozy new hometown: Blueberry Lake, Minnesota. "Good to see you too, Mom."

Bea (Beatrice, actually, but she'll throw you in the lake if you call her that) McGovern laughed, opened her arms, and gestured for me to fall into them. I did, letting my mother wrap herself around me and squeeze deeply. Despite the time that'd passed, she smelled exactly the same. Like the hint of lemon she spritzed into her mint tea and the cinnamon she sprinkled on her coffee. Like warmth and pound cake and whipped cream and home.

"It's winter, darling," she said, her lips pursing with concern. "You will break an ankle on black ice the second you step outside. You know your grandmother's old house isn't built for practicality."

Six hours ago when I'd stood in the LAX airport waiting to board, I'd felt perfectly in place. My shoes had been rocking, my purse was fluffed and fuzzy, my hair was curled and bouncy as I set off with all my belongings packed into the newest Victoria Strand luggage collection. Plus, my Louis

Vuitton handbag, which I'd obviously used as my personal item since I couldn't stand to be parted from it—lucky thing, seeing as the airport lost two of my three checked bags! (Did they not realize I had earrings from Lauren B herself in the case? Or a new MAC eyeshadow palette that had cost a fortune?)

Which is why I stood before my mother with my beloved Louis Vuitton and one measly little Victoria Strand duffle that held nothing but a collection of underpants and pajamas. It was a very good thing Victoria's Secret had been having their semi-annual sale the week before I left. At least everything in there was new and cute—especially that brilliant yellow set with the little ladybugs embroidered on them. How could I *not* buy them?

"I'd love to stick around and chat, but I am really wiped. I couldn't sleep on the plane, and then there was the issue with the bags, and the lady at the counter was really grumpy—not that I blame her, since who wants to get to work at four thirty in the morning? That's just ridiculous."

"Of course, of course. Sid, can you grab the key for Jenna?" My mother called upstairs to her new husband while simultaneously winking at me. "You are going to love Gran's old place. I'm so glad you finally decided to fix it up. Speaking of, we might as well head over to your grandmother's house now so you can drop your bags off."

My mother had married Sid exactly a year and a half ago. The two were still very much in the honeymoon phase, which was a huge part of the reason I hadn't been home in over a year. There was such a thing as living too close to your mother, especially when she was a newlywed. Full stop.

Sid is the reason we landed in Minnesota. Well, actually, it's all Gran's fault. Gran always lived in Blueberry Lake, along with my cousins and a few other McGovern family off-shoots. My mother and I had moved to California after my father passed away when I was four. I'd never asked her why she'd uprooted us and left, but I imagined the sting of being too close to his memory had a lot to do with it.

However, we'd never been able to truly stay away from the quaint town where I'd been born. Every summer, we'd packed our decidedly boring duffle bags and flew back to join Gran in her roomy, adorable Victorian house near the lake. I'd spent the time outdoors, running around with May and her troublemaking brothers. The humid July days had been filled with laughter and games, bonfires and sticky s'mores, grimy hands and scraped knees.

During those times, my problems had seemed simpler. In fact, the solution to just about anything had been to throw us in the lake. Sticky hands? Jump off the dock. Skinned knees? Stick on a Band-Aid and hop in the canoe. Tears from an argument? Go cool down with a nice back float.

After a brief drive from my mother's house, I found myself facing Gran's old house for the first time as a full-grown adult. I couldn't help but hope the lake still held that healing magic. I had plenty of problems to deal with, including a public breakup that had left me reeling (never date a movie star!), the small matter of a dwindling savings account (darn you, winter sales!), and the loneliness that came from living across the country from my closest family and dearest friends.

"Isn't it just like you remembered?" My mother anxiously glanced my way as she handed over the key. "I hope you're happy here."

I did my best to offer her a thousand-watt smile as I studied the house Gran had left in my care when she'd passed away three years back. "Yeah, pretty much."

My eagerness and excitement slipped like sand through my fingers. While the house itself was a gorgeous structure, all sweeping pillars, lopsided windows, and little turrets fit for a Midwestern castle, there was an air of abandonment that had settled over the place. Three years of sitting empty had made the house a lonely tower instead of the beaming ray of pink and purple siding that I had come to think of as summer.

"Actually, it does look, *er*, different," I said delicately, noting that the flower pots which hung from the long, luxurious porch were filled with dry leaves and snow instead of the blooms normally spilling around the edges. The vines that had so beautifully wrapped around the pillars and overflowed onto the sides of the house were a mess of brown and ugly. Even the layer of snowy white that blanketed the world couldn't hide the peeling paint or the cracks bleeding through under the early morning winter glow.

"I know it doesn't look like it did when your grandmother lived here." My mother wrung her hands. "I tried to keep it up after she died, but then Sid and I got married, and life got hectic, and... well, I'm sorry, Jenna. I hope it'll suit you."

"Of course it will," I said cheerily. "A little fixing up, and it'll be perfect by summer. I can't wait."

My mother's smile broadened. "Exactly! And remember, you've never seen the house in winter, or at least, not for a long, long time. When summer rolls around, it'll be perfect again."

I wasn't convinced she was right, but I gave a nod anyway. Digging deep, I searched for the wild sense of adventure I'd felt on the way to the LAX airport and the eagerness at the opportunity to start over.

I'd had all my worldly possessions packed into the trunk of an Uber car, and I'd felt like my twenty-nine-year-old-self had been given the world on a silver platter. *Wherever you want to go, Jenna McGovern, I'll take you there*—just say the word! That's what I imagined my Uber driver saying, when really, he asked if I needed the air conditioning turned down.

The eagerness faded some as a pit lodged into my stomach, and I wondered what I'd done—if this had all been one gigantic mistake after the next. I'd given up my studio apartment in a 'less-than-desirable' neighborhood of Los Angeles to move to a town where Uber didn't yet exist and there was one coffee shop on main street—and it wasn't a Starbucks.

To top things off, my shoes were impractical here. Impractical! Tears welled in my eyes at the thought. I'd built my life around styling fashion, and here I was, plopped into Blueberry Lake like a well-dressed fish out of water. Which was just silly because fish didn't wear clothes. A fact I'd discovered in second grade while trying to put Fred, the class goldfish, into a raincoat. Needless to say, I had been banned from taking class pets home after that.

My mother watched the change in emotions with concern, so I gave one huge sniff that ended my little pity party and decided to make the best of it. I had a gorgeous home that needed lots of repair (a good thing since it would distract me from the lack of movie premiers!), a caring family, and the opportunity to start over. Blueberry Lake was about to get a makeover.

"I'LL LEAVE YOU TO GET settled then." My mother stood at the front door of Gran's house. "I'll see you in an hour at the shop."

"An hour?" I gave my mother a bleary-eyed stare. "It's barely seven in the morning, and I haven't slept in approximately thirty-nine hours. Do you mind if I take a quick nap?"

"Actually," she said, shifting uneasily. "Maybe you could nap later?"

"What did you do, mother?"

She sighed. "I made you an appointment with Grant Mark."

"Does it have to be so early?"

"He's the best man in the Duvet wedding," she said, the words spilling out in a deluge of hope. "Please help, honey—we need his business. I just got in a slew of new suits and tuxedos, and it would be so great for the store if we could say we outfitted the best man. The Duvet wedding! It's the biggest winter wedding Blueberry Lake has ever seen. I heard Lana's father is spending almost six figures on it!"

"No offense, mom, but why would he be shopping at a thrift store for his wedding attire?"

"The bride and groom requested it. They're doing an old rustic themed wedding, and they want to use only local businesses for the event. Also, Lana had a bit of a falling out with Amy Flowers, and Amy's got the only tux rental shop in town. We're her only hope to keep everything local if she wants to boycott Amy's store."

"So, we're the last choice?"

"I'm afraid so," she said with a wince. "But these new suits will be perfect. He'll look marvelous."

My eyes widened. It *would* be a lot of money for my mother. And maybe I would get a small commission on it. The things I could buy! I could fill a closet with new shoes. I could open a makeup salon with all the foundations and eyeshadow palettes and lipsticks I could purchase. I could retire and buy a golf cart and live as a stylish old lady on Blueberry Lake for the rest of my days. Okay, maybe not the latter, but a girl could dream.

"Let me guess. You told him I'd help style his outfit?"

"Sort of." At my glare, my mother sighed. "I told him I was flying in a stylist from Hollywood who could guide him on the latest fashions. I told him he'd be so hip."

I smacked a hand to my forehead. "Please tell me you didn't use the word *hip*."

"Is that out of style now? See, Jenna—you're proving my point. I need your help. I'm an awkward old woman, and you're my gorgeous, successful daughter."

"You're just sucking up to me now, mother," I said. "And by the way, I flew myself in, thank you very much!"

"I..." My mother hesitated. "I sent your cousin to pick you up from the airport."

"I'll be there," I promised her. "Have all the suits and tuxedos pulled into a section when I get in, and it will make everything go faster. Oh! Let's also have a few suave outfits sitting in the dressing room as well—stylish jeans, formal but comfortable shirts, that sort of thing. He'll have a rehearsal dinner, some lounge times with the groomsmen, a bachelor party. We can help him with all of that."

My mother wobbled a little as she leaned against the door. "You're brilliant. Thank you, honey. By the way, don't forget—dinner is at seven tonight. Sid and May will be there, too."

I gave her a wave as she left and headed to her thrift shop, aptly titled Something Old. Ever since I'd been a child, my mother had collected things. She'd started with books, then moved on to interesting and oddly shaped planters, then graduated to furniture and records and a slew of anything that was older than her and smelled like dust.

After her move to Blueberry Lake, she'd decided to turn her passion into a business and had founded the town's first true thrift shop. She'd expanded into clothing and lamps and bookcases and all sorts of brilliant things that had once been in style and then been lost. The only unfortunate part of the equation was the lack of profit. She'd been burning through cash getting a foothold in the business, and the revenue just wasn't coming in fast enough to fill the hole.

Part of the reason I'd moved home was to see if I could help. I was under no illusions that I had a magical touch, but I'd already chased my dreams in Hollywood, and they'd sort of fizzled out and ended with a whizz-bang after a public dumping from my ex-boyfriend. After years of putting my needs first, it was time to help my mother see her dreams to fruition.

I spent the next hour puttering around and sweeping off the furniture my Gran had left behind. It was easy to see where Bea had halfheartedly tried to run a duster over the couch and swipe a paper towel on the kitchen counter, but as one obsessed by chaos and disorder and collections of old things, keeping a clean house was not high on my mother's priority list.

As the sun rose, it burned stronger through the windows despite the ridiculous temperatures. When the sunlight sparkled, I caught glimpses of the place that had been my summer haven. The place where worries had ceased to exist, and friendship and food and family had come together in a dream for several short, fleeting weeks.

There was no food around, but the electricity had been turned on and the heater left running to get the house warm for my arrival. Thank goodness for that, since the weather outside was in the single digits. One-degree Fahrenheit, to be specific. *Why does one-digit weather even exist in this universe?*

Due to the absence of food, I'd have to stop at the coffee shop and check out the array of muffins on the way to my appointment. My stomach was *growling*, and that was not the soundtrack to a professional styling appointment.

After tidying the kitchen, I moved to the living area where a bay window sat like a portrait along one side. A stiff window seat with squashy cushions filled the nook and made me smile. May and I had spent our evenings here eating popcorn and fresh blueberries—the town was named appropriately, after all—as we watched the sun set.

A darker swatch of woods sat behind the house, and it was amid these trees that the local neighborhood children had spent hours playing tag or hide and seek, called home only by the dinner bell that rang universally at dusk. It was under the tightly knit canopy of branches that I'd first broken my arm, and it was high above the ground where May had hidden on an attempt to run away from home for all of five minutes. (She'd only packed Twizzlers. She would never have lasted long.)

It was the place where, once upon a time, we'd believed fairies flitted above us and pixies peeped between sun-dusted leaves. I briefly wondered if the magic of the outdoors would persist now that I was nearly thirty years old and properly filled with cynicism. I hoped so—I'd never minded a good fairytale.

A quick glance at the clock told me time was ticking, and if I wanted that muffin, I'd better get moving. I decided to bring Louie (my purse) along for the ride, and because my shoes murdered me just a little bit with every step, I gently kicked them off and settled on the cutest pair of furry boots I'd gotten at a sample sale. Nineteen dollars, but they looked like a million bucks. I was my mother's daughter.

Blueberry Jam was the town café belonging to June Bixby—a woman who had looked exactly eighty-nine years old since forever and had been my grandmother's dearest friend. Even as a child, I remembered June looking as ancient as my mother's collections. As I stepped through the doors, I realized that some things never changed—including June.

"Well, well, if it isn't Greta Green reincarnated." June beamed a huge smile as I stepped, still shivering, into the warmth of the sweet-smelling café. "Jenna McGovern, how are you?"

My mother's maiden name and Gran's married name had been Green, a fitting name for a woman who'd spent her spare time as a botany hobbyist. Gran had run a small garden shop simply called Green's after her husband died decades ago. It was that business which had provided her with an income to live on and raise her children, even though the shop had been no more than a glorified shed and greenhouse combination in her backyard.

The structures were still there. I'd seen them on my walkthrough of the yard, though they'd fallen into a state of disrepair. I made a mental note to have someone come out to the house and see if they couldn't help me revive the glorious gardens at last frost. I'd love to coax back those knotted raspberry bushes, the thorny blackberries, and the tart little apple tree with a perfect reading nook between its branches.

I sighed. "When does summer arrive around these parts?"

June grinned. "Your vitamin D can't be depleted yet! You just touched down."

I smiled back and scanned the menu. "Speaking of, I'm starving. Do you have any of those muffins I love?"

"Blueberry glaze," she said confidently. "Fresh from the oven. Can I add a little butter for you?"

I was surprisingly touched by the gesture and her offer to add fat to my muffin. In Hollywood, if I'd ordered the same, I'd have been given a low-fat, crusty collection of Branflavored cardboard in a pre-wrapped package. There'd be no *fresh from the oven* warmth, nor would there be the personalized touch, the remembrance of an order from years past.

"I'd love that," I said, and pretended my lip didn't tremble. I really needed some sleep. My eyes were probably red, and my emotions were just bursting to come out through every tear duct this body owned. "Thanks, June. How have you been?"

She gave a shrug as she buttered it, and I noticed her hair had turned just a bit whiter. "It was hard to say goodbye to your grandma. We'd been friends since we were just girls. Watching you and May run around together all those years ago—it was just like seeing your grandmother and me all over again."

I forced a smile while simultaneously talking my own tears down from a ledge. As the newbie in town, I didn't want someone's first impression of me to be a snotty, sobbing mess in the local café. That would be perfect fodder for the local gossip mill, and my reputation might never recover if word got out. Small town talk could be brutal.

"Enough about me," June said. "What can I get you to drink?"

"Venti nonfat vanilla latte with two pumps of sugar free syrup—" I stopped at the look of horror on June's face and closed my mouth quickly. Squinting at the menu behind the counter, I saw a simple listing for coffee and orange juice. "Actually, I'll take a cup of coffee to go."

"I knew you'd inherit a prissy order being out there," June said, reaching for the Styrofoam cup and filling it with piping hot black coffee. "I'll make a deal with you, Jenna

McGovern. You try drinking this steaming hot black coffee every day for a week. In the meantime, I'll learn to make those fancy lattes you like."

"Oh, you don't have to do that, June."

"No, no, change is good," she said with a smile. "Plus, I reckon you won't find anything better than a cup of hot, slightly burned black coffee to warm you up in these winter months."

I raised the coffee and muffin in a salute as the door tinkled open and a slew of other customers strolled inside. "You're on, June—consider it a deal. See you tomorrow!"

Though I hated to admit it, June was right. As I plowed through six inches of yet-to-be-shoveled snow in my fluffy boots, which were rapidly de-fluffing, I watched the swirl of steam rise through the lid of the mug and freeze upon impact with the air. When the ridiculous temperatures outside had cooled the coffee to a safely consumable level, I took a sip, and sure enough, it warmed me straight to the core. I pictured the beverage sliding through my veins like mercury, and by the time I leaned against the entrance to my mother's shop, I had pink cheeks, soggy boots, and a grin on my face.

"What makes you so happy?" my mother said. "You look like a drowned rat. And those boots, darling, are not practical. Why don't you pick a pair of shoes off the rack and get changed? You'll catch a cold if you have wet feet all day! Hurry, though. Grant is already in the back perusing the men's section. Oh—" she paused for a noisy kiss to my cheek—"and thank you, honey, for all your help."

I happily complied with my mother's suggestions. I wandered first over to the cash register where a young woman sat.

"Hi, I'm Allie Martin." A woman who appeared to be in her mid-twenties, stuck her hand out, accompanying the gesture with a bright and shiny grin that had me unable to resist smiling back. "You must be Jenna. Your mom has been talking about you coming home for months! I could've picked you out of a lineup."

"Well, that just makes me blush." I shook her hand, watching her eyes widen at the sight of my purse. "Do you mind if I leave this behind the counter?"

"Is that a real Louis Vuitton?" Allie flicked a mane of shiny brown hair over her shoulder. "Not a knock-off purchased out of some weirdo's trunk?"

"It's real," I admitted, thrilled to be with a kindred Louie-lover soul. "Go on, you can touch it."

"Oh, my stars." Allie took the purse, cradled it to her chest. She flashed that contagious smile again. "This is gorgeous."

"It was actually a gift," I said, wrinkling my nose as I recalled the giver of it. "From my ex-boyfriend. I probably should've dumped it when he ousted me, but I couldn't give him up. The purse, I mean."

"You shouldn't have to," Allie said. "It's like...I dunno, keeping the dog or something. You wouldn't give away your gorgeous pup just because your boyfriend was a jerk, would you?"

"I'm glad we see eye to eye." I positively *trilled* with excitement at Allie's enthusiasm. Maybe I wouldn't be so out of place in Blueberry Lake. "Well, I guess I have a client, so I'll see you around. Thanks for watching over my purse for me."

"Say, I have a quick question for you."

"Sure, what is it?"

Allie's grin grew brighter. All soft curves and big, fluffy hair, Allie looked like the quintessential girl next door... with an allergy to fashion. Massive hoop earrings kicked off an ensemble that ended with scuffed combat boots on her feet, and the outfit in between looked like it'd been picked off the racks of my mother's shop in no particular order. Her highlighter-yellow turtleneck was offset by a pair of velour pants in an odd shade of purple. Both were just a smidgeon too tight.

"It's a little embarrassing," Allie said, running her hands nervously over her purple pants. "You style people, right?"

"Yes! And I would be very happy to style an outfit for you."

"Not me!" Allie recoiled and gestured to her rainbow clothes. "Look at this! I've got more style than most women can handle. But my mom's birthday is coming up, and she's always complaining about how she's got nothing to wear. Do you think I could hire you to do a quick styling session for her?"

"Consider it on the house," I said. "Mark it down in the planner."

"What planner?" Allie looked around at the counter, but there was nothing on it except knickknacks. "We schedule sort of loosey-goosey around here."

I reached over the counter, unzipped Louie, and pulled a cute little floral notebook from it. Flipping it open, I slid it across the counter. "Here's our new planner. You pick the date and time because I'm as free as a bird. Meanwhile, I'd better get over to Grant."

While Allie set to getting the planner ready, I swung by the women's shoe section, thinking I really needed to get this store outfitted with a computer. I'd caught sight of a large-print calculator on the counter and a stack of blank receipts. My mother still provided handwritten receipts and used a calculator. The year was 2019 for crying out loud. *Only in Blueberry Lake.*

In the women's shoe section, I found a gorgeous pair of powder blue vintage heels in a size eight and slipped them on. They were the perfect accent to my slim black pants and loose flowing top—also black. Black matched everything, but without a pop of color to spruce things up, it could get a bit drab. Then again, I hadn't much of a choice in what to wear since nearly all my clothes were lost in some airport jail in Aruba (or, more likely, LAX).

Newly outfitted, I sashayed to the back of the store, greeting customers as I went. To my surprise, the place had filled up nicely despite the early morning hour. Apparently, people were either stir crazy because of the snow, or everyone had plans this weekend and needed a new outfit. Either way, it was a promising sign for my mother.

I found a lost looking man somewhere between women's brassieres and men's boxers. "Hello," I said with a kind smile. "Are you Mr. Mark?"

"Er, no," he said, and then scurried away leaving me to melt into a puddle of embarrassment.

"Hi there, you must be Jenna." A deep voice sounded from behind me, accompanied by the opening of a fitting room door. "Call me Grant."

I could feel my cheeks coloring as I turned to face the correct client standing in the doorway. "Hi, sorry! He just looked lost, so I thought—my, you've gotten a great start already!"

"You think?" Grant had blond hair, a clean-shaven face, and a crooked sort of smile that led me to believe one flash of it could get him whatever he wanted. "I just threw on whatever your mother had set out back here."

"You look really great," I said, surveying the suit on him. "Are you thinking of wearing this for the wedding or the rehearsal dinner?"

"Neither. This one would be for work," he said in that smooth voice of his. "I'm a lawyer."

"Ah, well, I'm sure this will look great in the courtroom," I said. "Er—what sort of lawyer are you?"

"You're cute, you know." He laughed, ignoring the question. "Say, can you give me a hand?"

"Um, sure. Do you need something in a different size? I can poke around, but usually the things we have are one-of-a-kind."

"That's why I'm here." He took a step closer, his eyes scanning me over thoroughly from head to toe in a way that made me squirm in my new heels. "I'm not a fan of cookie cutter *anything*, really. You know what I mean."

"Sure."

"Your mother said you were a pretty thing, but I really didn't expect you to be this beautiful." Grant leaned back again, giving me welcome space to breathe. "Say, are you single? We should grab dinner sometime."

"Sorry, Mr. Mark. Though I'm flattered, I am coming off a bad breakup. I'm not looking to date right now."

"Come on," he said, reaching for my wrist. "Just one drink."

"No, Mr. Mark," I said coldly. "Please let go of me. As I said, I am flattered, but uninterested."

"Uninterested in *me*?" One perfectly manicured eyebrow raised in surprise. "But surely I can convince you to let loose. Come on, sweet cheeks. Why don't you come on in here and help me with the suit?"

"Let go of my arm," I said. "It's the last time I'll ask nicely."

Instead of listening, Grant walked his fingers up from my wrist to my elbow and then squeezed my shoulder, letting his hand linger there. "Don't be so uptight. I just thought we could have a little fun together while I'm here for the wedding—"

In one motion, I ducked. Slipping out from under Grant's arm, I hopped out of my shoes for better leverage. Without thinking, I nabbed the powder blue stiletto from the ground and brandished it like a sword. "I think it's time for you to leave, Mr. Grant."

He raised his hands. "Whoa, whoa—I was just being friendly to the newcomer."

My mother appeared at my shoulder, concern furrowing her frown. "What happened here? Jenna, why are you holding our customer hostage with a shoe?"

"Your daughter is a psycho," Grant said, picking up his clothes from the floor. He opened his wallet and pulled out a hundred-dollar bill. "I'll take the suit. Keep the girl—she's a moron."

As Grant left, I froze in my karate position. I felt the edges of stupidity creeping in at the realization that I'd scared off my first customer. By the time my mother wrenched the stiletto out of my hand, it was clear I was shaking.

"Honey, are you all right?!" She shook her head. "I would have never let Grant in here if I knew he'd say such a thing! What happened?"

"He tried to hit on me after I said no. Repeatedly." I took a deep breath and explained the situation more thoroughly. When I finished, my mother's frown lines grew deeper. "Forget it, mom," I said in conclusion. "He's a jerk. I should be used to guys like him after Hollywood. Don't let it ruin your business with the rest of the Duvet wedding."

"I think we should report it," my mother suggested. "Let Chief Dear know. Grant will be in town for a while due to wedding festivities, and I'd hate to think of him cornering another young woman like that. What if you had been alone and somewhere more private?"

Still trembling, I shook my head. "Don't report it, mom. I'm fine. He's gone."

"But, Jenna—"

"I just arrived in town this morning. I don't want to be thought of as the one who stirs up trouble wherever she goes," I said. "Just let it go. If he comes back, we'll call the cops."

She didn't look convinced, but Allie called her over at that moment to help with the register. Or more likely, the calculator, since the register was an antique piece of junk that probably hadn't functioned properly since 1962.

"Hey, mom," I said, grabbing my purse from behind the counter. "If you don't mind, I'm going to head home and take a nap. I'm exhausted. I'll see you later for dinner."

She gave a distracted nod while trying to ring up a pair of fluffy burlesque style handcuffs being purchased by a woman old enough to have no business using them. I recognized the customer as one of Gran and June's friends, and I waved a hello.

"I heard what happened back there with that slimy young man," Anne Trudeau said, waving the fuzzy pink handcuffs in my face while my mother sweated over the calculator. "If that man comes back here, I'll use these on him. Got it?"

"Thanks, Mrs. Trudeau," I said with a wink. "If I need backup, I know who to call."

Chapter 3

I woke from my nap feeling refreshed and energized. Whoever said sleep was important was probably right. Though I tended to ignore most of the advice given by professionals that wasn't convenient to my lifestyle, I wondered if I shouldn't pay more attention to that whole get-eight-hours-a-night rule.

When I'd arrived home from Something Old, I'd taken a warm shower to get rid of the clamminess in my toes that'd started after my stomp back in horribly impractical boots. I really did need better winter clothes, or I'd be one miserable (but fashionable) woman for the next three months.

Sitting up in bed, I glanced around the room where I'd slept with May for most of my childhood summers. It was a small space, snug and comfortable. Because of the high, sweeping windows that let in buckets of afternoon light, this was notably the warmest room in the house. Thanks to the freshly washed comforter and soft-as-silk sheets, I'd lingered in a dreamless sleep for hours.

A knock sounded on the door. Whoever was tapping was incessant, as if they'd been at it awhile.

Yawning, I slipped into the big, fluffy purple robe that had been in my pajama duffle. I peeped out the circular window from one of the turrets but couldn't see squat, so I hurried down the spiral staircase and padded over to the front door.

Since this was Blueberry Lake, I figured it might be a neighbor dropping by with cookies, or even my mother swinging over to check on me. But my mother would have walked right in, and a neighbor would have called hello, so I peeped through the curtains and found a man standing there. Over his shoulder, I glimpsed a police car parked a respectful distance down my drive.

I opened the door, keeping my cell phone close. "Hello, may I help you?"

"Are you Miss Jenna McGovern?"

"That would be me!" I grinned. When I received no smile or response of any sort in return, I hesitated, then repeated my question. "Can I help you with something?"

"I'm Cooper Dear, chief of police for Blueberry Lake." He didn't extend his hand for a shake, which I took as another bad sign. "I have a few questions to ask you."

"Um, sure. Come on in," I said. "Can I get you a coffee?"

"No, thank you," he said, which I took to be a third bad sign. "Unfortunately, I'm not here to welcome you to the neighborhood."

"Oh." I gave a nod of understanding. "My mother called you, didn't she? I told her not to tell anyone."

"Why would your mother call me?"

"Because of Grant!" I insisted. "She wanted me to confess the situation to you, but I didn't think it was smart. Small town and all that. People talk."

"I'm very confused, Miss McGovern." He ran a hand over his forehead. "You know Grant Mark, and you're ready to confess?"

"You mean the guy I had to fend off with a stiletto," I said, waving my hand. "Yes, of course. It was a shame for the shoe, I have to admit. It didn't deserve to be used as a weapon."

"You are admitting to threatening Grant Mark?" The police chief looked mystified. Then he grumbled something about his job being too easy.

"I wouldn't say *threatened*," I corrected, trying to infuse a bit of jolly into an awkward situation. "I was very uncomfortable, and I just wanted some space."

"So, you killed him?"

"Well, I—" I stopped talking mid-cinch of my robe and looked up at the chief. "Excuse me?"

"Where were you, Miss McGovern, between the hours of noon and two p.m. this afternoon?"

I glanced at my watch and realized it was three p.m. I'd laid down around eleven thirty after my shower and a blueberry treat from June's. "I was here. Sleeping."

"Alone?"

"Not that my sleeping situation is any of your business," I retorted, "but yes, I was alone."

"Nobody can verify your alibi?"

"Ali-*what*? Back up to the part about you thinking I killed someone. What are we talking about here? I thought this was about my shoes at the thrift shop."

"It is," Chief Dear said, and even though he was dancing around a dark subject, I couldn't help but notice the handsome five o'clock shadow on his face and the attractive touch of his rare smile. "Grant Mark was found dead at one fifty this afternoon."

"Dead?!" I backed away. "What are you talking about? I just saw him this morning. Met him for the first time, actually."

"And yet you admit to threatening him with the murder weapon."

"Whoa, *whoa*. Sticking a shoe in the face of an aggressive man and asking him to step back does not make the shoe a murder weapon."

"It does when the shoe is found lodged in his throat," Chief Dear said, and waited for the news to sink in. "Miss McGovern, welcome to Blueberry Lake. I suggest you find a lawyer."

I inched backward, my mind drawing a blank until the back of my knees hit a pink chaise lounge, and I fell onto it with a dramatic flair. I wasn't trying for drama, but it was impossible not to feel a little weak when being blamed for the murder of a man I barely knew.

"You're going to have to slow down," I said. "I was here sleeping all afternoon."

"Miss McGovern—" The chief stopped talking at a light tap coming from behind him.

Neither of us had bothered to close the front door tightly after the chief had stepped inside, and a hand reached around the frame as a second man poked his head inside. It was a testament to how distracted I'd been that I hadn't noticed the frosty chill working its way through the drafty house.

"Excuse me," the newcomer said, inching into the hallway while the chief and I stared dumbly at him. "I'm Matt Bridges, your new neighbor. I—ah, sorry to interrupt, but

I just got home from the station and saw the door open. Thought I'd check things out. Bea—er, Mrs. McGovern, asked me to keep an eye on the place after Gran passed."

"I'm Jenna," I said, forcing myself to my feet. "Sorry for my lack of hospitality. You caught me at a bad time. The chief was just stopping by."

"Is there a problem?" Matt flicked a glance toward Chief Dear, and if I wasn't mistaken, a look of challenge passed between them.

"Nothing to do with you, Bridges," Chief Dear said stiffly. Then, as if realizing he was being rude in front of me, he gave a nod. "Good to see you, Matt."

Matt gave a broad grin, and I was struck by the overall handsomeness of his features. In a room where I'd been just about arrested for murder, it was utter delight to find someone smiling brightly at me.

"Don't mind Cooper here," Matt said with a chuckle. "He's still sore about the guns versus hoses hockey game he lost last night out on the lake."

"Guns versus hoses?" My mind clicked quickly through until the meaning dawned on me. "Oh! A police versus firefighter game?"

Matt nodded. "It's supposed to be lighthearted, but some of us—" he gave an exaggerated cough and finger point toward Chief Dear—"take these things a bit seriously. I won't name names."

"I'm actually here on business," Cooper said to Matt. "Do you mind if I have a second alone with Miss McGovern?"

"Not a problem. If that's all right with the lady." Matt's eyes flicked toward me with genuine concern. "You gonna be okay here, Jenna?"

"Great."

"Well, I've got a dozen muffins to bring over later this afternoon. My grandmother—maybe you know June?—would kill me if I didn't welcome a neighbor properly to Blueberry Lake." He gave a friendly wave, then glanced back at the chief and spoke with a hint of challenge. "I'll be back in half an hour to check on things. Holler if you need anything."

"You have June's muffins?" My stomach growled. "I had one this morning. It was excellent. Actually, she was very close with Gran."

"I know," Matt said with a pleasant crinkle of laugh lines around his eyebrows. "I loved your Gran too. I was sorry when she passed."

"Me too."

"Oh, and you should know—the muffins aren't from June's bakery," Matt said with a hint of sheepishness. "Though it was June who taught me how to bake. She never cared that I had testosterone—she always said a man needed to spoil a woman with his cooking. Ain't that right, Chief?"

Matt thumped Chief Dear on the back, and the latter looked annoyed. The situation hovered on the brink of discomfort.

"Well, that sounds wonderful," I said to break the silence. "Thank you for the friendly welcome."

"Anytime." Matt stepped out the door, then called back over his shoulder. "Looks like I'm not the only one. You've got more company."

Chief Dear gave a deep, guttural sigh, then fixed me with a stare. "Do you mind if we talk in private? It's important, Miss McGovern."

"Call me Jenna," I said. "And sure, just as soon as I see who's at my door."

"Coop! What are you doing here?" May's chirpy voice asked as she barreled inside without waiting for an invitation. "Come to welcome my cousin to the neighborhood?"

"Actually—" he said, but he couldn't finish his sentence because May gave him a firm pat to the back and moved right past him.

"They still didn't find your bags, huh?" May asked, scanning me from head to toe. "That's an adorable robe, though. Where'd you get it? Maybe I should put it on my registry..."

"Registry?" I blinked, sifting through occasions I should be remembering. "You got married nine years ago, and you bought a new house last year, so..."

"Baby!" She threw her hands up. "Me and Joe are having a baby! I was *dying* to tell you on the car ride from the airport, but we were in such a rush to get you to your appointment, I had to wait until now!"

I gasped in excitement as my eyes flicked to her stomach. "When are you due? How far along are you? Can you just imagine all the cute clothes I can buy? I hope it's a girl. A little princess. Congratulations, May. I am so thrilled for you and Joe!"

"We're due in September. Things are still really early, so don't say anything." She grinned, raised a finger to her lips in the shushing signal. "You either, Coop—got it? No gossiping at that police station of yours."

"Er, ladies—"

"Can we have my baby shower here?" May spread her hands wide. "I'll help you whip this place into shape. We can start on the interior, and then when spring comes we'll bring the gardens back to their former glory. Gran will be so proud, and then we'll get Matt over here to help with the painting. He's real handy."

My head spun from the onslaught of news. As I processed, I caught the deadly look in the chief's eyes, and muted my overexcited response. "Actually, May—I think we might have a problem."

"What do you mean?" Her eyebrows furrowed. "Oh, shoot. I shouldn't have invited my baby shower here. That was so unthoughtful of me, especially as you're just getting settled. What if we—"

"No, May—the chief isn't here to welcome me to the neighborhood."

"Sure he is." May spun to face Cooper, her expression livid. "Aren't you?"

"Actually, I'm afraid she's right." Chief Dear's face turned a bit red under the pressure of two ladies staring him down—one of them a Puerto Rican pregnant lady with a legendary temper, and the other an emotional transplant with a penchant for deadly shoes. "We have reason to suspect Miss McGovern was involved with the death of Grant Mark."

May let out a spluttering breath that ended in a near hysterical laugh. "You're joking, right? Jenna would never kill anyone. Tell him, Jenna."

"I did," I said, wincing. "It wasn't enough."

"Come on, Coop. You can't be serious."

"I am deadly serious," he said, taking a step deeper into the room and regaining control over the situation. "What we have is a dead body and Jenna's fingerprints on the murder weapon. How much clearer would you like me to get?"

"YOUR FAVORITE." MY mother arrived at the table with relish, pulling the lid off a piping hot plate of fresh blueberry pancakes and brandishing it under our noses. "Breakfast for dinner. Welcome home, honey."

I swallowed and tried to force a smile. "Thanks, mom. I'm sorry, I'm just not really hungry. You didn't have to do all this."

"Honey, nobody thinks you killed that man!" My mother put a hand on her hip, surveying the rest of the table with a viciousness that demanded agreement. "Right?"

Sid nodded his head, his shaggy gray hair flopping over his forehead and reminding me of a Shih Tzu in need of a trim. He had that puppy dog sort of face, aged with wrinkles, that looked neither handsome nor worn. Just sort of floppy. His clothing choices were the same, and if I wasn't so upset about the accusations of murder against me, I'd quietly slip my mom a few suggestions for clothing that would better suit Sid's floppy figure.

May nodded vigorously. "Of course not! And I gave Chief Dear a talking to, don't you worry. I can't believe that's how he'd welcome Jenna to town!"

"Bless his heart; he's just trying to do his job," Bea agreed, "but he is wrong, wrong, *wrong*. Accusing my poor girl of murder—shame on Cooper."

"Thanks, you guys," I said, heaving a smile in their direction. "I guess I could stomach one pancake. Or maybe two. Can you pass the butter? And how about the syrup?"

On second thought, I reached for three pancakes. After all, if I was heading to jail in the most hideous jumpsuit ever created for man, I might as well do it on a full stomach. It wasn't like my mother would be able to deliver piping hot pancakes to my cell—and even if she did, I'd probably have to share with Donny-the-Art-Thief from one cell down.

Possibly my imagination had gotten to running wild after the scare this afternoon. Unfortunately, thanks to the neighbor on the other side of my house—Angela Dewey—the news had spread like wildfire through the community. Angela was queen bee of the gossip community and the proud owner of the worst hairdo ever created, but that was probably neither here nor there.

It did matter, however, that she hadn't bothered to introduce herself before getting out her walker and inching her way down to June's Blueberry Jam Café to whisper about my visit from the police chief. From there, disaster had struck.

All afternoon cars had driven by my new house at a slow crawl, stopping to stare for all the wrong reasons. I'd drawn the curtains, curled up in bed, and put Beyoncé on repeat, but even that hadn't shaken me from my mood. I'd tried to do some online shoe-shopping therapy, but my cellphone had spotty service in the bedroom and my internet wasn't yet hooked up. It was like living in Antarctica.

I'd huddled under the covers until my mother came over and dragged me out of bed and over to her place. She'd caught me by surprise, and since my luggage still hadn't been found, I'd been forced to wear flannel pants and high heels to her house thanks to my furry boots being soaked through and utterly de-fluffed. Which actually made dinner somewhat of a theme party, seeing as we were having my mother's specialty pancakes, and I was in pajamas.

"This would be a whole lot more enjoyable if it didn't feel like The Last Supper," I moaned, taking an absolutely mouth-watering bite and letting the tastes of syrup and butter melt and mix in my mouth. "I didn't kill him! I didn't even know the man. It was sheer bad luck that I happened to raise a shoe at him this morning."

"I know, dear," my mother said. "What if we talk about something else at the dinner table? Sid, how was work?"

Sid shrugged. "Fine."

Sid wasn't a man of many words. Normally, that was fine by me, but today, it just felt like a wet blanket draped over the conversation. He also had the most boring job of all time. Something to do with numbers—and we're not talking shoe sizes.

"Well, I have something to talk about." May preened, positively glowing with happy pregnancy. "And it's good news."

"Thank the heavens." My mother turned to her. "Have you picked out names yet?"

"Oh, this isn't about the baby. This is about the way Gran's old neighbor was looking at Jenna." She wiggled her eyebrow. "I think Matt is interested in your daughter, Auntie Bea."

"What makes you say that?" I gave a shake of my head and stabbed another pancake. "If anything, I probably scared him off. What sort of a first impression is it to meet your neighbor and find out they've been accused of murder?"

"I can take care of that itsy-bitsy problem." May waved goodbye to it, as if it were that simple to make problems disappear. "I'll have Joe explain everything to Matt."

"Oh, no—*no*!" I saw where she was going with this. "You are not meddling in my life now that your life is all situated and gorgeous, okay? Leave me out of this."

"Come on! I'm an old married lady. I need to have some fun."

"You are not old and married," I said to her. "You and Joe are more in love than anyone I've ever seen. It's ridiculous. And on occasion, gross," I said, thinking that I preferred not to sleep in a hotel room that shared a wall with my cousin. It'd happened at my mother's wedding, and I'd evacuated the premises to sleep on another friend's couch.

May wasn't the slightest bit fazed, and neither was my mother. Both of them were in loving, healthy, gloriously romantic relationships. Which meant they needed to fix me, the broken one.

"I am not broken," I said quickly, before they could get the idea that there was, in fact, something wrong with me. "I just got out of a serious relationship."

"You were never going to marry that loser," May said. "Forget about him, Jenna."

"He's not a loser," I said. "He's on every movie poster across the country."

"He's a loser," May said, "if he dumped you."

"Well, our schedules—"

"I call bull," May interrupted. "He dropped you the second he caught his big break and started going out with that floozie from his new movie. That's a douche-canoe move!"

I couldn't argue with her since the embarrassment was still fresh. I *thought* it had been love. The true, gushy romantic kind. We'd dated a year, after all, and lived together. I'd bought him headshots. He came as my date to red carpet premiers on *my* invitations. Hell, I'd introduced him to the connection that got him his breakout movie role.

"Okay, so he pulled some loser moves," I admitted. "But it's in the past. I'm over it."

"Great—then you won't mind if Joe sets you up on a date with Matt." May said it like a statement, not leaving room to argue. "How does Saturday sound?"

"Um, horrible? How will that look if I'm accused of murder and then seen dating my neighbor? Give this time to settle down first," I said. "One thing at a time. My skin looks all washed out in orange, so that's my first concern."

My mother gave me a sad sort of smile. "You're using this as an excuse, Jenna. You're pushing opportunities away."

Exasperated, I reached for a fourth pancake. Arguing burned lots of calories. Also, it's not like my shoe size changed if I put on a few pounds, though that little red dress in my bag might be tighter than I'd like. Which would probably never be a problem seeing as my bag might not find its way to Blueberry Lake—a scenario that was looking more and more real by the hour. To compromise, I put on half the amount of butter and syrup and called it even.

"Guess who else is single?" My mother spoke to May, as if I wouldn't catch the fact they were talking about me over the table. "Chief Dear."

"Wasn't he dating that girl from Butternut Bay?"

I rolled my eyes. "Do you guys live in a Dr. Seuss book?"

My mother ignored me. "He was going steady with her, but they broke up—it's very hush-hush. Even Angela Dewey hasn't gotten the gossip, and she's Chief Dear's great aunt once removed."

"Oh, golly gee, they must be close," I said dryly, "with a family tree like that."

"I'm just saying, he's a very nice young man," my mother said. "And very cute. The two of you were just darling when you'd play together over the summer."

"I knew him?" I frowned. I hadn't remembered that little tidbit, which was odd. I would have thought I'd remember him. (And *not* because he was cute, but because he was a giant pain in the blueberries!)

"Oh, sure, you guys played together when you were babies. He left the summer before you turned ten and just moved back a few years ago—actually, some say he moved back to be with Hilary. The girl from Butternut Bay." She whispered the last few words, as if it were a secret. "I think she broke it off with him, poor guy."

"Poor-*schmore*!" I said. "Did you forget I'm your daughter? You're supposed to love me more than him. We're mad at the chief—remember? He barged into Gran's house accusing me of slamming a heel into a man's throat today. Which—I would like to point out—I would never do. I would never ruin a pair of shoes like that."

May contemplated for a moment. "I could see that, but don't you think Chief Dear is a little too serious for Jenna? Matt seems more...friendly. Joe loves working with him down at the station. They get along like a pair of mischievous boys."

She had a cute smile on her face as she said this, and it was clear she adored her husband. I had a fleeting thought that their little nugget would be the luckiest baby of all time. Plus, this baby would have me as an aunt (*hello*, baby shoe shopping!). He or she would be spoiled rotten.

While I'd been lost in my musings, my mother and May had continued the conversation about my love life without me.

"I really think Jenna could use a little serious in her life right now, after that—" she held up a hand and hissed—"jerk!"

"He was a jerk," May agreed. "That's why Jenna needs Matt to bring some fun into her life. She doesn't want to sit around and mope with the chief all day."

"The chief isn't a moper. He's probably just sensitive!" My mother argued back. "And you have to admit he's very handsome."

"Matt is handsome too! And—" May paused, giving a salacious wink. "We all know how much I love a man in a firefighter's suit. I'm telling you, Jenna, you want to choose Matt."

"If the chief falls in love with her, then he'll see my daughter's heart of gold," Bea explained. "He'll know she can't have killed Grant, and the mystery will be solved."

"It doesn't work like that," I interrupted, but nobody listened. Sid gave me a sympathetic gaze. I liked Sid and his silence. "Okay, carry on without me. Don't worry about what I think."

"I'm her mother," Bea was saying. "I know what's best for her."

"But I'm her cousin, and I know Matt better than you do. He's perfect for her."

"Why don't you let Jenna settle this for herself?" Sid sounded exasperated at having his pancakes interrupted with talk of the bachelorette-hood. "She's an adult."

Okay, now I really, really liked Sid. I gave him a hearty nod of agreement and passed him the pancakes.

"Great idea," my mother said. "How about we both set Jenna up on a date, and then she can choose."

"How about we—" I started.

"Deal." May stuck out her hand, and they shook.

Sid looked disgraced, and he put the pancakes back. I gave him a shrug of apology and nodded for him to take one anyway. At least he'd tried.

"Sure—while you do that, I am going to retrace Grant's steps to figure out who killed him," I said. "Because if you were listening, my highlights will not look good against orange. I hate to mention that I won't be dating anyone if I don't find out how a stiletto ended up in Grant's neck with my fingerprints on it."

"Hang on a sec!" May raised her fork and drizzled syrup everywhere. She quickly set it down and continued with her breakthrough. "Joe is always pointing out how crime scenes are all wrong on TV. There's no way that the chief could know your fingerprints were on the stilettos."

I sucked in a huge gasp. "You're right! I styled Danny Sloane on NCIS for three seasons, and I picked up a lot of useless facts while he ran lines. It takes weeks for most reports to come back from the lab!"

"That means the chief was bluffing." May stuck her finger toward my mother. "I told you she'll choose Matt."

"Cooper was just doing his job." My mother pursed her lips daintily. "It means he's a good cop. Of course she'll choose him."

"Something must have happened in order for him to think my fingerprints were on the shoe," I said, thinking aloud. "Do you think the killer used a pair of *my* shoes? Maybe ones from my missing luggage?"

"How would he know the shoes are yours?" Sid asked. "Men don't pay attention to shoes."

"I know, Sid," I said lovingly, glancing at his feet. "I can see that."

Sid especially doesn't care much about shoes. He has the unfortunate habit of wearing those ugly ones with individual toes built right into the shoe like thick socks. I am ashamed to admit I generally pretend not to know him when he wears them to a public event. He hasn't done it yet this trip, so hopefully he's progressed past the toe-shoe stage of life.

"Then why would he think your fingerprints are on them?" May asked. "That's a pretty big bluff."

I snapped to attention. "The powder blue vintage heels! Mother, did someone buy them?"

"I don't know, I'll have to check," she said. "Why?"

"Those are the ones I threatened Grant with!" I exclaimed. "If someone bought them, then it might not be a bluff at all—my fingerprints could still be on them! I slipped them off at the store this morning. Anyone could have them."

"I'll check tomorrow," my mother said. "I leave the records there."

"We really need to get you a computer," I said. "But if you'll excuse me for the abrupt departure, I have a quick errand to run. Thanks for the pancakes. *No* thank you for pimping me out to your choice of single men."

"Jenna—"

"I'll be back," I hollered, running to the door and slipping into my high heels. "Can I take the car, mother?"

"Keys are in the ignition," she called. "See you for dessert, sweetie."

"Mom, lock your door!" I said, pulling it open. "And don't leave the keys in the car. There's a murderer on the loose!"

"Sure, honey," she breezed. "Chief Dear will protect us, don't you worry! Just remember that on your date with him, okay, darling?"

Chapter 4

C ooper Dear lived in a perfectly normal house, on a perfectly normal street, in a perfectly normal neighborhood. He had rose bushes along the sidewalk, an apple tree hanging over his lawn, and a yard situated cozily between two neighboring houses that looked equally normal.

In summer, I imagined it to be a bright and happy sort of place. Under a coating of snow, it looked a bit like Narnia with the glowing streetlamps and white flecks falling from the sky. (Speaking of Narnia, do they sell Turkish Delights in Blueberry Lake? Must check Flora's candy store.)

It looked like the sort of street where one might find a children's game of kickball going on at all hours of the day and well into the evening, until dinner bells rang from front porches at dusk. I imagined young couples out for their evening strolls, ice cream cones in hand and their dogs happily trotting beside them.

All of it surprised me. Chief Dear seemed too grumpy to live on such a perfectly normal street. I was expecting something more along the lines of a haunted mansion tucked onto a dead and gloomy old cul de sac where he sat on his throne in starched pants and stiff shirts, cackling while he sentenced innocent people to orange jumpsuits.

Too late, I realized my flannel pants didn't look all that appealing with the only pair of heels I had left, but I wasn't about to detour home to change. Tomorrow morning I'd grab some clothes from my mother's store. I'd been far too distracted so far, what with my narrow escape from Grant Mark's creepy little hands, to worry about whether flannel matched stilettos.

I hugged my jacket tighter and slipped from the car, slamming the door behind me to announce my arrival. I marched right up Cooper Dear's perfectly normal front walkway and rapped my knuckles on the solid wood door.

I took a step back, careful not to twist an ankle on the ice. I half expected a monster to be waiting for me, all grouchy and big and ready to slap handcuffs on me, so I took a deep breath and steeled myself for whoever—or whatever—waited inside Cooper Dear's lair.

However, when the door opened and there was no monster, I found myself disappointed. Instead, there stood a strapping gentleman a few years older than me, dressed in a threadbare black T-shirt with worn jeans that made his butt look like a cowboy's rear end. (Not that I have studied the subject matter extensively, mind you! P.S. If I have studied it on occasion, it was for *work*.) On impulse, I stepped backward.

"Oh, my," I managed to breathe, before my heel hit a patch of ice with my unexpected movement. And then I completely lost my balance.

I was heading down like the luge in the Winter Olympics—fast and unstoppable and weirdly fascinating. Without thinking, I yelped and reached out my hands, waving them wildly for something—anything—to latch onto for stability.

A pair of warm arms found me, wrapping around my waist and pulling me upward. The man belonging to the arms trapped me firmly against his chest, which at this moment felt like the most stable force in the world.

"Whoa, there," he murmured, his voice gentle and soothing in my ear. "You all right? What happened?"

I huffed unladylike gasps in his face. "Nice house," I said dumbly, hoping Chief Dear didn't recognize the change of subject for what it was: embarrassment. "Sorry about that. Er—usually I'm more graceful. I'm not used to the ice."

As I inhaled, I caught the scent of his breath—cinnamon and a hint of red wine?—and felt the warmth of his body. The man wasn't as much of a monster as I thought, which was a bummer. I almost liked this version of Chief Dear. He was handsome, mysterious, and he caught me when I fell over. The other, snarlier version was much easier to dislike, and I was *not* interested in crushing on the man accusing me of murder.

"What happened out there?" Cooper murmured, his hands still around my back. "Did you show up at my door just to fall into my arms?"

"I was just trying to help you earn your salary," I snapped. "At least when you're catching people, you're doing *good* work."

He blinked, shook his head. "What are you talking about?"

I tapped his chest again which gave a hefty sort of *thunk*. "Excuse me, your arms are still around my waist."

"You fell into me and didn't seem keen on moving."

I reached behind my back and unclasped his hands at the same time he released me. As I stepped away, I found myself subconsciously missing the warmth shared between us. (Though I'd *never* tell my mother that, or she wouldn't stop gloating.)

"I have some unfinished business with you," I said, tottering as I regained my balance four inches above his floor. "Hold on a second, will you?"

My heels might make my calves look great, but there was a hunk of ice stuck to one that was being very stubborn, and eventually, I had to kick off both shoes and retreat to ground level to avoid falling again. Though a second trip into Cooper Dear's arms wouldn't have been the worst part of my day.

"That's better," I said, pulling out my finger and giving it a wiggle. "I need to talk to you about what you said this afternoon."

Chief Dear was taller and broader than me in shoes, so without them, I felt like I was sinking into quicksand. At five feet, six and three-quarters inches tall, I landed on the chart just above average height for a female. (Reaching five feet, seven inches is a yet-to-be-accomplished item on my bucket list.)

"What did I say this afternoon?" He crossed his arms over that glorious chest (scratch the *glorious* part and replace with *average*, or my mother will cackle to her grave), and leaned against the wall. "I hope you're not here to talk about the investigation. I shouldn't be socializing with suspects."

"Well, that's just stupid." I dropped my finger and gave a shrug. "This is a small town. Everyone's a suspect. June is a suspect, so I better not be seeing you getting a muffin from her until the murderer is caught."

"And you have enough experience to teach me how to do my job?"

"Not exactly, but I have done makeup for half the actors on NCIS, and I've picked up a thing or two."

He cracked a grin, which split his face into a nice-looking portrait.

"In fact, I'd be happy to style you sometime," I said, changing the subject—albeit briefly. "If I could just have a thousand bucks and your measurements, I can have you a new closet in a week. You'll be red carpet ready by Monday."

His smile lost its luster. "Hollywood doesn't interest me, Miss McGovern. Neither does your sales pitch."

"I'm sorry, it's just—you have the body for it, and..." I hesitated, my face heating with embarrassment. "I'm sorry. You're not interested."

If nothing else, my awkward blunderings had brought his grin back, which made me happy, oddly enough. He ran a hand through chestnut brown hair, leaving it standing on end. It should've made him look like a slob. It didn't.

"I happen to like my clothes just fine," he said. "But I'm touched by your concern."

"Anytime." I looked down, grinding my toe into the mat to avoid eye contact. "Anyway, I have a bone to pick with you."

"Pick away."

"Like I said, I worked on crime shows, and I know you can't tell just from looking at a pair of shoes that my fingerprints are on them. Whatever heel you found in Grant

Mark's..." I hesitated, feeling queasy. "The murder weapon, I mean. You were bluffing."

"Maybe," he said with a shrug. "But I suspect we'll find a match when we get results back from the lab."

"How are you so certain?"

"Possibly because I have four different people telling me they saw you hours before Grant's death brandishing the murder weapon in front of his face. Usually, that'll do it."

"But those aren't *my* shoes. I left them at the store," I said proudly. "I only had those heels in my possession for a hot second."

"For a what?"

"A hot second," I said. "You know, only a little bit of time. Like I told you, my bags were lost. I only had these super cute fluffy boots that had any hope of surviving in the snow, but when I wore them, they got all soggy, so my mother let me pick some heels to wear for my appointment with Grant so I didn't catch a cold. I found these fabulous chunky ones: powder blue, vintage—a perfect fit. It was like Cinderella in a thrift shop."

"Go on, princess."

"I left the shoes behind at the store after my confrontation with Grant. I was so sure my bags would be here by now that I didn't even consider buying them to wear later." I frowned. "I wish my bags were here. Remind me to call the airline, will you?"

"Um—"

"Anyway, if you find the person who purchased the shoes, you'll find the killer."

"You're claiming that the shoes were not in your possession at the time of the murder?"

"Of course not!" I spread my arms wide. "I was snoozing in my old room at my Gran's. Er, well, it's my place now. If walls could talk, they would verify my alibi."

He gave me a patronizing smile. "Walls can't talk, but people can. I have you as the last person seen with Grant before his death."

"That can't be right because I didn't kill him," I said vehemently. "Have you never watched a crime show? Someone is framing me!"

"In Blueberry Lake." Cooper looked skeptical. "Someone knew you'd lose your bags, wear the wrong shoes, and then not have an alibi for the time of the murder?"

"Okay, so maybe it wasn't all premeditated," I said. "But I still think the shoes are the key. If we follow them, I guarantee they'll lead us to the killer. Whoever killed Grant had them in their possession. And we know they were at the store earlier this morning, so it had to be someone who came in during or after my session with Grant."

"Does your mother keep records?"

"Records?!" I thought back to her dinky little calculator. "She has something better than records."

"Dare I ask what?"

It was my turn to smile at Cooper's uneasy frown. "Mrs. Beasley."

"Mrs. Beasley?" he asked, skeptical. "She owns the knitting store across the street. She also just celebrated her ninety-first birthday. How can she help?"

"She's one of the women who lunched with my grandma and June every afternoon at the Blueberry Jam Café, which means she's a gossip," I said with confidence. "You can bet Mrs. Beasley was watching my mother's store like a hawk. One visit to her, and you'll have a full list of suspects."

The chief exhaled a long, slow sigh and raised his hands. "Thank you for your concern, Miss McGovern."

"Call me Jenna, please."

"I hope you know this doesn't clear your name."

"Oh, but it will."

"But it doesn't yet."

"No," I said patiently. "But it will. Trust me. You'll be handing me a detective badge before this is over, Chief Dear."

"It's Cooper."

"Excuse me?"

He smiled, softer. "Call me Cooper when I'm off duty. We have to cohabitate in this small town, so I suppose we might as well try to be friendly."

"Cooper," I said. "Thanks for the warm welcome to the neighborhood."

"Your cousin is probably ready to kill me."

"She said Joe might have a word with you."

"Your mother called me," he said, an eyebrow inching up. "Just before you got here."

"Really?" I feigned innocence. "What did she want?"

"To know if I was interested in playing Bingo on Sunday."

"Oh."

"I'm going," he said. "You're welcome to join if you'd like. Everyone will be there."

I watched him carefully. "Are you asking me on a date?"

He visibly blanched. "Of course not. I can't date a suspect—I'm trying to redeem myself and be civilized to you before May sends Joe to smother me in my sleep."

"Thanks for the half-assed invitation from my mother. I think I'll pass."

"Jenna, wait—"

"Good luck finding the murderer," I said, slipping my feet into my shoes and turning to leave. "You're wasting time if you continue to look at me."

"Jenna, look out!"

I took one step, missed, and went flying face first on a different ugly patch of ice. The snowbank hurtled toward me, and I landed with a soft thump in an upside-down snow-angel position.

"I tried to warn you," Cooper said, climbing down and helping me to my feet. "Can I get you a sweatshirt? Hot chocolate?"

"N-no," I said, shivering. "Just find the murderer before these shoes kill me, will you? I don't want to be laid out at Franny's Funeral Parlor in handcuffs. My mother would die."

Chapter 5

The next morning dawned bright and sunny in a way that only the coldest, snowiest winter day can. Rays reflected from the sun off the gleaming white banks, sending fractures of light careening into my eyes.

I sunk lower in bed, hugging the thick, fluffy comforter to me and wondering how anyone in their right mind had possibly chosen to live in Minnesota. Why hadn't all our ancestors moved to warmer locations? Snow was nice in a cute, festive sort of way, but more than that was just plain inconvenient.

Pulling my phone closer to me, I huddled deeper into the warmth and told myself I was being productive by calling the airline company. (Spoiler alert, they hadn't found my bags.)

With a sigh, I watched as my phone lit up again with my mother's picture on it. Or rather, her nostrils. Last night at dinner she'd attempted to master the art of selfies and had inadvertently taken a photoshoot of her nose and locked it as her contact photo.

My mother, May, Sid, and I had finished the night off with dessert—a chocolate lava cake that was devilishly delicious and equally high in calories. Something I'd never have found in Hollywood. If I didn't watch myself around these parts, I'd waddle back to Los Angeles after my mother's shop was up and running looking like the Macy's Thanksgiving Day Parade float version of Jenna McGovern.

"Do you need a ride this morning?" Bea barked into the phone. "Sid plowed our driveway, so I'm taking the truck if you want. Isn't he a doll?"

I wouldn't call Sid a doll, but I'd take the ride. "Sure—what time are you swinging by?"

"I'm outside your house right now."

"But mother! I'm still in bed."

"It's seven thirty!"

"In L.A., that means it's five thirty. I'm still jetlagged."

"Well, then, I'll wait out here."

"Give me two minutes," I whined. "It's not like I have a plethora of outfits to choose from."

Groaning, I hauled myself from bed, lamenting every shiver and blink of snowflake that spiraled past my window. My trip here had been wrought with disaster so far, and my future wasn't exactly looking bright.

This morning, I was going to my mother's thrift shop to give the place a second chance. After all, my first one had ended in an inadvertent grope and a murder accusation. With any luck, I could find out who had purchased the shoes.

At the very minimum, I could find out who had been in the store yesterday morning, which would help in gathering a golden list of suspects. All I would have to do was match up that list of suspects with a person who wanted Grant Mark dead, and *voila*! Case closed; jumpsuit catastrophe avoided.

If only my mother had a true receipt program instead of a clunky old calculator, we could've tracked the murderer down over chocolate lava cake yesterday evening from the comfort of her house. As it was, I'd need to check the written record or ask Allie. My mother was hopeless at recordkeeping, and she hadn't even realized the shoes had been sold.

Sometimes I wondered if my mother wasn't a bit of a lost object herself—fitting, considering her passion. There were days she wore her shirt backwards for hours. I loved her, but the woman would forget her head if it wasn't glued on tight.

I slipped into the outfit May had brought over last night. My cousin had a few more curves in the hips and bust than I did, so the jeans were a little loose and the shirt a tiny bit baggy, but it was better than digging in my mom's closet or my grandma's attic. They'd work until I picked out some clothes off the racks today.

May had also apologized for her hand-me-down boots. They were hideous, and it was no wonder she didn't use them anymore. It pained my very trendy little soul as I slipped one foot and then the other into them. But May claimed they were effective, which was more than I could say for my heels.

I grabbed Louie and locked up the house before skidding my way down the front path to Sid's ridiculously huge truck. It was a far cry from the new Tesla models that populated the streets of Los Angeles, all robotic and electric and futuristic. This was just one big fat truck that could cruise through two feet of snow without wincing. I was in a whole new world.

"Good morning, darling. Ready for a better day?" Bea, the perpetual sunshine, grinned at me. "I brought you a treat!"

My eyes landed first on the blueberry muffin and second on the piping hot cup of coffee sitting in the cupholder. "Both are for me?"

She nodded, reversing out of the drive. "Dig in, buttercup."

"This is not healthy," I said, digging into the muffin. "I'd be having a fruit smoothie out in California, not more carbs. You already stuffed me to the brim with that lava cake!"

"You can stand to gain a few pounds," my mother said. "Relax. Enjoy. You need to fatten up for winter—it's how we stay warm."

"But my clothes," I moaned. "None of them will fit."

"Like it matters," Bea said. "Don't give me that look. If your clothes are never found, you'll have to buy a new wardrobe anyway. Just buy it in Minnesota sizes."

I harrumphed. Luckily, we arrived at the store shortly after. I sized up the Something Old sign, which was quirky in and of itself. My mother had fashioned it out of single letters she'd pulled from other various objects. The result was a mismatched hodge-podge of capital letters and small ones, big sizes and little sizes, and looked as if it'd been stapled above the store by a kindergartener whose definition of a straight line was sketchy at best. It was an OCD mathematician's worst nightmare. I thought it was adorable.

"Here we are," my mother said. "Are you excited to put your detective hat on?"

I gave her an odd sort of look. "I'd rather nobody was dead in the first place."

"Yes...but Matlock." At my blank stare, my mother gave me a look of incredulity. "We used to watch Matlock together every afternoon, and you always solved the case before he did. You should really consider detective work for your next career."

"I'll leave that to the police," I said, thinking of Cooper Dear and his hoity toity badge. "I'm more of a *fashion* police sort of gal. Speaking of which, mother—the blue and orange color scheme you've got going on with your clothes is from the seventies. Can I please dress you?"

She pulled off an orange scarf as we entered the store and frowned. "No. I like being quirky."

"You can be quirky and modern."

"I'm not young and hip," she said. "Let me be old and quirky."

"You're barely fifty."

"Well, I do have more romance in my life than you," she said, giving me the side-eye. "I don't know if that means I'm young or you're old."

"Romance has no bearing on age!"

"I sure hope not," she said. "Because you're almost thirty. Didn't Cooper look nice when you went to visit him last night? He's living all alone in that single-family home. Do you hear the words *single* and *family*? Family, dear. He's looking to start a family, and he just needs the jelly to his peanut butter."

"I'd like to shove jelly somewhere special for him," I said bitterly. "He accused me of murder, mother."

"He's just doing his job. A very noble profession, I might add," she said. "His move into a single-family home—again, do you hear my words?—is very telling. He's subconsciously wanting a family, even if he doesn't know it yet."

"Nope!" I hummed. "I'm not hearing any of your words anymore. How are you this morning, Allie?"

The door jingled as the bright-eyed employee entered the store, looking very vibrant in her choice of clothing. The brightness reached new heights as Allie slipped off her jacket and displayed pants that resembled some sort of complex illusion with all the jagged white lines and black swirls, topped with a rosy pink sweater. It made me dizzy if I stared at her thighs for more than a few seconds at a time.

"I'm great. My cat isn't though. Freddie had the grossest hairball this morning." She nonchalantly brushed fur off her sweater before looking up. "Besides that, all is good. What about you?"

"Been better," I admitted. "I assume you heard about Grant Mark's untimely demise?"

"Oh, yeah. Someone got him good, they're saying." Allie leaned forward and whispered. "What if he was smuggling drugs across the border and someone blew him up?"

"I don't think that's what happened," I said gently. "But it's an interesting theory."

"Oh." Allie's shoulders slumped. "Well maybe he was a terrorist, and someone forced him to eat a cyanide pill and before he could die, a sniper shot him in the face."

"I don't think—" I started, but my mother interrupted.

"Allie, are these plots of the books you've been reading?" Bea cocked one eyebrow in a very motherly way—that sort of eyebrow cock that encouraged only the truth. (I'd seen it a few times myself.) My mother turned to me. "Allie is quite the bookworm. Her imagination is...active."

Allie gave a huge sigh. "It's just that regular old murder is boring."

"Unfortunately, not boring enough," I said. "If I had it my way, there would have been no murder at all."

"I mean, Grant Mark basically attacked you yesterday," Allie said, looking skeptically at me. "You're not at all happy he's the one who ended up dead?"

"What sort of question is that?" I whirled on her. "Of course not. I wouldn't wish anyone dead. I might have wished him a bad case of the stomach flu, but that's the extent of it."

"That would do it." Allie nodded knowingly.

"Since we're on the subject, I actually had some questions for you."

"Oh, *oh*! This is the amateur sleuth moment, isn't it? You're going to go all Nancy Drew on me." Allie gave a sly nod. "I read you. Well, if you need a sidekick, I'm available for duty."

"Thanks, but—"

"Who do we think killed him?" Allie asked quickly. "Frankly, if this were my book, you'd be the first person I'd look at for murder charges. You had a huge, public fight with the victim right before he ended up as toast."

"Thanks," I said dryly. "You're a real great sidekick."

"I'm just saying—objectively," she added. "But it would be nothing more than a red herring. It's *never* that obvious."

"No offense, Allie, but it doesn't matter what you think, or even what I think. What matters is proving to the police that I didn't do anything." I eased out of my own jacket and hung it on the old-timey coat rack behind the register. Popping around to the other side, I faced Allie across the desk while my mother began tidying up behind me. "There was a pair of powder blue heels here yesterday. Right over there."

Allie's eyes followed my pointed finger, landing on the empty space on the wall where the shoes no longer sat.

"Yeah, the ones you were wearing," she said. "I remember."

"Yes! Exactly." I felt myself visibly brighten. Maybe my mother didn't need anything but a dinky old calculator; maybe it was better to have humans who could remember things. Particularly budding mystery novelists on the lookout for clues. "This is very important: I need to know who bought them and when."

"That's easy," she said, grinning at my huge sigh of relief. Which all went away at her next statement. "I did."

"You did what?"

"I bought them," Allie said. "I saw them on your feet and they made your ankles look so rad. I mean, all slim and bony and really cute."

"Sorry, what?" I massaged my forehead as I tried to understand what this meant for me, and then for the investigation. "You bought the powder blue heels that I selected yesterday?"

"Yes, ma'am, I did," she said. "I bought them the second after you popped them off your feet. I thought it was sort of cool how you used them for a weapon. A little James Bondish, don't you think? But in your case Jenna Bond because obviously James wouldn't wear heels."

"Obviously," I agreed wryly. "Do you know where those shoes might be now?"

"Er—" She raised a finger, pressed it to her lips. "You know, that's actually a good question. I realized when I got home last night that I didn't have them with me."

"Did you leave them here?"

"No," she said, "I must not have. I mean, you're welcome to look around, but I don't see them anywhere. I locked up yesterday evening, and you guys opened this morning, so if they were here last night, they should still be here this morning."

"Unless someone stole them," my mother said, chiming in from across the room. Her face went pale. "What if someone broke in here last night?"

"Uh, you guys are forgetting one important fact," I said, raising a hand to stall the conversation. When I had the attention of both ladies, I raised my eyebrows. "Grant Mark was murdered yesterday afternoon. Which means the shoes must have been taken some time between my departure from the store and Grant's murder."

"Why?" Allie frowned. "I mean, how do you know that? It's not like the murderer is broadcasting the fact they were walking around in stolen shoes."

"Actually," I said, biting my lip as I glanced at her. "She was."

"It was a she?"

"I have to imagine so," I said. "Because the weapon that killed Grant Mark was one of those very shoes."

"So, it really wasn't an explosion?" Allie looked visibly disappointed. "Huh. I guess I did let my imagination get the best of me. Well, that makes things easier."

"Easier?"

"Yeah," she said with a grin. "It's a classic twist on Cinderella. Find the missing shoe, and you've found your murderer."

I blinked, considering this, and then leaned across the counter and pulled Allie into a hug. I dusted a huge fat kiss on her cheek, feeling a flutter of excitement unlike anything I'd experienced since arriving in Blueberry Lake.

"That's brilliant, Allie," I told her, clapping my hands. "I knew you'd be on my side. Except..."

"Aw, no," she groaned. "Don't make this more difficult."

"How do we go about finding a missing shoe?"

"Like Prince Charming! Go around asking," she said. "There's not that many people in a town this size."

"Right, but nobody's going to fess up to having the murder weapon's identical twin," I said, sinking back into despair. "Hold on—let's get back to the last moment the shoe was in your sight."

"Sure. After you wielded the heel like a light saber, I quick bought the shoes, put the cash in the register, and packed them up in a bag. I set the bag behind the counter like we're allowed to do," Allie said with a quick glance at my mother, "and then I went back to work. I still have the receipt in my pocket."

"Did you see anyone hanging around the register?"

"Well, there was a huge influx of customers right after you left," Allie said to me. "The entire bridal party came in, and of course there were some of the regular Saturday shoppers. I stashed a few bags behind the counter for the customers as they shopped. Do you think it's possible someone picked up the wrong bag on accident?"

"I think that's entirely possible," I said, grasping at the faint thread of hope. "And I think if we find out who got the bag, we find our murderer. Allie, let me buy you a coffee. I'm going to need a list of everyone you can remember who stepped foot in the store yesterday."

"Ooh, a suspect list," Allie said. "And a coffee from Blueberry Jam? Count me in."

Chapter 6

"Spring is coming," June said the second Allie and I reached the front counter at the local café. "Do you smell that?"

"Spring?" I wrinkled my nose. "It looks like wet slush out there to me. Feels like it, too."

June's face crumpled into a smile. "Just a few weeks and the snow will be gone. It'll be swimsuit weather by May this year—mark my words."

I glanced at the barely-above-freezing outdoors behind me. "Sure, June. Whatever you say."

She gave a tinkling laugh. "Are you planning to revive your grandmother's garden shop?"

"I'm more about shoe shopping. You know, things that don't require care. I have a black thumb," I said with a frustrated bob of my shoulders. "But yes, May and I are planning to have someone come out to help us return Green's to its former glory."

"You're a McGovern!" June gave a knowing cluck. "I bet you just might find yourself surprised if you give it a try."

"I tried keeping a lucky bamboo alive in my apartment in California," I said, leaning on the counter and giving a scan over the fresh-baked goods. As much as I loved discussing my lack of talent for keeping plants alive, my stomach was grumbling. "How about a blueberry muffin and some cornbread pancakes?"

If June was surprised by the size of my order, she didn't give any indication of it. "You should be starting your vegetable seeds soon, I'd think," she said. "I'm urging you to give it a try. A little flop with lucky bamboo doesn't mean all that much. What can I get you to drink? That fancy latte machine isn't coming until next week."

"Then I'll take a black coffee for today," I said. "Though I am determined not to be happy about it."

June chortled again as she rang me up. "Is that all?"

"For me, but add whatever Allie wants to my tab," I said, moving aside so Allie could order. "We're together."

"Lemon rosemary scone with coffee for here, and a jasmine tea to go?" June asked before Allie could speak.

Allie gave a single nod, and June plunked away on the keys.

"I guess you're a regular here," I said to Allie. "I didn't see lemon rosemary on the menu."

Allie just blinked. "Everyone's a regular at June's."

June reached across the counter and pinched Allie's cheek. "I could just eat you up, doll. Your order will be right out, girls. Oh, and Allie, I just love those pants."

As I studied Allie's quirky outfit, I couldn't help but think Blueberry Lake had an entirely different style palate than Hollywood.

I was beginning to doubt my skills as a stylist here and began to think harder about getting Gran's shop up and running again. I had money for a few months of living expenses, but come the end of summer, I would need to find a steady stream of income. Otherwise, I'd be unable to afford even a single earring, let alone that Briana Bartone bracelet that would be going on sale this fall.

Allie and I grabbed a table in a bright, sundrenched corner. We each took a side of the booth and perched on worn, yellow cushions with a lemon pattern printed on them. A young server came by with two mugs, one of them slightly chipped, and a pot of coffee. He filled up both our cups and then vanished behind the counter, leaving the two of us alone to watch the steam rise and curl from our beverages as soft snowflakes began to drop outside of the window.

"Spring, huh?" I commented, pulling the chipped mug close to me. "I think June might be wrong this year."

"Oh, June's never wrong," Allie said happily. "Not about the weather, at least."

I glanced down at my chipped little mug and felt a burst of kinship with it. Just a little bit broken, but still functional. I figured there was a lesson in there for me somewhere, but the second I sipped the coffee, all deep thoughts left my skull and drifted away in swirls like the fat flakes falling outside. I was left with the buttery warm taste of coffee, the chaotic, quiet cozy of the café, and the sight of someone's gorgeous new boots stomping through the door.

I was squinting at the boots on a leggy female, struggling to read the label, when Allie waved a hand in front of my face. "Earth to Jenna! Did you hear me? I said you shouldn't doubt June's ability to predict the weather. It's quite weird—she can sense spring better than most groundhogs."

"I'm pretty sure groundhogs are a myth," I told Allie. "I mean, the fact that their shadow can predict spring, and all of that."

"Oh, you're one of *those*." She gave me a knowing nod. "I bet you don't believe in unicorns, either."

"Um..."

Allie picked up her own mug and shrugged. "It's fine. Your loss."

"Right. Well, maybe we can start discussing business," I said. "Obviously, I need to clear my name—and the best way to do that is to give Cooper a list of suspects."

"You're on a first name basis with Chief Dear, huh?" She raised her eyebrows. "That was fast."

"Excuse me?"

"I put my money on Matt. You know, forced proximity and all that." She gave me a dumbfounded stare. "Seriously, read a book or something. You and Matt are both beautiful people, you live next door to one another—it's only a matter of time before things start heating up between the two of you."

"Exactly what *sort* of things are you talking about?" I asked. "I have no plans to—"

"Oh, are you discussing the pool?" June asked, carrying three plates of food between two hands. She deposited them gently on the table. "I put my money on the chief. I'm leaning more toward the whole enemies-to-lovers thing they have going on."

"See? June reads books," Allie said, as if that explained everything.

"I'm more concerned about the whole *money* and *pool* aspect of this thing," I said. "Is there a bet going around?"

"I wouldn't call it a bet," June said. "More like gentle encouragement for you, dear. We've all been wanting a nice woman to come along for both Matt and Cooper. And now you're here, and you're already involved with both—but you're only one woman. We're very excited about the whole thing. I hope you choose quickly."

"Do—er, the men know about this?"

"*Who?*" June asked. "Oh, the boys—Matt and Cooper. Who knows? Possibly. But men are oblivious. My husband wouldn't have noticed I got a haircut if I dangled it in front of his face. Love him to death and God rest his soul, but he had other talents that didn't include perceptiveness."

"How about we leave my love life alone?" I volunteered the suggestion, but both Allie and June gave me blank stares as if I'd suggested we launch my car to Mars. "Yeah, all right—never mind. You both should know, though, that saving your money is best. I'm not looking to date."

"Sure." June patted my head sympathetically. "And spring isn't right around the corner."

I glanced at the quickly accelerating snow outside and thought that nothing looked further from the truth. I was willing to bet money I could safely live in an igloo for the next six months.

After June left us alone with our food, Allie and I took a moment to turn off any ladylike manners and completely dive into the spread before us. I made it halfway through the muffin and was elbow deep into the short stack of cornbread pancakes before I surfaced for air.

"She's right, you know," I said, taking a moment to swallow my food and wash it down with freshly poured hot coffee. "I'm going to gain fifty pounds on June's food alone."

Allie shrugged, her lemon rosemary scone already gone. I noticed she hadn't offered to share, though I'd invited her to take a pancake for herself.

"If you gain a few pounds, we can share clothes," she offered. "I've got a little more meat on my bones than you do."

"Speaking of clothes," I said. "Let's discuss who you saw at my mother's shop yesterday. Starting from the time I left until late afternoon."

Allie sunk into thought. "Well, on one hand it's going to be hard because the store was packed. I mean, Friday afternoon—we get a lot of women blowing off work to go look around before they pick up the kids from school. A few minutes to themselves, you know?"

"Are any of them regulars?"

"Sure," she said. Then she hollered over my shoulder. "Mrs. Beasley, we need your help!"

"Mrs. Beasley?" I glanced behind me with horror as the coffee shop froze. It seemed I couldn't get away from causing a scene even when I was trying my best for discretion. "Oh, Allie—we don't need to break up their meeting."

"It's just knitting club," Allie said, and then raised her voice for the whole shop to hear. "Mrs. Beasley, would you rather discuss murder suspects or knitting club?"

"Go on over." Angela Dewey, my tattletale neighbor, flicked her wrist at her friend. She spoke rather loudly (probably a result of the annoying hum coming from her hearing aids that was audible from across the room) and gave a hungry look in our direction. "Get the scoop, Marge, and then report back."

Marge Beasley stood and grabbed her walker. It took approximately seven minutes (during which I finished the rest of my muffin and a partial pancake) for her to arrive and perch on the chair at the end of our table. "How can I help you girls?"

"We're trying to put together a list of people who might have killed Grant Mark," Allie explained. "We think it's someone who was in Mrs. McGovern's shop between—oh, nine in the morning and one thirty in the afternoon."

"That's easy," Mrs. Beasley said. "I watched the comings and goings all day and my memory is the best in the business."

I wasn't sure what business she meant, unless she was discussing the rabid gossip community of Blueberry Lake, but I dug deep into my purse and pulled out a bejeweled Kate Spade pen and matching notebook. "Okay, who did you see enter the shop?"

"You have your regulars," Mrs. Beasley said. "Mary, Jane, Susan, and Jennifer. They're there every week on the lunch hour. The first three are married, but Jennifer is divorced and on the prowl. She was wearing leopard print leggings and looking desperate, poor thing. I think her eggs are shriveling up."

Allie nodded sympathetically. "She was at the shop to flirt with Bob Hannigan."

"Bob has no teeth," Marge Beasley said. "Even I wouldn't date Bob."

"Um, okay," I said, urging things along. "Who else?"

"Well, the entire bridal party was there," Allie offered. "They came in just after you left. Your mother wasn't around—she came down to June's on her lunch break while I held down the store. It was crazy."

"There were..." Mrs. Beasley counted on her wrinkled fingers. "At least eleven of them."

"Eleven people," I said. "And I bet a good chunk of them knew Grant."

"I probably should have said the bridal thing first, huh?" Mrs. Beasley said. "On account of it's probably not one of the locals. I'll bet whoever killed him was from the wedding party and knew him well."

"We just need to find out who disliked Grant," Allie said. "We can match it up with a motive for murder, and opportunity, and *voila*—you're a free woman, Jenna McGovern."

"Great. Back to the bridal party," I said. "Are you familiar with the names of the ladies?"

Mrs. Beasley and Allie exchanged looks as if that were the most useless question they'd ever heard.

"Of course," Allie said. "We'll start from the top. Lana Duvet is the bride. She's from Blueberry Lake and lives in that rich-looking white house at the end of Ivy Road."

"I know her," I said grimly, thinking of the week my mother had sent me to summer camp. "Unfortunately."

"Then, there's her sister and mother—Eliza and Bridget Duvet, respectively," Mrs. Beasley said. "They were both there. Bridget Duvet divorced William Duvet—Will is married to a new woman, Brenda, but she wasn't there."

I made notes on my makeshift family tree. "I'm looking just at the people who were there. It had to be someone at the shop to have access to the shoes."

"You know, Becky was there too. She packed a few bags behind the counter. She peeped into all of them when she left though, so she couldn't have taken the wrong one by mistake. I'll bet it was her. Maybe Lana asked her to off Grant. Everyone knew Lana didn't want him in her wedding."

"Really?" I asked. "Why not? I mean, I have my guesses because of his personality, but still."

"Lana didn't think Grant was a good influence on her husband," Allie said. "I heard them talking about it yesterday. Patty Blarney had been drinking at the lunch hour, and her lips were flapping."

"Who's Patty?"

"She's...er," Allie stilled. "Well, she dated Grant for a short while."

"Was Grant from the area?"

"He was from the next town over," Mrs. Beasley said. "He lived on Shepard Way over in Butternut Bay. But the ladies from knitting club say he worked his way through Butternut Bay, so he had to come sow his seeds over in this direction, if you know what I mean."

"Ew," I said. "Too much information."

"Birds and the bees," Mrs. Beasley said. "If you ask me, it was Patty. I think Grant dumped her. Patty likes her cocktails, too. Maybe she had a little much to drink and got carried away."

"No," Allie said, shaking her head. "That's not what I heard. Yesterday, one of them was saying how Grant wouldn't stop following Patty around even after *she* broke things off."

"My, oh my," I said. "There are a lot of motives in this bridal party."

"I think you need to get the inside scoop," Allie said. "Go undercover. You can slip in unnoticed to the bridal shower happening tonight. They were talking about it all day yesterday—I guess the caterer cancelled after the dead body was found. Huge big uproar."

"Yeah, that'd be a great idea," I said with a dry laugh, "if it weren't impossible. I'm new around here, and I have no way of getting into that party without seeming suspicious."

"Not unless you start thinking outside the box," Mrs. Beasley said. "I might just have an idea for you."

"I think I'm good on ideas," I said. "They haven't done very well for me lately."

"Well, mine's a real doozy. Do you have one of them cell phones?"

I pulled out the phone and handed it over. "What are you doing, Mrs. Beasley?"

She held up a finger for me to wait as she dialed a number by heart in a painfully slow fashion. Then she raised it to her ear and cleared her throat, waiting as the phone rang. "Mrs. Duvet, this is Mrs. Beasley."

I blanched at the thought of my number appearing on the caller ID of the bride's mother. If Chief Dear found out about this, I'd be in deep trouble.

"Good morning, ladies."

Speak of the devil, I thought, as a low, rumbling voice slid across the table. I looked up to find Cooper Dear standing over the table.

He smiled down at me. "Enjoying breakfast?"

Attempting to split my listening between Mrs. Beasley's conversation and the chief was a daunting task that didn't end well. I mumbled something that sounded like *hewp* and realized I was a failure at multitasking unless the tasks were applying makeup and driving down the 405 at eighty miles an hour.

"Excuse me?" Concern pinched Cooper's brow, as if he suspected I might be suffering a stroke. "Was that English?"

"I meant—ah, we're just enjoying breakfast at June's," I said. "Snowy day out there, huh? Apparently spring is around the corner."

Cooper didn't look impressed with my small talk. "I'd like to speak with you both," he said, nodding to Allie and me. "I swung by the store this morning, and your mother—" he gave me a pointed glance—"very happily directed me here."

"Dang," Allie said. "I knew I should have put my money on the cop."

Chief Dear looked mildly concerned, so I hurried to cover up the awkward silence with a cough. It started as a fake cough, then turned into a real live choking hazard that had my eyes watering until Cooper thumped me on the back.

"I'm done now," Mrs. Beasley declared. "How do you hang up this dratted thing?"

She handed me the phone mid-call, and I quickly hung up and pocketed it before Cooper could glimpse the number. "Er—Chief, we're just finishing up our meal. Maybe we can meet you outside in a second?"

Cooper looked outside at the pelting snow. "I'll see you at the front door."

Mrs. Beasley blatantly admired Cooper's backside as the chief walked to the counter and ordered a piping hot coffee from June. "I wouldn't blame you if you chose the chief," she said, turning back to face me. "By the way, that was Lana's mother on the phone."

"I gathered as much," I said dryly. "What were you doing calling her?"

"Well, you wanted an invite to the bachelorette party, didn't you?" she asked. "You're too new to secure an invitation for yourself, so I did it for you."

"I don't understand," I said. "How'd you secure me an invitation?"

She flashed her pearly whites. "Allie just said they're down a caterer. So, I volunteered your cousin for the job. You can go along as her server."

"What?!" I visibly blanched. "I haven't asked May if she's free! What if she's busy? What if—"

"Tell May I'm asking nicely," Mrs. Beasley said. "Plus, the Duvets have offered to pay a sizeable amount." Mrs. Beasley nabbed the bejeweled pen from my hand, jotted down some numbers on a napkin and slid it across to me. "Have her look at that before she turns down the job."

"Well, even I can bake a cake for that much." I eyed the number on the napkin. "That sort of pay would hold me off for a few months. I could redo the greenhouse and get those new yoga pants I've been eyeing from that fancy new line at Macy's."

"It's up for grabs—if you can convince May, the job is yours." Mrs. Beasley stood, leaned on her walker, and began toddling away. "Now go cuddle that cop of yours before I get to him first."

Chapter 7

As it turned out, Cooper wasn't in a cuddly mood. Then again, neither was I.

After leaving a hefty tip and polishing off the last of my pancakes, June shipped us out the front door with a fresh cup of coffee for the road for me, and a piping hot jasmine tea for Allie. Cooper, Allie, and I all huddled for warmth around our individual beverages as the snowstorm picked up the pace.

"You must've found Grant's body perfectly preserved if he was killed outside," Allie chirped, breaking the silence as we walked. "I mean, with freezing temps, all the evidence must've been intact."

Cooper gave her on odd look. From behind Allie, all I could do was shrug my shoulders. The interestingly dressed bookworm was a mystery to all of us.

"I'm actually here to ask you a few questions," Cooper said to Allie. "I would prefer to do it someplace warm, but—"

"We're fine," Allie interrupted. "But how about we walk and talk because my break is going to be over when we get back to the thrift store, and Bea doesn't appreciate when I sit around talking instead of working."

Cooper cleared his throat. "I'm looking for the owner of a pair of shoes."

"They're not just shoes," I interrupted. "They're gorgeous, powder-blue vintage heels."

"Right." Cooper gave me a glance. "What she said."

"They're mine," Allie said. "I mean, I bought them. Unfortunately, I don't still have them."

Cooper gave her a quizzical stare. "I'm going to need you to expand on that."

So, Allie chattered the rest of the way back to the store—a walk that should have only taken four minutes but took thirteen—thanks to the near white-out blizzard that snuck up and surprised Blueberry Lake.

My legs were exhausted from trudging through snow by the time we reached the store, but I said a quick *praise be* to the shoe gods for May's foresight to give me a pair of ugly, warm Eskimo boots. My socks were somehow still dry, a feat that spared me from intense pain as I began to thaw.

We stepped inside Something Old as Allie finished up her story. She explained how someone had probably mixed up her bag with theirs or, alternatively, stolen it to frame me. She launched into several tangents about the suspects she was considering in her amateur sleuthing, but Cooper didn't seem amused.

"Thank you for that, ah—thorough assessment," Cooper said, trying to ease himself away from Allie. "I think I have all the information I need."

I flexed my fingers until they regained sensation in a very painful way. Little pricks poked every inch of my hands until I was convinced they were dying, one knuckle at a time.

"Is this normal?" I held up my hands. "I can't feel them."

Cooper leaned closer and examined my mittens. They were cute, knitted things I'd gotten from a stoner on Venice Beach in California. I'd foregone the thick puffballs May had given me because they just didn't look good—and the dexterity in them was horrible.

"There are holes in here," he said. "These gloves are just for decoration."

"They're also for warmth," I said. "Why else would they be called mittens?"

"These are not mittens. These are bits of string sort of looped together."

"It's called knitting, Cooper," I said. "Go ask Mrs. Beasley about it."

"I don't think Mrs. Beasley would recommend wearing these during the winter."

I huffed my disagreement and tucked the gloves behind my back. "So, did you get what you needed?"

Cooper glanced around the store, which was delightfully busy thanks to a new shipment of supplies. My mother had already gotten Allie started unpacking some oddly shaped mannequins near the back of the store while a few ladies perused a stack of chunky sweaters along one wall.

When the chief spotted Allie in the distance, he lowered his voice. "Essentially, she thinks half the town could have committed murder."

"Yeah, but did you notice who was absent from the list?" I raised a hand, made a pointer finger, and gestured to my head. "*Me*. My name wasn't on the list. I was already gone by the time the shoes were taken. You have a witness saying she saw the shoes after I left the store. I didn't come back, and both Mrs. Beasley and Allie can vouch for that—so how could I have gotten ahold of the murder weapon?"

"Fine."

"Fine?" I became a little screechy. "What does *fine* mean?"

He scratched at his cheek. "I don't need to discuss this with you any longer."

"Come on, I'm not a suspect anymore." When he didn't answer and merely squinted at me, I got suspicious. "Wait a second—you still don't think this clears my name? How is that possible?"

Cooper shifted his weight from one foot to the next, then took a step backward. "There are other possibilities to consider."

I took a step closer. "Give me an example."

We were very close now—so close I could smell the light scent of our coffees swirling up in a mixture underneath my nose. I caught a whiff of his cologne, as well, and I hated to admit it sent a batch of warm tingles through my body. He smelled like pine, like the hearth of a home and a crackling fire, and freshly chopped wood. I could sniff him all day, but since that would be considered awkward, I refrained.

Cooper had fallen under a similar spell. His head jerked up as I snapped to reality and stepped away. He glanced around, as if surprised to find other people still in the store.

"An example," I prompted. "Theoretically, how could I have gotten the shoes?"

"I don't have to discuss this with you."

"You don't have to, but you're being ridiculous," I told him, which earned me a small smile from Cooper. "If you're so convinced that you're right, then help me to understand why I'm still a suspect. You heard Allie—I'm the red herring."

"This isn't a book, Jenna. This is real life," he said. "Blueberry Lake is nothing like Hollywood—understand?"

His words stung. I hated that they got to me, but it was true. I was new here, and I didn't belong. It's not like I had a ton of friends around these parts who knew and trusted me, believed in the goodness of my heart, and were willing to vouch for me.

Sure, my mom and May defended me, but they were family. That was pretty much a requirement. Allie might believe I wasn't guilty, but she had a puzzle for pants and a well-known imagination, so there was that. Maybe June or Mrs. Beasley had converted to my side, but that was just because they were more interested in my love life than my criminal record.

Cooper blurted out his next question. "Are you coming to bingo tomorrow night?"

I blinked, caught off-guard. "How does that have to do with my innocence or guilt?"

"It doesn't. It's just a question."

"You're trying to distract me," I said. "I'm still waiting to hear how you can possibly believe I got past Mrs. Beasley's hawk-eyed stare back into the shop, stole the shoes, killed Grant, and then made it home in time for you to wake me up from a nap."

Cooper watched me for a long moment, and then he leaned forward and surprised me with a smile. "I'll tell you tomorrow night. See you, Jenna."

He turned and, without another word, disappeared out the door. I moved to the window to watch him walk away, but I lost sight of him after a few seconds. The last thing I saw was him hunching into his coat against the wind as he disappeared into the blizzard.

"Did anyone else just hear that?" I turned to face the rest of the shop and scanned the thin crowd. Slowly, my mother, Allie, and the three ladies pretending to be invested in sweaters all raised their hands to acknowledge their eavesdropping ways. "Good. Then maybe you can tell me if that was him asking me out on a date?"

My mother's shining face said it all. "Oh, darling. I'm so happy for you!"

"That wasn't a clever way to ask a woman out," one of the ladies said, holding a sweater in front of her body. "A man's gotta take control and make it clear he's interested."

"Oh, he's interested," Allie said from behind the counter. "You should've felt the heat radiating off the two of them on the walk over. I stood between them and didn't need a jacket. They were melting snow as it came down. It was like a breath of Hawaii, an afternoon in Greece, a—"

"Enough with the analogies," I said. "There wasn't *that* much heat. In fact, there wasn't any heat at all, thanks to my stupid knitted mittens that are adorably cute and hopelessly useless."

My mother took one look at my pout and shook her finger at me. "Turn that frown upside down, Jenna McGovern. Tomorrow you have your first date with the chief of police."

"I don't know if that qualifies as a *date*," sweater-lady argued lightly. "If I were you, darlin', I'd make him ask me out right and proper. I want flowers and a car door opened for me."

"I suppose it's a good sign either way," I mused. "I mean, if he really thought I killed Grant, he probably wouldn't want to sit next to me at bingo."

Sweater-lady clucked her tongue. "Well, I didn't know you were his *suspect*. That changes everything! It's forbidden love! The cop drawn to a killer."

"Hold your horses—I'm not a killer," I said. "That's what I'm trying to prove."

"Girlfriend, I got your back," Allie said. "I told him you were the red herring, and then I gave him a list of a zillion other suspects that are way better than you. No offense, but you can't even dress yourself for winter weather. I doubt you could murder a man in cold blood."

"Er, thanks?" I said. "I think you've helped plenty today, Allie."

She gave a smug smile. "Oh, I know. You're welcome."

"It's romance," my mother said finally. "He can't stay away from you, dear—not that I blame him. You're irresistible. I mean, I made you myself, so I'm biased, but I think you're great."

"Thanks, mom," I said, rolling my eyes. "But you're just hankering to win the bet against May."

"I was going to put my money on Matt," sweater-lady said, "forced proximity and all. Allie had me convinced you'd pick the neighbor, but after seeing this burst of flames up in here..." She made a hand gesture in the general vicinity of me. "I think I'm changing my tune."

"What are you going to wear tomorrow?" my mother asked. "Shall we pick out an outfit? You can't wear those awful heels with your pajamas."

"Oh, no," I blanched. "I'm not actually going to bingo."

"*What*?" Every head in the store swiveled to face me, but it was sweater-lady who broke the silence first. "Oh, honey, you have to go. If for no other reason than to prove you're not a murderer."

"And to fall in love," my mother added. She pulled a slim dress off a rack and held it against her chest, letting it fan out over her legs. "What do you think about pink? Pink says innocent, doesn't it?"

Chapter 8

My mother succeeded in her mission. She sucked me into the process of trying on every single dress in the store and purchasing ten of them. Then again, it wasn't like I had a ton of clothes to choose from at home—what with my bags being eaten by the airlines.

Allie had tried to encourage me away from dresses and to choose more practical items, but I'd had enough change in my life lately. I couldn't add chunky sweaters into the mix and throw my entire wardrobe off, so I stuck to what I knew best, and that was dresses.

That was how I ended up clomping my way into May's restaurant in a flowing red dress, thick tights, and the worst droopy hair of my life.

"Look what the cat dragged in," May drawled from behind the counter. "Are you alive under there? What happened to the clothes I gave you this morning?"

"They're in the car," I said. "I did some shopping at the store and couldn't carry everything home, so I wore it."

"Uh-huh," May said, sounding unconvinced. "Joe, come say hi to your cousin."

I spun around to find an entire table of men who looked like firefighters staring right at me. Firefighters had a specific look to them—the everyday man with an extra dash of handsome thrown in, probably due to their ability to save cats and babies and women in danger. The shirts that had ***Blueberry***

Lake Fire stamped across them probably helped in my deduction, but I preferred to think I was partly psychic.

Not that I was a woman in need of saving, but if my house caught on fire and I was locked upstairs in Gran's bedroom, I wouldn't mind if one of the strapping young gentlemen sitting at the table climbed through the window to haul my (well-dressed) butt out of the house. That's half the reason I packed an entire duffle bag full of nice pajamas.

One of the men in particular, however, caught my eye. Matt Bridges, June's grandson and my brand-new neighbor. And the other man in my apparent love triangle, thanks to my mother and May. I smiled at Matt because it wasn't his fault he'd been dragged into this mess with me.

While I was awkwardly studying Matt, May's husband rose from his chair and crossed the room. Joe gave me a firm squeeze, and I held him tight as I whispered *Congratulations!* in his ear. I spoke softly because I wasn't sure the news was public, and he responded in turn with a whispered *thank-you* that proved my theory correct.

"It's so good to have you back in town," he said, stepping back and gesturing toward the table. "Do you want to sit down and have a bite to eat? Meet the guys?"

"I've already met one," I said, giving a polite finger wave to Matt. "Howdy, neighbor."

Matt laughed and gave a bigger wave back. "Take a seat—May's food is incredible."

"Don't I know it," I said. "You all are lucky—she tested the worst of her recipes on me back in the day. I recall one very specific mud pie that gave me a stomachache for weeks..."

"She lies!" May called from the kitchen. "I was born to be a chef!"

In a way, she had been born for her career. May had found her niche, opening a homey restaurant that specialized in a Puerto-Rican fusion with American food. While the restaurant served a little bit of everything, May leaned heavily into her family's history and had soon become famous for adding a spice of Latin flavor to the middle of Minnesota.

She served specialty twists on *mofongo* and *arroz con gandules*, as well as a traditional take on *asopao*. For dessert, my favorites were the *coquito cupcakes* and *arroz con dulce*. The thought made my mouth water, despite my excess fullness from June's pancakes and muffin.

I found myself wondering if I'd regret buying a size six in all my new dresses earlier this morning. I'd never be able to give up June's baking or May's cooking. Then again, if I gained weight, I could always buy a whole new wardrobe—and there was nothing I loved more than an excuse to shop.

"I'm stuffed actually," I said. "I just came from June's."

The men groaned in agreement.

"That sounds like an excuse," Joe teased. "I didn't take you for a quitter."

"That is true," I said, "however I'm here on business today."

"Business already? You've barely landed," Joe said. "Don't you want to take a few days to recover?"

"I would, but unfortunately, it's not in the cards," I said. "I have to chat with May, so I'll leave you gentlemen to it."

"You're here on business?" May asked while I took a seat behind the counter. "That can't be good."

"It might be good," I said, digging in my pocket for the napkin on which Mrs. Beasley had written out the large dollar amount. "What do you think about making this much cash?"

"Is that a trick question?" May asked. "I can always use money."

"Think of the baby," I hissed. "You could buy a top of the line stroller with this."

"What's the catch?"

"When I tell you, just remember you fed me mud pie that made me sick for weeks," I said, and then winced at May's stare. "Fine. I need your help catering an event tonight. And by that, I mean—I need you to cater an event tonight, and I'll be in your debt for the rest of my life."

"No," she said shortly. "There's no way. It's Saturday night! We are booked solid with reservations. One of my sous chefs called in sick. I have a server that I was going to fire tonight, but now I can't because we'll be understaffed if I do. I'm sorry, hun, I just can't do it."

"Can I buy all the food and cater it myself?" I asked. "Pretty please?"

"I really could use the money, so I'd do it if it was at all possible," May said, looking genuinely remorseful. "I'm sorry, Jenna—it's just not in the cards. Why is it so important to you, anyway?"

"Long story short, Mrs. Duvet's caterer cancelled last minute on Lana's bachelorette party. Mrs. Beasley made a phone call and got you the job."

"You mean, she got *you* the job—you just need me to do the work."

"You can have all the money!" I waved the napkin around like a magic trick. "I'm not doing it to be paid—I just need to get inside that bachelorette party."

"Is this about Grant's murder?" she asked, lowering her voice. "Jenna, I think you should stay away. Cooper will catch the killer. Everyone knows it's not you, so it's only a matter of time before the truth comes out."

"Maybe," I said. "But just think of the cash. And I'll do whatever it is you need me to do. I'll cook, I'll wear a tutu and serve meals, I'll rub your shoulders so you don't kill me with that look you've got in your eyes right now."

She laughed. "I can't."

"Crap."

"Maybe. That's all I can do for you, okay?" May relented, glancing at the napkin on the table. "We do need a crib, a car seat, and a stroller for starters—and the thought of shelling out for all that is making me ill."

I pushed the figure closer. "It's all yours. I don't want a penny. Plus, look at it this way—everyone in that wedding party is super skinny! I bet they don't eat anything. Mrs. Beasley said to prepare a few appetizers and a dessert. That's it."

"You'll be the server, and you're baking the cake," she said. "I don't do cakes."

"You know I don't bake," I said. "I don't do anything with food except eat it."

"Well, *you* figure it out," she said. "If you do the dessert, I'll agree to cater the rest."

"Fine," I said with a huge sigh. "Maybe June can help with something."

"Or maybe Matt can help," she said, waggling her eyebrows. "Your neighbor is quite talented in the kitchen."

"So I've heard."

"Might as well find out if it's true," she suggested with a wink. Before I could stop her, she called across the restaurant. "Matt, are you off this afternoon?"

"Just finished my shift," he said. "Why?"

"Jenna needs help baking a cake," she said. "Is it all right if she knocks on your door with any questions?"

"I won't have any questions." I spun around and shot Matt an exasperated look. "I know how to bake a cake. Obviously."

For some reason, I didn't want Matt to realize the extent of my undomesticated abilities. It's not as if I was *interested* in him per say, but he was a strong, stable sort of guy. A real man's man, a hard-working fellow who seemed ready to have a family. He could probably build a house *and* bake a cake. I could shop bargains like nobody's business, but I didn't know the first thing about baking.

"Sure thing," Matt said. "Come on by if you need anything—I'll be around."

"There you have it," May said with a smug smile. "I'll get my money and you get your guy."

"You get the money, and I get the gossip at the bachelorette party," I said. "I don't need help with a cake."

"No running off to June and asking her to bake it for you."

"I wouldn't dream of it," I said, annoyed that she'd guessed my exact plan of attack. "See you tonight?"

"Meet here at six," she said, and then gave me an indulgent wink. "Have fun, *sugar*."

Chapter 9

June turned me down flat.

It was almost as if she took *joy* in telling me that she didn't have time to help me with a cake. As I walked home through the storm, huddling against the cold, I couldn't help but wonder if May had called June and told her to reject my pleas for help at all costs in order to force me into Matt's kitchen.

I was probably being completely paranoid, but the closer I got to home, the more I wondered if May and June had been conniving behind my back. *I'll show them*, I thought, kicking open my front door with additional force since it'd all but frozen shut. I'd bake the best darn cake they'd ever seen—all by my lonesome.

At least, that was the plan.

That was also how I ended up outside of Matt's house, my shoulders slumped in defeat as he pulled the door open with an unsurprised grin. "Can I borrow an egg?"

"Just one?" he asked, a smile twitching his cheek upward.

"More like four," I said, scrunching up my nose. "I'm out of eggs. I haven't gone to the store yet—I've sort of been living off your grandmother's muffins."

Matt disappeared, then returned with a carton of eggs. "Take whatever's left—Mrs. Marigold brings by fresh eggs every Tuesday."

"Thank you so much," I gushed in relief. "I swear to you though, I can normally bake a cake."

"I wouldn't care if you couldn't."

"But I can," I insisted. "I definitely have more talents than shopping."

"I didn't know shopping was considered a talent." He leaned against his doorway looking mighty handsome in his firefighter T-shirt and a pair of worn jeans. "Only because I hate doing it myself. Hence the reason I wear this sort of thing."

I found myself studying his physique and the way the clothes hung over his body. "You look great as is," I said, and then blushed. "I mean, you don't need fancy clothes to decorate when your body looks like..." I stopped abruptly and cleared my throat, then raised the carton in a display of gratitude. "Thanks for the eggs."

Matt laughed easily, the sound a nice sort of warmth from the frigid snowfall. "Anytime."

I hurried down his front path in my borrowed boots, careful not to slip and fall this time around. Scurrying back inside my Gran's house, I pulled up a Google recipe titled *Child-proof Vanilla Cake*. I quickly scanned the list of ingredients and began pulling them from the cupboards.

I found flour and sugar. My mother appeared to have stocked a few necessities, but that's where she'd stopped. She had probably remembered how little I actually cooked and therefore left most of the cupboards bare. I couldn't blame her, seeing as reading some of these recipes was like trying to decipher a Russian textbook.

"Mix on low," I murmured aloud to my phone. "What does that *mean*? With a spoon? A fork? Can I substitute an electric mixer for a whisk?"

I dug around under the cupboards and found a mixer, but I determined just seconds later that I was missing butter and powdered sugar. I wasn't sure where to look for baking powder. (Or was it baking *soda*? Was there really a difference?)

This cake was going to be a disaster.

There was no way I was making it to the store, seeing as the snow was drifting and swirling white in every direction. I'd be able to borrow my mother's truck when she got home from work to get to the bachelorette party, but until then, I was stranded.

I was just preparing to crumple in front of the fire and let loose a stream of tears when a knock sounded on the door. Thinking it was my mother here to deliver the car keys early, I whooshed a sigh of relief and stood. I could still *possibly* make it to the store and back, and somehow manage to whip up white-cake-for-dummies before it was time to leave.

"Thanks, mom—you're a lifesaver," I said, pulling the door open. "I love—"

Matt stood on my front steps, snow dotting his dirty-blond hair with flecks of white. "I brought you something."

I tore my eyes away from his face and found a grocery bag filled with supplies in his arms. Inching onto my tiptoes, I peeked inside and quickly read a few labels. Sugar, baking powder (or soda?), and the silvery glint of a pan. Something I hadn't even considered yet.

"What is this?" I asked. "You didn't have to come over here—really, I can do it myself. It's a simple cake."

"May I come inside?" He gave a lopsided smile. "It's chilly on your porch. If you don't want me to stay, I'll head home. I thought you could use some additional ingredients. No getting to the store without a big ol' truck in this weather."

"Oh, um—yes, come inside."

Matt slipped off his boots on the front mat and marched into the kitchen. He dropped the bag gently on the counter and began pulling out a few supplies. Once he had everything organized on the counter, he neatly folded the grocery bag and tucked it under his arm.

"Well, I'll be going now—keep the pan as long as you'd like, and I don't need any of the ingredients back." He smiled in my direction. "If you need additional help, you know where to find me."

"Matt—I don't know what to say." My hands came up and clasped my cheeks of their own accord as I studied the perfectly laid out ingredients. "This is amazing. It's too much."

"Just neighborly assistance," he said, looking uncomfortable at my gratitude. "It's what we do around here. Your grandma would've done the same thing for me."

"That's really sweet," I said. "Are you sure you don't want to stay for a cup of coffee? It's freezing out there."

"I was going to offer my hand in baking, but you seem like you're not too keen on having help." He stood in the kitchen doorway making no move either in or out. "But if you'd like a few tips I picked up from June, I'm available."

"I'm sorry—you probably think I'm the worst neighbor. If you're not busy, I would love some help if you're willing to give it," I said with a wince. "I just didn't want you to think I expected it. May sort of foisted me on you earlier, and I didn't want you to feel pressured into giving up your time this afternoon."

"May didn't foist anything on me," he said, stepping further into the kitchen. "I'm here because I want to be. Believe it or not, I'm a big boy—I can say no. Shall we get started?"

Half an hour later, my kitchen was a disaster. Largely due in part to my inability to correctly work a mixer. My new dress was covered in my own handprints, and Matt's shirt was a poor excuse for clean clothes.

"Look at you," I said, reaching over to brush a handprint from his shoulder. "I'll wash your things. If that's not weird. I just meant, well, I'm sorry I made such a mess of you."

"Stop apologizing." Matt watched as I brushed the handprint away. "I had a great time today."

"Me too." I grinned, meaning it. We'd worked like a team in the kitchen—or, more like a mentor and a clumsy rookie. "I wouldn't have been able to do this without you."

"We don't know if we've done it yet." Matt reached for the bowl of batter and pulled it close to him. "Ready for June's final test?"

"Test? I hate tests."

"You might like this one." Matt dipped a clean spoon into the cake batter and raised it to his lips. He tasted it with his tongue. A slow grin spread across his face, a delightful little smile. "I'd call it a raging success."

"I want to test," I said, looking for a spoon. "I think I can pass a test like this."

Matt had already secured a second spoon and dipped it into the bowl. He extended it to me with a second hand hovering underneath to guard the floor against drips. "Go on, Jenna."

I leaned in, my heart beating faster at the sheer proximity of us. I closed my lips around the spoon. My eyes shut at the brilliant taste of creamy sweet, and I gave a sigh of pleasure.

"Wow," I said. "We made that?"

"We didn't make that," he confirmed. "*You* did."

I rocked with laughter. "Yeah, right. I'd have replaced milk with melted snow and eggs with—I don't even know what. Thank you, Matt. You really are a lifesaver."

"Last step is to pour this in the pan we pre-greased and pop it in the oven. It's already pre-heated, and I'll set the timer before I head out. Just don't fall asleep or leave the house, and it'll be fool proof."

"Nothing is fool proof when I'm involved," I confessed. "Knowing me, you'll be back here to put out a fire before you've taken your boots off."

"It'd be my pleasure." He stopped, crooked an eyebrow. "I mean, don't set anything on fire. If you need a hand, I'd like to help before your kitchen goes up in flames."

I laughed again, enjoying the lightness of my afternoon with Matt, especially after the heaviness of murder that'd clouded my time in Blueberry Lake. Between Cooper's accusations and the airline mishap with my bags, I'd been more stressed than I'd let myself believe.

Add in my lack of income and my rapidly depleting savings account, and I'd become a bundle of nerves. My afternoon in the kitchen with Matt had been refreshing—filled with laughter and sugar and warmth while the snow plunked lightly down outside.

"I think I could get used to having you as a neighbor," I said as I walked Matt to the door. "Thanks again for everything."

"I'm glad to hear it," he said with a wink, "because I don't plan on going anywhere. For what it's worth, if I had any idea Gran's granddaughter would be as..." he hesitated. "As fun, and kind, and as beautiful as you, I would've asked for an introduction a long time ago."

"Gee whiz, I don't know what to say."

"I have two questions for you," Matt said as he slipped into his boots. "May I?"

"Shoot."

"Do you always wear a dress out in a blizzard?"

I glanced down at the red frilly dress I'd picked up at my mother's thrift shop. "Nope, but the airline ate my bags, so I had to buy replacement items."

"And you went with a dress? Don't get me wrong, you look stunning, but..." He glanced over his shoulder. "*Brr.*"

"I'm still on California time. And temperature," I admitted. "And attire. In fact, June told me that spring is just around the corner, so I'm being optimistic."

"June is never wrong about the change in seasons."

"So I've heard. What's your second question?"

"What's the cake for? I mean, I had a blast making it, but I'm sensing some urgency with it. Are you celebrating something?"

"Sort of," I admitted. "I'm helping May with a catering job later tonight."

"It wouldn't be the bachelorette party, would it?"

"How do you know about that?" I narrowed my eyes at him. "Will you be there?"

His eyes twinkled. "Of course not. If you haven't realized, everyone knows everyone's business around town. Lana Duvet hasn't been quiet about wedding plans."

"Figures." I let out the eyeroll before I could help it. Matt saw it, judging by the little smirk on his face, so I quickly continued. "Let's pretend you didn't see that."

"Not a huge fan of Lana?"

"Eh," I said. "I don't want to speak ill of anyone. Like you said, the town's small."

"Gossip goes a long way around here," he said. "Which is why I'm wondering if this has anything to do with Grant Mark's murder?"

"I don't feel like commenting on that."

"I helped with the cake," he said. "Don't I deserve to know what it's for at the very minimum?"

I gave a deep sigh and crossed my arms. "Fine. You seem trustworthy enough, so I'll give you the short story. I'm not a huge fan of Lana because she pulled down my shorts during summer camp. Which is mortifying when you're a kid and wearing underpants that spell the day of the week on them."

"Yeah, I'd imagine that's not easy to live down."

I rolled my eyes. "I was called Tuesday for a year."

He laughed, then covered it up with a muffled cough. "I'm sorry—that's not really funny."

"It's fine." I gave a dry smile. "It's funny now, but it wasn't then. So yeah, I wasn't exactly pleased to hear about her wedding when I came back. Then her best man goes and gets himself killed, and I'm a suspect in his murder? The whole thing is unpleasant. I feel like the only way to get a fresh start in Blueberry Lake is to uncover the truth about what actually happened."

"I don't think anyone believes you killed Grant," Matt said. "I spend a good amount of time with June, and she thinks you're innocent. If June's on your side, you've got the weight of Blueberry Lake behind you. Her vote is important on matters of public gossip."

"Well, that's good to know. Thank goodness for your family, or I'd be a leper," I said. "In a red dress because I can't even clothe myself properly for the seasons."

"For what it's worth, I think you look perfect," he said. "I am just worried about your knees getting frostbitten the second you step outside."

A moment of awkward silence took over. Matt's eyes flicked to my face and lingered until I looked away. I wasn't exactly ready for romance, but Matt was giving off some interested vibes. It's a shame I was still recovering from a bad breakup. Otherwise, he would've been perfect dating material.

Finally, he broke the silence and turned the door handle. "I'm going to head home, but if you need anything—give me a call. I left my number on the counter."

As he stepped outside, I waved goodbye and closed the door behind him, thinking it looked like a true winter wonderland outside. The fresh coating of brilliant white on everything—the greenhouse, the yard, the deck—made me think of Christmas all over again. In a way, it was as if this quiet blanket was laying the groundwork for a fresh start in all things: romance, hometown, and career.

With a smile, I turned to the oven and glanced at the timer. Twenty-four minutes to go, and I'd have a perfect cake courtesy of my next-to-perfect neighbor.

Humming a little ditty, I ran upstairs to shower quickly before the cake finished. While the snow shone brightly outside, all that glittered was not yet gold. There was still a murder to be solved—and so long as Cooper hadn't arrested anyone, I wasn't in the clear.

Worse yet? I *knew* I hadn't killed anyone. Which meant that whoever had killed Grant Mark was still on the loose. A murderer hid among us—roaming free through Blueberry Lake. Was it only a matter of time before he or she struck again?

Chapter 10

"Oh, this is *so* not a good idea," May grumbled as I pulled up in front of the address to the Duvet residence. "There's no way this ends well."

"Since when have we ever gone along with all the good ideas?" I chirped. "We seem to excel at the troublesome ones."

"Yeah, but this is the Duvets we're talking about. They're rich and snotty and powerful."

"June is more powerful," I said, regurgitating the line Matt had used on me earlier. "If anyone's opinion holds weight in this town, it's June's. And she was there when we organized this whole thing. Mrs. Beasley is the one who got you the job."

May gave me a perceptive glance. "You're right. But I'm suspicious—who told you all that about June's word being the voice of reason in the gossip mill?"

I realized my misstep too late. Under my cousin's dark and threatening stare, I exhaled loudly and spilled. "I begged Matt to help me bake the cake this afternoon."

"I knew it!" She pointed a finger at me as I threw the truck into park. "I knew you didn't bake that beauty all on your own."

"No, but I frosted it. Sort of," I said, which was also a lie. Matt had conveniently popped back over with some misplaced mail just in time to help me frost the thing. We'd both pretended it had been fate, when really, I knew it was his thoughtfulness. (Or pity, but I'd take it all the same.)

"Right," May said, her voice edging toward conspiratorial. "So, tell me about it! What happened?"

"What do you mean?"

"Was there hand holding? Kissing? Romance in the air?" she asked. "That's how people fall in love, you know, doing these little things that turn into big things. Isn't he a hunk?"

"He's a good man," I agreed, realizing I was drawn more toward his sturdy gentleness than his looks, though he wasn't exactly an eyesore. "He's really nice, but I'm not looking for anything romantic at the moment."

"Don't tell me you're into Cooper!" May rounded on me. "You have Matt practically bending over backward to help you get this cake ready—if you give me the *he's too nice* argument I'm going to flip out. You want to marry the nice man, Jenna. Not the bad boys."

"First, Cooper doesn't strike me as a bad boy. Second, who says I go for bad boys, anyway?"

"Your last boyfriend was *such* a nice guy."

"I thought he was," I said defensively. "You know, for a while at least."

"Uh-huh." May hopped out of the truck and began gathering trays of food into her arms. "Sure. Look me in the eyes and say that."

"He was nice on our first date," I said. "And then things moved along really quickly. We had chemistry."

"I'm not going to lecture you, I'm just saying—be open to a different sort of guy." May gave me a wink. "You might find he's just what you're looking for. Take my Joe for example. He's nothing like the boys I used to date. He's a real man, you know? He's smart and sexy and all that, but he's also there for me. He's going to be the best father."

"I know all that! Joe is great for you, but I'm not looking for anything at all. That's the difference."

"That's when you always find it," she said knowingly. "Grab the appetizers—we'll leave the cake out here for a minute because it'll stay frozen anyway."

The two of us picked our way through the freshly shoveled walkway up to the looming front door of the Duvet house. Though the path had probably been shoveled less than thirty minutes before, there was already a light dusting of snow in which our footprints lingered.

I had chosen to wear my (freshly laundered) outfit that I'd worn on my flight to Minneapolis. Black pants, black shirt—it was the most official looking attire I had with me that also covered my legs, helping to avoid frostbitten knees. I still wasn't completely certain if Matt had been making a joke, but I didn't want to take the risk. (Wouldn't that be horrible if my knees turned all knobby and black because I'd worn a dress and tights in a blizzard?)

May had opted for a similar outfit except she'd gone with a starched white shirt instead of my flowy black one. This wasn't her first rodeo at catering events, and she handled everything with pure professionalism. I owed her a huge favor, and I told her so again. I had no doubt she'd make me pay her back in a big way. I groaned at the very thought of it.

The door opened to reveal Mrs. Duvet standing before us in an outfit of smart black and white—a tight pencil skirt leading into a breezy top with long, gauzy sleeves that flared out at the wrists. She could either be going to a charity gala or a job interview, but not hosting a bachelorette party. Unless all the bachelorette parties I'd been to so far had been doing things wrong.

"Thank you for covering at the last minute," Mrs. Duvet said crisply, speaking only to May. "It was a relief when Mrs. Beasley rang this morning after our original caterer cancelled."

"Yeah, it was quite a surprise," May said dryly, choosing not to look at me. "But it's my pleasure. Where should we set up?"

Mrs. Duvet led us through her home—a place that lacked any of the charm of Gran's old farm house and all the sleek fixings that could be found in a Pottery Barn catalogue. I wondered if she hadn't paid a staging company to come in and make her house look like a studio set. It had that same empty, unlived in feeling.

"Here we are," Mrs. Duvet said, gesturing to a long white table covered by linens so expensive my fingers longed to touch them. It was all prepped for wine spills and sauce stains. *Pity.* "The guests will be arriving in half an hour. We'll do cocktail hour first, and I'd appreciate if you—" she paused to give a pathetic sort of glance toward me—"wouldn't mind carrying trays of the signature cocktail around?"

"Of course not," I said, bowing my head. (Don't ask me *why* I bowed—I don't have an explanation.) "It'd be my pleasure. What would you like me to serve for the signature beverages?"

"Champagne flutes and The Lana," Mrs. Duvet said. "We had an adorable custom mimosa concocted for the bride-to-be. "It's over in the kitchen. I'll leave you to set up. Oh, before I forget—I have this for you."

Mrs. Duvet slid May a tidy envelope which I imagined housed a check. Once the hostess disappeared, May cracked open the envelope and peeked at the sum written on the line.

"Well?" I asked. "Is it all there?"

Her eyebrows raised slightly. "With a nice tip. *Fine*, I won't make you pay for throwing this on me last minute. We'll be able to get that fancy new jogging stroller I've always wanted."

"I thought you didn't jog."

"I don't," May said smoothly. "But I'm optimistic that might change."

"Touché," I said. "Maybe I'll try jogging with you."

May and I exchanged glances with one another and then burst into laughter.

"Yeah, okay," I said, wiping tears from my eyes. "That was fun. Now, direct me, boss. What should I set up?"

The setup time passed quickly. May was just fixing cutesy little umbrellas into the tops of the finger foods when the doorbell chime sounded and guests began flooding in one by one. I leapt for the silver tray on which I'd loaded halfway with champagne flutes, and halfway with The Lana signature cocktail, and rushed toward the top of the steps.

The drinks teetered precariously. I clamped my lips together, balancing them steadily with every atom in my body. The last thing I needed was to get kicked out of the house for clumsy catering just when all the prime suspects were arriving.

"Oh, *there* you are—give me one of those prissy things," a brash voice called. "Yes, you, with the alcohol. Bring me two, why don't you?"

I slid closer to a woman with fiery red hair and brilliant blue eyes. "Which would you like?"

"What in the world are those?" she asked, squinting at the bubbling pink drink. "Looks like a love potion to me."

"It's called The Lana." I cleared my throat, trying not to feel silly. "Would you like to try one?"

The woman gave me a quizzical look. "That's about the last thing I want. Give me one of the champagnes. Nah, make it two."

I handed over two and sidled closer to her as the hallway flooded with a burst of guests. "I'm Jenna, the caterer's assistant. How do you know the bride and groom?"

"I'm the groom's cousin—Patty," she said. "I moved to town for a man, oh, five years ago. I lost the man but kept the house, so I'm still here."

"I'm sorry," I said, watching as she sucked down the first glass. "Do you live in Blueberry Lake then?"

"Oh, it's no loss for me. I'm over in Butternut Bay," she said, waving a hand in the general direction of the door. "As a matter of fact, I lived right down Shepherd's Way from Grant. The fellow who ended up dead."

"I heard it was gruesome," I said, hoping to fuel the gossip flame. If I remembered correctly, Allie had mentioned that Patty had been drinking before the thrift store trip the other day and had acquired a set of loose lips. I reached out and took the empty champagne glass from her hand as she reached for another. "Horrible, huh?"

"I suppose, but the man had it coming."

"How do you figure?" I asked, completely ignoring the rest of the guests as I leaned closer to Patty. "I only met him once and he seemed—" I hesitated, trying not to speak ill of the dead. It was difficult. "He seemed a little pushy."

She gave a croaking laugh. "Difficult, sure. You mean a creep who couldn't keep his hands to himself? That's more like it. Ask me who wanted the man dead, and I'll give you a list as long as my arm."

I paused in the discussion for a moment to quickly offer a round of Lana beverages to the rest of the bridal party as they arrived. By the time I'd finished, Patty was ready for me to collect her second champagne flute while she started on the third. "Does that mean you have some idea who might have killed him?"

"Idea? I have ideas—plural," she said, squinting as she glanced around the room. "Probably someone here tonight, frankly. Unless it was Greg."

"Greg is..."

"The groom," she said. "My cousin. Greg can be very jealous, and Grant was known to be handsy. If Grant ever took a pass at Lana, I could see Greg flying off the handle."

"What about the women?" I asked, dancing delicately around the question as I super-secretly herded Patty toward the corner of the room for a more private chat. "Do you think any of them could've done it?"

Patty pursed her lips as she swallowed a big gulp. "Yeah, sure. Any of them, really. Who would you like me to start with? Why are you so curious, anyway?"

"Just making small talk," I said quickly. "I'm new to town and don't know many people. It's hard for me to get acquainted in such a small town where everyone already knows everyone else. Why don't we start with Mrs. Duvet?"

Patty blinked. "Didn't expect you to go straight for the jugular, but yeah—the mother of the bride would be one of my prime candidates. She does anything her baby girl wants—apparently going so far as to name a pink drink after her. I'm telling you, Lana does no wrong in her mother's eyes."

"How does that have anything to do with murder?"

"Well, I'll tell you this—Lana was *not* happy when Greg named Grant to be his best man."

"Why not?" I asked, stealing a glance at the bride as she entered through the front door amidst a flurry of hugs and cheek kisses and white streamers. "What'd Grant do to her?"

"What'd Grant do to her *sister*, you mean," Patty said, pointing to a pretty, brown-haired woman standing in the corner by herself. "That's Eliza Duvet—she's a sweet thing, I have to say. Somehow she didn't inherit the stick shoved you-know-where like the rest of the Duvet family."

I caught sight of May giving me a dangerous-looking stare as I bit back a laugh, but I quickly ducked from her gaze and swiveled back to Patty. It was hard to say how much longer she'd last before taking a nap on the couch, and I had to maximize my time with her.

"What happened between Eliza and Grant?"

"He asked her out on a date," Patty said, lowering her voice. "And got too grabby at dinner. Eliza was pretty upset about it. In fact, it caused a huge row between Greg and Lana—they almost called off the wedding when Greg named Grant his best man."

"How did Greg and Grant know one another?"

"College buddies," Patty said with a shrug. "Old bros. Greg didn't back down. That's why I think either Lana or her mother could've done it—they both wanted him out of the wedding badly enough and made it quite public."

"Yikes. That's one messy bridal party."

"You don't even know the half of it," Patty said. "See Becky over there? She dated *both* Greg and Grant."

"The groom and the best man?" I asked, squinting at the nondescript blonde shaking hands with Lana's mother, Bridget. "Why is she a bridesmaid then?"

"She was Lana's roommate. I guess quite some time has passed since she dated Greg, but I think she just broke up with Grant a few weeks back."

"Is there anyone who *didn't* have a reason to kill Grant?" I asked, trying to contain my shock and awe. "I sort of understand what you meant when you said the man had it coming."

"I don't think Eliza did it—she's too much of a quiet little mouse. And Becky seems completely over both men, so I doubt she had a real reason to kill anyone. That there—Brenda Kern—well, the *new* Mrs. Duvet, I should say. She's Lana's stepmother, and probably the only other person here with a pity invite."

"What do you mean, other person?"

"Well, I've got the pity invite!" Patty roared with laughter. "If I weren't related, there's no way I'd be here. And Brenda's only here because she married Will."

"Will is Lana's father?"

"You've got that right. Nobody was surprised when he left the wicked witch."

"You mean Mrs. Duvet?"

"The one and only," she said. "Bridget was always too...uptight for him. Not that I know them well, but even I could see from a mile away they were headed toward a divorce."

"How long ago did Lana's parents get divorced?" I asked. "Like I said, I've just arrived in town, so this is all breaking news to me."

Settling into her role as gossip-giver, Patty grinned. "I like you. Why don't you have a little sip of The Lana? Let me know if it's ghastly."

"Er—"

"Nobody will care," Patty said. "I've been dying to try it, but to be honest, I'm terrified."

Feeling a strong pull to taste test The Lana beverage for my—or rather, for May's clients—I dutifully took a sip. Sizing it up, I gave a nod, pouted my lips. "You know, not all that bad. Little sweet—oddly sour. I wonder if there's grapefruit juice in there?"

"Ah, all right then—let me have one."

I handed over a Lana to Patty and waited as she took a few big gulps.

"I think it was three years back now," she said, resuming the Duvet divorce story without further ado. "It wasn't a surprise to anyone, but it was still news. I mean, they're a very well-to-do sort of family, so every time they sneeze it seems to make the local news."

"Was it amicable?"

"I suppose as amicable as it gets," she said. "I'm not sure they ever loved each other—their marriage was one of those sorts of 'clock's ticking, dear' sort of things."

"Was Bridget upset when her ex-husband remarried?"

"She wasn't happy about it, but at the same time, Brenda is a nobody in her eyes. A real step down in terms of the social ladder. It probably annoyed her more than anything."

I studied Brenda Duvet—the replacement wife—for a second, then turned my gaze toward the former Mrs. Duvet. Where the latter was all starched clothes and black and white colors, Brenda was rounder and more colorful, with a frumpy sort of sweater-dress in a shade of green that clashed totally with her hair-color.

"I'm itching to get my hands on her wardrobe," I said, nodding to Brenda. Then I swung the nod around to Bridget Duvet. "Hers too, actually. I think a change in clothes could really do wonders for both women."

"Hey, you're that Hollywood chick!" Patty stared at me with wide eyes. "What are you doing slinging drinks at a cocktail party?"

"I'm helping out my cousin," I said nodding to May. "New to town, still deciding what I want to do for work. That sort of thing."

"Wait a second—aren't you the stylist who threatened Grant right before his head popped off?"

"I don't think his head popped off," I said. "But yes, I did see him that morning—"

"Only the killer would know his head didn't pop off." Patty lowered her voice, leaned in close. "Tell me—did you do it? I won't tattle on you. Frankly, the man deserved it. I already told you that."

"I didn't kill anyone!" I said, though my voice came out slightly too shrill and the rest of the room glanced at me. "—er, with kindness." I struggled to recover. "Kill them with kindness, ah—who wants more Lanas?"

I raised my tray and left Patty's side, scurrying around the room to deposit the beverages while attempting to avoid May's murderous stare. When I was fresh out of drinks except for the one I'd personally adopted, I made my way over to the buffet table where May was replenishing the appetizers.

"What was that all about?" she hissed. "I thought you were going for discreet. And what is that in your hand?"

"Um, The Lana?" I raised the half-empty glass. "I was having a chat with Patty! It's a social drink."

"This isn't social hour," May said. "You're working."

"Working with the *intent* to solve a murder," I said in my most convincing voice. "You won't have help catering if I end up behind bars, dear cousin."

"You won't have a job if you keep sipping while you work," she said. "And what is with the dead body talk? At least keep things discreet."

"It's the topic *du'jour*," I said. "Everyone's curious. Why don't you try this?"

I extended the pink drink to May who looked utterly appalled and shook her head. "Pregnant, remember?"

"Oh, right. That's why I should have yours. I mean, if the customers ask me what it tastes like, how am I supposed to describe it to them?" I ignored her huge eye roll and took a sip. "Don't you agree?"

"Just get the cake from the car. It'll be properly chilled by now. I still can't believe you and Matt pulled that thing off."

"Yes, well," I said, raising a glass of The Lana toward May. "Magic."

Chapter 11

The appetizers were a raging success. The main course went over with rave reviews. By the time we displayed the cake on the table, the party was well underway with a pleasant little hum. Glasses of The Lana and flutes of champagne had been passed around generously while the guests had inhaled May's cooking.

With full stomachs and beverages in hand, the festivities split into little pockets of chatter as May and I set to cutting the cake. Matt had a way with baking, that much was clear. Though we'd only had a few hours to prepare the dessert, he'd fashioned something worthy of a Beverly Hills bakery in my humble (and very barren) little kitchen.

He'd crafted a cute little phrase that said: *Sip, Sip, Hooray*! onto the cake, along with a tiny little bride and groom figure he'd mysteriously pulled from somewhere. Apparently, it wasn't his first bridal party rodeo.

"He gets roped in to help with cakes all the time," May explained, straightening the happy groom and bride figurines. "June probably stashes all of her decorating supplies at his house. He did an incredible job."

"I helped," I said with a faux-pout. "I taste-tested it."

May gave me a sideways grin. "I'll bet you helped—by keeping Matt's morale up. Are you going to see him again?"

"I'm sure. I mean, he's my neighbor. I can hardly walk out to the car without seeing him if he's in his yard."

"You know what I mean."

"This wasn't a date," I argued. "It was dire circumstances, and he was a true hero. He's meant to be a fireman."

"Right. Just like Joe. And he makes great husband material, if I may say so myself."

"We baked a cake together for crying out loud! We're not moving in with each other," I said. "*Yeesh*. I'm fresh off a breakup. Give me some space."

"Fine, but you're almost thirty."

"And you're..." I hesitated, striking out. She was almost thirty, but she was happily married, pregnant, with a good career well underway. "You're perfect. It's not fair."

She laughed. "Not in the slightest—I just like meddling in your life. Okay, time to start serving. People are getting antsy for sugar."

Photos of the cake had already been taken by the time I began cutting into it. Mrs. Duvet wandered over and tried her best not to look impressed. "Which bakery provided the cake? It was short notice."

"Yep, *ah*—it's a new place," I said, glancing over Bridget's shoulder at May. "You probably haven't heard of it."

"What's the name?" Bridget raised a perfectly manicured eyebrow. "I'm always looking for a new bake shop to supply desserts for book club, town halls, you name it."

"Er—yeah, it's a small shop," I said, struggling for a name. For some reason, I doubted she'd be impressed if I told her I baked it in my kitchen after begging my neighbor for help. "Matt *à la Mode*."

"You're right, I've never heard of it. I'll have to look them up," she said, sneaking a piece of cake from the table and bringing it to her lips. "It smells... edible."

Mrs. Duvet made her way back to the cocktail tables situated discreetly against the living room window. I watched with curiosity as she took another sniff of the frosting and looked mildly interested. Then she reached for a dainty, pearl-encrusted fork and sliced off the tiniest bite known to mankind. She tasted it, puckered her lips delicately, and swallowed. Then pushed the cake away from her.

"That's about the highest compliment you'll get from her," May said, inching next to my shoulder. "If she says something is edible, that's the equivalent of earning your Michelin stars."

"She only had a nibble," I said. "Now she's off talking to her daughters."

"She normally won't even hold a slice of cake in her hand," May whispered. "How do you think her hips are so trim? Here, go drop these off to her daughters. Bride gets cake first, even though she won't eat it either."

"What a waste," I said with a pout. "I worked really hard on this."

"Sure you did," May said. "You and *Matt à la Mode*."

"I had to scramble, okay?"

"And that's the best you could come up with?"

I grabbed the two proffered plates of dessert and made my way over toward the bride, the maid of honor, and their mother. As I neared, a snippet of conversation filtered across the room that had me stopping dead in my tracks.

"—don't know why she's still here," Lana was saying. "She's only in the wedding out of courtesy."

"Why'd you invite her in the first place?" Eliza asked. "I told you it would be a bad idea."

"She was my best friend and roommate. It would have been obvious I didn't like her if I left her out."

"She's dated everyone in the wedding party," Mrs. Duvet said. "It would be understandable. But then again, you've already asked her to be your bridesmaid—and there would be tongues wagging if you gave her the boot now."

"What if *she* did it?" Eliza asked. "Like that cop said, it might be someone we know. Can you imagine?"

"I can't have a murderer in my wedding party," Lana said, but her voice sounded flat. "That would be a disaster."

I sucked in a breath as I realized the women were likely discussing Becky, the pretty blond woman who'd been seen peeking in the bags at my mother's thrift shop. The same woman Patty had just told me had dated both Grant and Greg.

I blinked, forcing my attention back to the conversation between the Duvets. Eliza sounded adamant in her belief it was Becky who'd killed Grant. I couldn't say if Becky was innocent or guilty since I'd never spoken with her, but if I had to guess, Eliza was innocent. Judging by her shoes, which were way too cute to belong to a killer.

Lana hadn't seemed all that interested in pursuing the topic of Grant's murder, which I took to mean she was either completely clueless and bored of the subject, or she was trying to squash any further discussion of it. Could Lana have killed Grant?

"Is that piece of cake for the bride?" Bridget asked when she saw me standing in the middle of the room staring dumbly at the three of them. "Bring it on over, will you?"

I hurried forward, trying to gauge whether she guessed I'd been listening. A chill slid over my spine as I realized I needed to pay more attention—for my own safety. If the murderer really was in this room and sensed I was onto them, that would equal bad news for me. Instead of an orange jumpsuit, I might be caught flaunting a power suit during my own funeral.

I couldn't fathom the idea of being buried in a power suit. I made a quick note to edit (or rather, create) a living will that banned my mother from dressing me in a suit in the unlikely event of my death. I would prefer to be buried in new Louis Vuitton heels, Brenda Blake accessories, and could she *please* make sure to touch up my roots. I'd make that part official the second I got home.

"Miss Duvet," I said, extending a piece of cake toward Lana. "Congratulations to you! And Eliza, here's yours."

I distributed both cakes. Thankfully, it didn't appear the three women had been paying me any mind at all except as hired help. With a breath of relief, I headed back to get plates of cake for the rest of the ladies. I came to a halt as I felt a set of eyes on my back. When I turned, I found Becky staring at me. The unblinking eye contact threw me off kilter, and it was all I could do to tear my eyes away and return to May's side.

"Do you think anything is off with that woman?" I gave a subtle head nod toward Becky. "I think she was staring at me."

"Um, because you're dangling dessert in front of everyone's faces and not delivering it?" May shoved a silver serving platter full of cake slices toward me. "Get to work handing these out and people will stop drooling over you."

"I think she's onto me." I adjusted the tray on my hand and lowered my voice. "I think she knows I'm here looking into the murder."

"You're being paranoid." May shooed me away from the table as she began cleaning up the finger foods. "Everyone is having a lovely time and just wants their sweets!"

I began passing out desserts (two pieces for Patty, one for the rest of the ladies), saving Becky for last. Something about the way she'd been staring at me had felt too personal. As if she'd recognized me or suspected me of something. Maybe May was right and I was just being paranoid, or maybe she'd heard the Duvet women talking about her and assumed I had been, as well. Whatever the reason, it gave me goosebumps that hadn't quite vanished by the time I approached her.

"Would you like a slice?" I asked, extending the remaining plate to her. "Saved the best for last—that one has a particularly good bit of frosting on it if you ask me. My favorite part."

She raised a hand in a stop gesture. "I think I'll pass."

"Wedding diet?" I said, trying for a smile. "Diets are the worst."

Becky was still staring curiously at me. I glanced around, but Becky's hand snuck out and rested on my wrist, pausing me in my tracks.

"Were you the one who saw Grant before he died?" Becky asked in a low tone. "You look familiar to me, but I can't recall your name."

"Jenna McGovern," I said. "Greta Green's granddaughter."

"Right. I heard you went out with Grant on a date."

"A date? No, not even close." I visibly blanched at the thought. "I met him briefly, yes, but we were nothing more than strangers."

Becky made a noise of disbelief in her throat.

My frustration got the better of me, and in true Jenna McGovern form, I failed to keep my mouth shut. "I'm sorry, but you don't seem to believe me. Did someone say otherwise?"

"No, no," she said loftily. "I'd just heard you two were acquainted."

"From who? Did you talk to Grant recently?"

"No, of course not," she said sharply. "I haven't seen him for months."

"How did you know him?"

"We dated," she said quickly. "In a very brief capacity. Like you said, we were almost strangers."

I didn't believe her, but I couldn't put my finger on why. Becky's whole demeanor was just a bit off—a bit too aggressive. Something wasn't adding up, but I sensed now was not the time to press.

I glanced over toward May, relieved to find her wrapping up leftovers and preparing to head out. We'd almost made it through the party unscathed, and I couldn't ruin things now.

"Well, I guess I should help May clean up," I said. "It was nice to meet you."

"You're not staying for the gifts?" she asked, sounding innocent. "That's the best part."

I gave a dry laugh. "I don't think we can stick around. May keeps quite busy at her restaurant, and it is a Saturday night."

"What about you?"

I had one foot stepped away already, but her awkward question held me in place. "Me? I'm not so busy on a Saturday, but we rode together. Speaking of, it sounds like I'm needed. Enjoy the party."

I sidled over toward May and pretended to putz with a roll of cling wrap.

"How well do you know Becky?" I asked.

"You're being paranoid," May intoned under her breath, picking up a stack of leftovers. "Grab the other bunch—we'll put them in the fridge."

"It's not paranoia," I said as we shuffled through the crowd and stocked the Duvet's fridge with enough food to feed a family of five for a week. "She gave me strange vibes."

"Fine. Either way, it's time for us to go. How about getting the rest of those drinks off the tray?" May nodded to the last of the champagnes and The Lanas. "I'm going to load the dishes into the truck, and then I'll come back inside to say goodbye. No more pestering the guests, okay? Let them enjoy the wedding festivities."

I grabbed the silver tray, this time determined to follow May's directions to a tee. Unobtrusively, I worked my way into the living room and began passing out beverages to those standing around the corner.

"First gift is from my sister, Eliza," Lana said with a brilliant smile. "Thank you, hun."

"Open it," Eliza said with a giggle, "and then thank me."

"Don't tell me it's edible underpants," Patty blurted out. "That's what I got her."

Mrs. Duvet frowned. "I sure hope you're kidding. This is my daughter we're talking about."

"Mother," Eliza said, blushing. "It's a bachelorette party. Relax—have some fun!"

Mrs. Duvet dug around in the presents, presumably looking for Patty's gift, and quietly kicked it under the couch. The rest of the group's attention was on Lana as she pulled open an exquisite lingerie set of white lace and frills.

I couldn't help but gasp as I recognized the label. "La Perla?!" I held a hand to my chest and the drinks wobbled. "That is gorgeous. Can I invite you to my bachelorette party when the time comes? I have been wanting one of those sets for ages."

"Don't be ridiculous," Mrs. Duvet said. "You don't have a boyfriend. Who would you use any such thing on?"

"Herself!" Patty blurted. She was three sheets to the wind and halfway to cross-eyed. "The woman doesn't need a man in order to wear nice lingerie. Look at me! I've got on...let's see here, what have I got on?"

Mrs. Duvet inhaled a sharp breath as Patty peeked down her pants to determine exactly what she was wearing underneath. Most of the group was looking at the commotion, save for one set of eyes that were stuck on me.

I glanced over to find Becky watching me carefully. Her eyes were wide, and her lips formed a nasty little pout. Was I really the only one to think there was more to Becky than what met the eye?

Remembering May's warning, I did my best to look away and ignore her, unloading a few more Lanas off to the bride and her maid of honor. But a call from across the room drew my attention as Becky raised her hand.

"Excuse me, I think I got skipped," Becky called. "May I get another champagne?"

"Er—sorry about that," I said, and picked my way carefully through the tissue strewn floor. "Of course. I have three champagnes and two Lanas. Which would you prefer—*ooomph*!"

I saw Becky's foot kick out toward me, but it was too late for me to recover. Becky's little stockinged sole planted itself right in my path and swept forward. Just enough to wedge my legs off balance and send the tray shooting forward while I tumbled beneath it.

I scrambled to catch the beverages, but I didn't have a chance in Hades at success. The silver made a loud crack as it clattered into the wall, and two of the five flutes shattered instantly. The other three glasses spilled golden and pink liquids across the white carpeting, leaving glaring stains in the shape of blood spatters.

"Oh, goodness," Becky said. "Are you okay? Must have snagged a toe on the carpet or something, there. Did you hurt yourself?"

Becky extended a hand to help me up, but I refused, shrinking away from her. "You tripped me," I said under my breath. "What did I ever do to you?"

"Jenna?" May's horrified voice rang out over the hallway as she returned from loading up the car. "What happened here?!"

"I didn't—did anyone else see that?" I scrambled to my feet, waving an arm. "I was tripped! She tripped me!"

Mrs. Duvet appeared livid, while the rest of the party looked mildly uncomfortable at the confrontation. Nobody vouched for me, and while that wasn't a surprise, I felt my fingers trembling at the sheer unfairness of it all.

"What did I ever do to you?" I turned to Becky, trying to keep my voice low. "I was just trying to bring you a drink. You didn't have to take my legs out from under me."

"Jenna." May's voice was firm. "I think it's time for us to go."

May climbed the stairs while dipping a hand into her pocket. She removed the check Mrs. Duvet had handed her at the beginning of the party and returned it without a glance.

"Please use this to get your carpets cleaned and purchase replacement glasses," she said politely. "If the bill comes to more, send it to the restaurant, and we'll take care of it."

I had no choice but to follow May out of the house. Despite her businesslike handling of the situation, I could feel her frustration bubbling under the surface. The worst part was that I didn't blame her one bit.

As we climbed in the truck, May took the keys from me, and I slid into the passenger's seat. I could barely look at her as I began my profusive apologies.

"I'm so sorry," I said, feeling tears prick at my eyes. "I know I screwed up in a big way. I shouldn't have foisted this event on you, and I shouldn't have made you cater something on a Saturday night when you were already so busy."

May's fingers gripped the steering wheel tightly, but her face gave away no emotion.

"I shouldn't have been talking to all those people at the party, and I maybe shouldn't have had two Lanas."

"Two?"

"Moving on," I said. "I really apologize for making a mess of things in every way, but I swear to you—I didn't fall. Becky purposefully tripped me."

"I know."

"I swear, May—wait." I turned to my cousin. "What did you say?"

"I said I *know*." She gave a reluctant grin. "I believe you."

"I thought you were angry?"

"It's annoying we don't get paid for the gig, but I think you're right. Something weird is going on in that house." She shifted slightly and pulled her purse out from between the seats. "Open that."

I carefully unzipped May's purse and spotted a piece of paper on top with neat handwriting on it. Squinting, I studied it for a moment—wondering why the words there looked so familiar. Then, it hit me. "Wait a minute—that's my address. *Gran's* address! Where did you find this?"

"Look at what's underneath it."

I pulled the paper out and found a photo underneath. I blinked and shook it, as if expecting the image to change like a freshly printed Polaroid. "What is this? And where did you get it?"

"I found it when I went into the bedroom to get my coat. Mrs. Duvet tossed all our jackets together, and so I had to dig to the bottom to get mine. This was hanging out of the pocket of another coat."

"It could have been anyone's coat!"

"It was a pink fluffy one. It belongs to Becky."

"Becky has a photo of me? Why?"

"Exactly what I was wondering," May said with a smug smile. "When I said I was loading up the car, I thought I'd check things out a bit. After you said Becky was acting oddly, I watched her myself. She seemed weirdly keen on staring you down all evening."

"So, I'm not crazy?!"

"I don't think so," May said with a small smile. "I'm sorry I didn't believe you right away. It's just, I've never heard a lick of gossip about her except that she was Lana's roommate and dated Greg and Grant in past lives."

"Apparently, Grant wasn't such a past life," I said, holding the photo closer to my face and studying it. "Do you think she was following him around?"

"Either him or you," she said. "Why else would she be taking photos through the windows of your mother's thrift shop?"

I glanced once more at the image of Grant and I facing off near the dressing room. The photograph had been snapped from outside the shop through the windows. On my face was a look of surprise—it must have been right after Grant had tried to flirt with me and before I'd registered disgust. Grant, however, had his hand on me and was looking mighty interested.

Something a jealous ex-lover might not be excited to see, I thought.

"Do you really think Becky could have killed Grant?" I asked. "I didn't think she had it in her."

"A woman scorned..." May frowned. "I can't remember the rest of it. But you catch my drift. Something about fury and whatnot."

"Love hath no fury...?" I frowned. "We really should have paid more attention during the plays we put on at summer camp."

May laughed.

"I'm sorry," I said again. "It means a lot that you believe me, but I still can't help feeling like I ruined our night. I'll pay you back as soon as I get a job, I swear. I don't have all the funds yet, but I'm good for it—you know where to find me."

"I'll tell you what: If you host the baby shower at Gran's, I'll forgive your debt," she said, glancing over my way. "It'd mean a lot to me to have this little bean welcomed into the world with a party at her place."

Tears of relief and joy burst onto my cheeks. There was probably a bit of frustration and fear laced in there as well, seeing as a slightly psychotic woman had a photo of me and her ex-boyfriend in her coat pocket.

"That would be lovely," I said. "I might even order a cake from *Matt à la Mode*."

Chapter 12

I woke the next morning in bed, blissfully seeping into reality as the sunlight hit my face. Snuggling deeper under the blankets, I could *almost* pretend I was back in California waking up to a perfectly bright, seventy-degree day in the middle of February.

The sun beamed on my face. I was warm and clean and cuddled up in bed. If I imagined hard enough, I could picture the giant latte I'd order down the street as I completed my morning ritual with a stroll in a magnificent summer dress. I'd have on flip flops and a swishy skirt and swing by the Sunday Farmer's Market for fresh fruit on the way back home.

As per usual, I'd awkwardly shuffle the strawberries and blueberries between my arms because I could never remember to bring my stupid reusable bag. (It's not stupid; recycling is brilliant and all, but the fact that I can't seem to remember the bag whenever I leave the house sort of defeats the purpose.) Then I'd whip up a quick lunch and wait for my boyfriend...

My daydreams screeched to a halt. My eyes flashed open, and instead of seeing gently waving palm trees on a backdrop of cloudless blue sky, I saw the branches of strikingly white-laced trees whipping against one another outside my window—and reality came crashing back. It'd snowed again overnight.

I sat up in bed, rubbing my eyes and realizing for the first time that even if I returned to Los Angeles as I'd thought I might someday... things wouldn't be the same. I didn't have my job any longer, nor did I have my boyfriend. I'd be a lonely old spinster sadly juggling fruit in her hands because she couldn't remember her reusable bag. Except I wouldn't be able to afford my fancy lattes and fresh fruit without a job, so that daydream was bunk, too.

Glancing at the clock, I was startled to find it was already nine. Pulling myself out of bed, I padded downstairs in a cutesy set of flannel pajamas and began my new morning ritual: boring black coffee and no fresh fruit.

I frowned, glancing in the cupboards. The last few days I'd walked up to June's café for all forms of sustenance, which meant I still hadn't gone to the store. I spotted a coffee maker in one cupboard and reached for it, only to remember I had no filters. The thought of popping next door to ask Matt to save me again was somewhat appealing, but it was too soon. I couldn't be a damsel in distress all the time over a lack of food. That was annoying, not cute.

As I puttered about the kitchen, I found the cake pan we'd used yesterday. I needed to return it to Matt. An appealing idea hit me as I rinsed the pan out in the sink. Maybe I could take it over and charm my way in for a cup of coffee. Just one little mug so that I could come back, crawl into bed, and read a magazine for an hour before actually facing the world.

The only item on my agenda for the day, aside from calling the airlines again, was to revisit my notes about the ongoing investigation into Grant's murder. (My mission was now fondly dubbed: Operation Keep Jenna Free!) If I felt like it, I could possibly drag myself to bingo later.

I still wasn't sure about this half-date I'd gotten myself roped into with the chief of police, but I knew it'd keep my mother happy, and I might be able to glean some information from him while listening to numbers being called out to the senior citizens of Blueberry Lake.

I groaned, picked up the cake pan, and slid my feet into boots. I was all for procrastinating on the day's events for as long as possible, and I could start with my hunt for coffee.

I tramped through the fresh snow to Matt's, knocking as soon as I arrived. The panic hit a second later. It was a Sunday morning. What if I had arrived too early? What if he was at church? What if he was sick of me coming over and—

"Oh, hello," I said, battling the worries back as the door opened. "I hope I didn't wake you. I didn't even think before I came over here."

That seemed to make Matt smile. "Come on in—can I grab you a cup of coffee? I just made a fresh pot."

Oh, thank you, coffee gods. I murmured a silent prayer of thanks as soon as Matt's back was turned and followed him into the house. I slid off my boots but not my coat (didn't want him to think I was planting myself in his house for the day) and carried the cake pan along with me.

"You didn't have to invite me in," I said. "I was just swinging by to thank you for all your help yesterday. The cake was a raging success. Oh, and here's your pan."

"It was my pleasure." He reached above the sink and pulled down two sturdy mugs. The hot liquid percolated in the pot next to him, and the smell of freshly ground beans still lingered in the air. He hesitated, then crooked an eyebrow and tilted his head. "Did you hear something? I swear I just heard a door slam."

I paused, frowned, but the only thing I could hear was my stomach screaming for coffee. "No."

He shook his head and brushed it off while I studied the house around me. Matt the firefighter lived in a neat little dude-house. By dude-house, I meant that it was definitely male. There wasn't much in the way of flowers or bright colors sitting out, and the furniture and decorations were sparse and functional. The curtains were plain, the couches and chairs operational and pointed toward the television. There was a bookshelf in one corner, of which I wildly approved, and on top of it were a few trophies displayed proudly.

"What are those for?" I gestured to the trophies. "Third grade mathlete competitions?"

"Nah," he said with a laugh. "Fire versus police rec sports games. We're neck and neck for wins over the last ten years in kickball."

"Oh," I said. "And I'm sure thirty adult males most definitely need trophies."

"It's a big point of pride in Blueberry Lake," he said somberly. "We take our kickball seriously."

"I see," I said, sinking onto a bar stool at the island in the center of the kitchen. "I've got a lot to learn about this town."

"Be honest," Matt said, pausing as he poured piping hot coffee into both mugs. He slid one across the island to me, then raised his glass in a cheers sort of gesture. "Did you go hunting around your house this morning for a reason to come over here?"

My jaw dropped open. "That's cocky of you to say, Mr. Matt."

"Oh, I'm not under the illusion you wanted to see *me*," he corrected. Leaning over the counter, we went nose to nose in a challenge. "I think you wanted my steaming hot coffee."

"How dare you," I said. "I wanted to thank you for your cake services. Because of you, Blueberry Lake's biggest winter wedding survived its bachelorette party."

"Mmm-hm."

"And I wanted to return your pan to you before I forgot," I said with a little pout. "Isn't that thoughtful of me?"

"On a Sunday morning in your flannel pajamas?"

I glanced down, fighting back mortification. "My bags haven't arrived yet! My wardrobe is limited."

"I'd say that was kind of you, but..." he hesitated. "This isn't my pan."

"What?" I glanced at the long, thin thing I'd found on my counter. "But it isn't mine."

"It is," he said. "I pulled it out yesterday and must have forgotten to put it back. My pan is round."

"Oh."

He laughed, gave a small shake of his head. "Just admit you wanted my coffee."

"Never!"

"Admit it."

"You can't force me to say anything!"

"Admit it: You realized you didn't have beans. Or maybe filters. You decided to take the first pan you could find and march on over to my place." He made little marching fingers down his arm to punctuate his point. "Normally, you would've gone to June's, but it's a snowy Sunday morning and you had high hopes of climbing back in bed once you'd achieved full caffeination."

I burst into fits of laughter, clutching my coffee cup close to my chest and possessively taking a sip. "Fine! Fine—I admit it. I came over here for your coffee."

"Well, whenever you feel like returning random pots to my house, please feel free," Matt said. "I certainly enjoy your company."

I cleared my throat, searching for a response, when a loud knock sounded on the front door and interrupted the fun and games. Matt's face registered surprise as he moved to the entryway and checked through the peephole.

He gave a low grunt as he pulled open the door, blocking the visitor from view. "Morning, officer. May I help you?"

My heart pounded faster as I stood from the stool and slunk deeper into the kitchen. Until the sound of my name brought me to a dead stop.

"Have you seen Jenna McGovern recently?" Chief Dear's voice sounded crisp and businesslike. "More specifically, have you seen her after midnight yesterday?"

"Why?"

I wanted to hug Matt for sounding so defensive. During this trying time of being lauded as a murder suspect, it was nice to have someone on my team. Even if he had no good reason to believe me except for the fact he'd liked my Gran.

"I'm concerned for her safety," Cooper said. "The back door to her house was wide open and the lock was broken. I saw it while on patrol this morning and stopped to check it out. No answer when I called. I popped inside, but it doesn't look like anyone's there."

"The lock is busted?" Matt asked. "Someone broke into Jenna's house?"

"Looks that way," Cooper said. "But more importantly, we need to find her. Any idea where she might be? I called her mother, but—"

"You called my mother?!" I slapped a hand over my mouth at the outburst, instantly regretting it. "Er—*oops*. Surprise," I said weakly, easing out into the hallway. "I'm right here."

Matt stepped back from the door and revealed Cooper's tall, broad figure behind him. The two men were equals in size and strength, though Matt was a tiny bit taller and slenderer while Cooper was built like a brick wall. If he'd just let me dress him in something other than his uniform, he could look really stunning. In an objective sort of way.

"Jenna?" Cooper asked. "What are you doing here?"

"I believe that's her business," Matt said. "She's safe—that's all that matters."

"No, it also matters that someone broke into my house." I stepped out of hiding and took a long drag of coffee for courage. "I didn't leave my back door open when I left."

"Would you say you left sometime last night to come over to Matt's," Cooper asked, "or was it this morning?"

"I can leave my house whenever I want."

Cooper stared at me. "I'm not trying to pry into your personal life; I'm trying to pinpoint the time of entry. I imagine you'd like me to look into this?"

"Yeah, that'd probably be good," I said, feeling my cheeks heat up with discomfort. "I—er, I came over here this morning. About ten minutes ago."

Cooper gave a thin smile that seemed to irk Matt.

"I worked Lana's bachelorette party with May last night," I said to ease the smirk off Cooper's face. "Then I came home, and I went to bed. This morning, I woke up and decided to head over to Matt's to return his pan."

"*Your* pan," Matt said. "It's not my pan."

"I'm confused," Cooper said. "Whose pan were you returning?"

"It was really just an excuse to see me," Matt said with a proud grin. "Right, Jenna?"

"Not really," I said, annoyed he was lording my neighborly visit over Cooper. "Remember? I wanted your coffee."

Cooper snorted at that.

"Don't look so happy," I told him. "Matt's a great neighbor. I wouldn't have tried to mooch coffee from *you,* Chief."

Instead of boosting Matt up, my comments seemed to knock him down a few pegs. I couldn't understand why. Being a good neighbor was something to be proud of, but for some reason, even Cooper looked pleased with the development.

"Would you like to come take a look around your place with me?" Cooper asked. "I'd like to be there while you glance over your possessions to see if anything's missing."

"Fine, sure," I said. "Though most of my clothes and prized possessions aren't around, anyway, so I can't imagine what this person might have stolen."

"I'll come with you," Matt said. With a pointed glance at Cooper he added, "for protection."

"I'll be with her," Cooper said dryly. "I think she'll be fine. I already spooked the intruder."

"It would be best if she had someone with her—"

"Hello!" I waved a hand between them. "How about I get a say in my own life?"

Both men swiveled their gazes toward me as if they'd entirely forgotten I was there.

"Um, of course," Matt said. "What would you prefer?"

"I'm going to go with the chief—just the two of us—and we'll do a walkthrough of the house. Like he said, whoever broke in was scared off. I doubt they'll be back."

"But—" Matt frowned as I cut him off.

"I appreciate all you've done for me, Matt, and I appreciate your offer to come with. If I feel at all unsafe, I'll give you a call."

"If you're unsafe," Cooper said, "you should call the police."

"I'm her neighbor," Matt said. "I can arrive more quickly."

"You were a little too busy to notice the intruder in her house this morning," Cooper said. "So, as I said—"

"Ugh!" I shoved my feet in my boots, pushed past both men, and stomped through the snow toward home. They could have their macho talk all morning long if they wanted, but I was going to do something about whoever had broken into my home—flannel pantsuit and all.

Behind me erupted a staccato exchange of unpleasantries as Matt and Cooper finished their argument. I was back at the front door to my house by the time I heard footsteps behind me.

"Wait up, will you?" Cooper called. "Someone just broke into your house."

"Yeah, and like you said—you scared them away." I glanced back at him. "Which means they're not here anymore. I want to find out what they were after. Also, I don't want any part of whatever's happening between you and my neighbor."

"Are the two of you dating?"

"Is this part of the investigation, or is this just small town nosy?"

He didn't let my sass flummox him. "I thought we had a date tonight."

"A date? Oh, no," I retorted. "You *sort of* asked if I *maybe* wanted to *show up* at bingo. You didn't even ask if I wanted to sit next to you. And it's all because my mother called you and suggested it. I wouldn't call that romance central."

"I told you because of the investigation—"

"I'm not dating anyone right now," I said, waving my arms to signify the argument null and void. "At all. Not you, not Matt, not anyone else. I'm off the market."

"Are you otherwise taken?"

"Yes, by *myself*," I said, putting a hand on my hip as a frigid wind blew over my face. "Now can we please get this part over with?"

Without waiting for an answer, I turned the key in the lock and pushed through the front door. I ignored the feel of the cop's eyes on the back of my head as I stepped into my house and felt a huge draft of cold. I shivered, in part due to the temperature, and in part because an unwelcome visitor had been in my things.

"Do you think it was the same person who murdered Grant?" I kicked my boots onto the rug, then picked them up as I headed straight for the rear entrance. It was still chilly inside, but I was feeling claustrophobic and confined. "Do you think a murderer was in my home?"

"Jenna, listen—things are going to be okay." The chief's voice took on a soothing quality, lulling me into a temporary calm as he followed me through the kitchen. "I will have an officer drive by every few hours—whether it be myself or someone else—until this case is closed."

"You have more than one officer in a town this size?"

"Three," he said with a dry smile. "And help when needed from Butternut Bay. We have a few volunteers who assist, too. The city's small and our budget can't afford much more than that."

"Not to mention, you probably don't have murders happening around here left and right."

"Correct," he said with a thin smile. "The most exciting call I had last week was a burnt-out Christmas bulb in one of the parks."

"I hope you brought your gun with to that one. It sounds thrilling."

We shared a quiet smile which broke the tension. So long as he was by my side, it felt like nothing bad would happen in my house. I was preemptively dreading the moment he took his leave. I shivered just thinking about the emptiness combined with the knowledge that someone else had been in my private space—uninvited.

"Are you cold?" he asked as we came to stop near the back entrance to my house. "We can look at the outdoor tracks later and start with the inside if you'd prefer."

"No, I'll be fine."

Cooper explained in patient detail how the intruder had forced the back lock open and gotten into the house. He pointed out the trail of footprints that led beyond my backyard and into a thin layer of forest. On the other side of the tree-filled plot was a street.

"I spooked the person who was here by knocking," Cooper said, looking frustrated. "I should've just gone around back to look, but in case you had the door open for a reason, I didn't want to pry."

"It's not your fault," I said. "If you hadn't noticed the door open in the first place, who knows what would have happened. Do you think they were planning to wait for me?"

"I don't know," he said. "By the time I came around back, I heard a car starting up on the other side of the woods. I assume the intruder came from there, trekked through the snow, and into the house."

"What about footprints?"

"They're messy," the chief said. "There's a lot of wind and drifts going around today, and the snow is still coming down."

"Can't you take a cast of them or something?" I gestured toward the trail of rapidly disappearing snow-footprints. "I worked as a stylist for NCIS for a few seasons, and—"

"This is Blueberry Lake, not Los Angeles, Chicago, New York, or even the Twin Cities," the chief explained. "I'm afraid we don't have the same resources as the bigger departments. Not to mention, it was snowing outside, and the prints are already compromised. But that doesn't mean I'm not going to do the best I can to figure out who was inside. Shall we see if anything was disturbed?"

Cooper expertly navigated the investigative waters, keeping me calm and in check as we closed and locked the back door behind us.

"You'll want to get that lock replaced," he said. "If you need help, I can pop by this afternoon and do it for you."

"You'd do that?" I asked. "Sure—I mean, I could ask my mother or Sid, but if you're not too busy, I would appreciate that. I'll pay you."

"It'll take me ten minutes, and I'll do it on my rounds," he said with a quick wink. "Police work at its finest—changing locks is more interesting than switching light bulbs."

I came to a halt as I faced the interior of my house. "You know what's weird?" I glanced down and found a small pool of water on the floor near the back door. "The intruder must have taken their shoes off. This little puddle here, it's from shoes. There's no water over the rest of the house. Which means the intruder was probably a woman."

"How do you figure that?"

"Manners," I said simply. "They didn't want to get my floor dirty."

Cooper laughed. "You don't think men have manners?"

"Not if they're trying to murder me!" I said. "Not that I think anyone was trying to kill me, but you never know."

Cooper sobered quickly. "Can you think of anyone who might have had a reason to attempt a break-in this morning?"

My memories flashed back to the previous evening and Becky's odd behavior. Her name was on my lips, but I held back. It was one thing to have a tiff with a woman who'd tripped me, and another to accuse her of breaking into my house or murdering a man in cold blood.

"I don't know," I said. "It doesn't make sense."

"You were going to say something." Cooper was more perceptive than I'd given him credit for. "Someone is on your mind. Why are you protecting them?"

"I'm not protecting anyone! I'm just—I'm not sure."

"It's my job to be sure, not yours." Cooper frowned. "It's your job to give me all the information you have. I hunt down evidence."

"Look—I don't know if you believe me or not, but I didn't murder Grant Mark. Yet I was accused of doing so, and it was really upsetting," I said. "I'm not going to turn around and accuse someone of something they might not have done because it sucks. I know from experience."

Cooper sized me up. "I think we should finish the walk-through of the house, and then you can decide."

I gave him a thin smile. "Let's just get this over with, shall we?"

From the back door we moved into the kitchen, past the front door, then came around to the living room. Nothing looked remotely out of place.

"I guess that means we head upstairs?" I looked to Cooper for confirmation.

When he nodded, I started toward the spiral wooden staircase—full of delicious creaks and pitiful moans—and stopped three stairs up. I halted so abruptly the chief ran smack dab into my back, apologizing profusely. I was too distracted to notice because my attentions were elsewhere. Namely, on the shoe someone had left on my floor.

"I think I know what they wanted," I said, easing to the side to give Cooper a clear view of the powder-blue, chunky vintage heel. "They got one step closer to framing me for murder."

Cooper leaned forward and squinted. "This shoe can't be the murder weapon as we have that bagged as evidence, but yes, if we found the other shoe in your home, it would point in your direction..."

"Cinderella," I said with a sigh. "What a tragic retelling."

Cooper gave me a funny look. "You're certain this wasn't in your house before?"

I narrowed my eyes at him. "Don't tell me you're trying to revisit the idea of me being a murderer."

"My job is not to—"

"—assume, I know," I said. "But the answer to this question is obvious. No, that is not my shoe. Yes, I've seen it before and tried it on. My fingerprints might still be on it, but I doubt it. I bet whoever left it here wiped the whole thing clean so their fingerprints would disappear, as well."

"It's possible—"

"—possible I left it on my own step and staged the break-in?" I gave him a deadly stare. "Sure. I have an alibi for the time of break-in, for starters."

"Obviously. You spent the morning with Matt."

I ignored his jab. "I know about four people in this town. I'm sure you can verify the whereabouts of May, my mother, and Sid. None of them were in on this. I have no accomplice.

I'm not even a criminal! Except for that one time I forgot to pay for the nail clippers from my manicurist, but I think the statute of limitations has run out on that."

"What about your mom's front desk clerk? Might she have done it?"

"Allie?" I shook my head. "No, this wasn't her either. I'd practically swear it. She doesn't seem like the murdering type. And neither am I."

"Jenna, listen." Cooper took a step back, retreating down the staircase. "I don't believe you put it there. I don't think you murdered Grant. Are you satisfied?"

I felt the prickle of something similar to satisfaction crawl down my spine. "Do you mean that?"

"I mean it," he said. "However, I still have to do my job and ask all of the right questions. And if evidence turns up that points toward you, I'm still going to investigate it."

"That's fair. I wouldn't ask you to not do your job, I was just hoping..." I hesitated. "I don't know why, but I was just hoping you would believe me. I know we're strangers and all, so it's fine if you don't, but I didn't do this. I am trying everything I can think of to convince you of that."

"I believe you," he assured me. "Now let me gather up the shoe. I'm going to take it down to the station and add it into evidence. I'll be back in a bit to replace that lock. If you need anything at all, call the station—they'll reroute to me. I'd give you my cell, but I'd prefer to ask for your number when I'm off the clock."

I found myself smiling oddly at his thoughtfulness. "Thank you, Cooper. I appreciate all you've done for me."

He gave a nod and set to work on his police duties. He searched the rest of the house, took a few photos, and completed whatever technical things he needed to do. By the time he finished, I felt better about everything. Ironic, since I was technically as unsafe as I'd ever been. Someone had broken into my house to frame me for murder. It was a Hollywood script waiting to happen.

"Hey, chief," I called after Cooper as he headed toward his cruiser. "So, are we on for bingo tonight?"

"I thought it wasn't a date," he called back with an easy smile. "I only asked you because it seemed like you could use a friend."

I laughed as he climbed into his cruiser, grinning as he waved goodbye.

As I closed and locked the door, I realized the house did, indeed, feel a bit emptier without him. And no matter how much I fought it, I couldn't help but feel the slightest twinge of excitement for tonight. I really needed to get a hold of myself.

I had time to kill between now and my lock change, so I hopped upstairs and took a quick shower, a little embarrassed I'd been in my pajamas during all that had transpired over the course of the morning. Pre-coffee, it hadn't registered with how truly silly I looked. Post coffee, I was properly mortified.

The snow had stopped by the time I got out of the shower, so I picked a long-sleeved sweater dress and slid into it. The thickly knitted pattern was pretty and warm, and I prided myself on being functional as well as stylish. May's thick boots matched the ensemble and managed to look some-what less-than-ugly.

I stepped outside and found my mother's truck waiting for me in the driveway. She'd said I could use it as much as I needed for the first few weeks until I got on my feet and bought my own car. She and Sid could get by in their four-wheel-drive second vehicle. I hopped in, aimed the nose toward June's, and hit the gas pedal.

I hadn't mentioned Becky's name to Cooper, though he'd pressed once more before leaving. I had one more round of investigating to do myself before I dragged her name through mud. At the moment, I didn't have a strong case against her—a few weird looks and a potential tripping did not a murderer make. My best piece of evidence was the photo she'd taken of me with Grant, but I hadn't exactly come about the photo in a way I wanted to make public

I hadn't entirely figured out how I'd begin compiling evidence on Becky, but one thing was certain.

Coffee, first.

Then murder.

Chapter 13

"That latte machine is on back order," June said when I got in line. "You're going to have to settle for a black coffee again."

"You're doing this on purpose," I chided the old woman. "All you need is something to make froth with! You can pick a frother up for twenty bucks at Target."

"Getting to a Target in this weather is like hiking the Sahara," June said. "The roads are slippery, there's none within a forty-mile radius, and the—"

"Excuses," I said with a laugh. "I recognize this for a pile of excuses. You just don't want me to be right. You didn't even order that machine, did you?!"

June broke into a broad grin. "Is the black coffee growing on you?"

I grudgingly shook my head. "It's really good. It does warm the soul."

"Go on and sit down," June said. "I'm bringing you my specialty this morning."

"Oh, I was hoping to grab a quick coffee to go—I have some things to take care of, and—"

"It's the Lord's day!" June said. "Take a seat on that there window seat and eat some breakfast with your coffee. There's no place you have to be so urgently on a Sunday morning, I promise you."

She was right, oddly enough, so I took a seat near the window without further argument. I had no particular place to rush off to in search of evidence against Becky, and I didn't really want to sit in Gran's big old house by myself.

May would be cuddling Joe and their little butterbean baby on this snowy winter morning, and my mom and Sid would be doing something similar—something I didn't want to spend another moment thinking about. With a sigh, I realized that I was a true loner. I had nobody to snuggle on a Sunday morning except for the latest copy of Vogue.

"What are you sighing about?" Allie plopped herself across from me and unloaded her scarf and mittens without asking permission to join me at the window. "Oh, is that the new dress from the store? It's cute. Is it true you ruined Mrs. Duvet's entire house last night?"

"What? No!" I blinked, horrified. "Where'd you here that?"

She shrugged. "Word has a way of getting into my ears. That, and I like to gossip with the old ladies."

Fortunately, the conversation stalled when one of June's servers appeared with a pot of hot coffee and poured out mugs for both of us. I pulled my spring green cup toward me and took a sip, preferring to burn my tongue rather than delve into last night's fiasco.

"Say, remember you said you'd help style my mother?" Allie blurted. "I was wondering if we could set something up. I didn't pick a date on that planner thing before you left yesterday because I wanted to check with my mom first. I offered to style her myself, but she told me I was nuts. She has a different taste in clothes than me. Maybe *demure* would be the right word for her style."

"Halleluiah." Today, Allie had gone for faux-leather pants and a hot pink turtleneck. It was certainly interesting. "What I mean is that I'd love to set something up on the calendar. Pick a date and let me know."

"Okay," Allie said. "Now, tell me more about the total destruction of Mrs. Duvet's house."

"There wasn't total destruction! I tripped over someone's foot and spilled a few drinks. We're paying for carpet cleaning."

"Did you find out anything more about the *you-know-what*?" Allie asked, lowering her voice. "You know, the whole reason Mrs. Beasley set you up to work there in the first place?"

"If you mean Grant's murder, then, no." I wasn't about to tell this little conspiracy theorist about the break-in at my house. I was beginning to suspect she was behind half the gossip in the community. "It's a slow-moving investigation."

"I heard Grant took a lover a couple weeks ago." Allie spoke in a constrained, dramatic hiss. "That seems just like him, don't you think? What if this mystery woman killed him?"

"Where'd you hear that? I don't think it's true."

"Well, he dated Becky Turner, didn't you hear that?"

"Um—"

"You need to spend more time *listening* when you're at June's." Allie shook her head. "The gossip is all here, ripe for picking—you just have to know where to reach for it."

"What do you know about Becky Turner?"

"Well, she dated Grant. She says things weren't serious, but I don't believe her."

"Why not?"

As I pondered this, I realized Becky's stalking behaviors would make a lot more sense if things had been more serious between her and Grant than she'd let on. Especially if she'd thought I'd been the first woman to date Grant after they'd broken up...and she wasn't ready to move on.

"Well, Becky seemed very upset by the breakup," Allie said. "Which didn't make any sense, really, because she told everyone that *she* broke things off with Grant. I mean, we all know Becky is a little nutso to start with, so we all just thought that was her way of dealing with it."

"Did she say why she broke things off?"

"Something about Grant not being interested in taking things to the next level."

"How do we know if that's true?" I mused aloud. "Considering the gossip that's been circling around town about me—I'm hesitant to believe much of anything I hear secondhand. We need to find out if Grant dated someone *after* Becky from the source."

"The police force is basically one man and some bored volunteers." Allie spoke in hushed tones and glanced over her shoulder. "I bet they secretly want our help. After all, they haven't found anyone, which means there's still a killer on the loose!"

"I'm not so sure—"

"We could sneak into Grant's hotel room. He was staying over in Blueberry Lake for a bachelor weekend with his buddies."

"Sorry, what?" I made a gesture to reverse with my pointer finger. "Back up and start over. How would we be able to sneak into any hotel room? And wouldn't the police have already searched it?"

"Yeah, but like I said—they've got one man on the job," Allie persisted. "I can get us the key to the hotel room. What do you say we give a quick peek around in case there was something he missed?"

"That sounds like a bad idea," I said. "Sneaking into hotel rooms isn't really my thing. What are you expecting to find?"

"Love letters, phone numbers, lingerie," she said with a shrug. "Who knows? It's worth a shot, isn't it? Especially since I can get us the key to the room."

"How can you get us the key to a hotel room? That has to be illegal in so many ways."

"Not if the receptionist has a huge crush on me," Allie said proudly. "He'd lend it to me for five minutes. Plus, what is it going to hurt? Grant's already dead—nobody's going in or out of that room anymore."

"Exactly, which is why we shouldn't, either."

"Fine." Allie leaned back as the server came over and planted two huge plates with a Belgian waffle on each in front of us. "I'll go alone."

"That sounds like a terrible idea."

"Let me clarify." She dumped a spoonful of butter onto her plate. "I'm going just as soon as I finish my waffle. You can come with me or not...it's up to you."

"THIS IS A HORRIBLE idea," I said. "And if we end up in prison, I am never styling you *or* your mother."

"I don't want you to style me," Allie said. "I have perfect style."

"Not for breaking and entering!" I whispered as we strived to walk nonchalantly down the hallway toward the room at the end of the first floor. "You're squeaking with every step you take."

"It's the leather pants. They're a massive distraction. Nobody will ever suspect me of being a spy."

"Because you're not a spy!"

"Lighten up, will you?" Allie paused outside of room 102. "Brayden said this room has been checked out through the end of the week—you know, for the wedding. He thinks all of Grant's stuff is still in there, minus whatever the police took."

"Who's Brayden?"

"The front desk guy," Allie said impatiently. "I told you, he's got a thing for me. How'd you think I got the key to Grant's room?"

"I didn't think you had a key!"

She pulled out a thin keycard and flashed it in my face. "You can say a massive thank-you to the way my behind looks in these pants. I told him I'd lent Grant a few things and wanted to get them back."

"He still shouldn't have given you a key."

"Probably not, but who's gonna tell? The police have already been through here and taken what they wanted, and Grant's not coming back."

She did have a point, so I shut my mouth and tried to convince myself that I was doing the town a favor by investigating a murderer. I focused on room 102, surprised at the lack of caution-tape and flashing lights. Then I realized this wasn't exactly a crime scene, nor was it a movie set, and the hotel probably hadn't wanted to draw attention to the fact one of its guests had been killed.

"Go on," I said. "Before someone spots us standing out here."

"Calm yourself." Allie plunked the keycard into the door. "We'll be out of here in a second."

Once we were both inside, I let the door close behind me and turned to face Grant's belongings. It was odd being in a dead man's room, knowing he would never be back to collect his things.

His suitcase sat propped open with the contents haphazardly thrown around, as if he'd dug through it before deciding what to wear at the last minute. A few nicer pieces of clothing hung in the closet, and a backpack was situated at the end of his bed.

Other than that, the room was close to empty.

I began with the drawers, the closet, and the large spaces first. There was nothing in the most obvious spaces—which wasn't surprising. Most people who had something to hide weren't going to leave it sitting on their pillow.

I began the more careful task of digging through Grant's backpack and then his suitcase while Allie took charge of the bathroom. I didn't find much aside from normal clothing: workout attire, socks, boxers, and a pair of jeans lined his suitcase.

Grant had a book situated in his bag—the latest John Grisham novel in hardcover. It was in great shape, and I briefly flirted with the idea of adopting it for my own shelves, but I decided that was a step too far. A shame because books like this one were costly, especially on my shoestring budget.

I carefully closed the cover and began returning it to the bag when Allie popped out of the bathroom and startled me.

"Find anything?"

"Cripes, you scared me!" I whipped around so quickly the jacket of the book flew off as I rested a hand over my heart. "I'm jumpy being in here. Give me some warning."

"Warning for what?" Allie gave me a quizzical glance. "Next time I talk?"

"Yes."

"Well, there's nothing worth mentioning in the bathroom. You should've said you found something!" Allie bent over, pulling a few scattered papers from the ground. "These look like notes."

I frowned. "They weren't there a second ago. They must have—oh, *look*." I held up the Grisham book where a similar looking note protruded from behind the dust jacket. "Our man Grant tucked a few love letters in here."

"Right," Allie said, her voice quiet as she read the letters. "Except this doesn't sound much like love to me."

"What do you mean?"

"*I wish you were dead,*" Allie read aloud. "*You'll get what's coming to you—mark my words.*"

My eyebrows raised. "Looks like he might have had a mystery woman after all."

"And she wasn't very happy," Allie said. "However, there's no signature."

"There are more notes," I said. "Maybe we'll find one of them that's signed. Let's keep digging."

"We've probably only got about ten minutes," Allie said. "Despite the fabulousness of my leather pants, Brayden doesn't like me that much. If we take too long, he just might realize something's fishy."

"In that case," I said. "Let's do things this way."

I pulled out my phone and quickly snapped a photo of each letter. Then I replaced them carefully behind the book's dust jacket and tucked everything back where I found it. Allie and I were just stepping out of Grant's room when I heard a familiar voice at the front desk.

"Close the door!" I hissed to Allie. "Hurry!"

Cooper Dear came around the corner just as we reached the halfway point in the hallway. "Well, long time no see," he said, scanning his eyes over the pair of us. "To what do I owe the pleasure of finding the two of you here?"

"Exercising," I said. "With all the snow, we couldn't walk outside. And with all of June's cooking, I won't be able to fit into my clothes if I don't get in some cardio."

"Right. And what will I find if I pull the security tapes?" Cooper looked me in the eye. "Any thoughts on that, Miss McGovern?"

"As a matter of fact, yes," I said, biting my lip and searching for a clever answer while I wondered if my hair would look good on camera. Security tapes had a way of making me look all disheveled no matter how much effort I put into my hair. Since I couldn't come up with an answer, and I didn't want the chief to pull tapes and see me all out of sorts, I opted for the naked truth. "You'll find something that I wouldn't want you to see...*if* you pull the tapes. But maybe we can call a truce if I tell you that there's something worth noting in Grant's room. We didn't move anything from its original place—I swear."

"We already searched the room."

"Then why are you here?"

"A birdie told me two young women were strolling the hallways of the hotel," Cooper said. "I thought I'd do my duty and check it out."

"Forget about us," I said. "But if you'd like my advice, search Grant's room again. This time, try the dust jacket on the latest Grisham book in Grant's backpack. You might just find something of interest."

We left the chief staring after us as Allie and I scurried out the front doors. I exhaled a sigh of relief once we reached fresh air.

"Dang," Allie said once we were outside. "That enemies-to-lovers plot is really heating up, isn't it? I'll tell you what...if you let me win the pot, I'll share the money with you."

"You are ridiculous."

"Don't you want to know how much it is?"

I considered. I did want to know because I was cursed with curiosity. But I was also cursed with stubbornness, and I didn't need to know *that* bad.

"Nah," I said finally. "Ignorance is bliss."

Allie and I climbed back into my truck, and I turned us back in the direction of my mother's store. Allie was the first to break the silence.

"Who do you think wrote the notes?" she asked, staring out the window. "Do you think it was the murderer? Could it be Becky? Or a mystery woman?"

"I don't know," I said. "But we know for a fact some-one—or some *ones*—wanted him dead. We just have to find out who made good on their word."

Chapter 14

The last thing I wanted to do was return home to an empty house that'd been broken into by a homicidal maniac with a thing against shoes. I'd have to go back sooner or later, but in the meantime, I decided to stall while dropping Allie off at Something Old for her shift.

"I'm late," Allie said when I pulled into the parking lot. "It's twelve fifteen."

"Yes, well, I'll explain to my mother." I turned the car off and slid down from the seat. "Come along—I can't stay all day."

"What else do you have to do? More murder stuff?"

"Keep your voice down," I said. "Maybe, but I can't tell you. Top secret."

Allie pushed the door open. "Hi, Bea. Sorry I'm late; I was helping Jenna out on some—"

"—recon work for the store," I said. "Shopping the latest fashions, that sort of thing."

"Right, sure," my mother said, midway through stocking a rack of scarves. "Hop on the register and open things up, Allie. Then you can straighten the bra rack, please."

Allie leaned closer to me and lowered her voice. "I bet James Bond never worked a day job straightening bras."

"Nah, he's more of a flipping burgers sort of guy," I whispered back. "Thanks for your help this morning, Allie. And

160

tell your mother my schedule is wide open whenever she'd like to come in for an appointment."

My mother waited until Allie was caught up in the undergarments before sidling over to me and dropping her voice. "More *murder* stuff?" she asked quizzically. "Tell me I heard Allie wrong."

"You heard Allie wrong," I parroted.

"Now, *mean* it when you say it."

"Mother, I'm still not out of the woods on this case!"

"Chief Dear is not going to arrest you. He's taking you on a date tonight!"

"You need to stop spreading rumors. We do not have a date tonight—we are simply both going to be in the same place at the same time. It'd be a sin to miss the event. The entire bridal party is going, and I need to keep an eye on what's happening with them."

"Are you going to sit next to him?"

"Who?"

"Cooper! Who else?" My mother waved a hand. "I'm not interested in that murder stuff—we know you didn't do it, so leave that to the professionals. I'm interested in ensuring my daughter's happiness."

"You just focus on your own happiness."

"I have Sid. I'm overjoyed."

"I know, mother. You and Sid don't exactly keep quiet about your *joy*." I rolled my eyes and tapped my chest. "My happiness is coming from within."

"You keep rolling your eyes, and they'll get stuck like that. Then you'll never find happiness from within because your eyes will be staring in all different directions."

"That's a physical impossibility."

"You never know!" My mother shrugged one shoulder. "I think you should reconsider about this evening. Make it official."

"Cooper didn't ask me on a date. He just asked if I was going to bingo."

She frowned. "Maybe he's just shy."

"Nope," I said. "I don't think so. Just leave it alone, okay?"

"Fine, then how about your job?"

"What?"

"If I can't comment on your love life, I need to worry about something else. It's my motherly responsibility."

"I relieve you of your motherly responsibility," I said, reaching for an empty clothes hanger and touching each of my mother's shoulders with it, knighting her. "I absolve you from worrying about my private business."

My mother shooed the hanger away. "It's not so much *your* personal business if it involves *my* shop." She gave me a knowing stare. "I'm worried about you, Jenna. Gran's place will need some repairs this summer; Sid and I will help out if we can, but..."

Her meaning was clear. *Jenna, get your act together,* she said with her eyes. *Stop moping around and do something with your life.*

"I get it," I told her. "I came home to support you and the store. What can I do to help you?"

"I can't afford to hire another full-time employee," my mother said. "I wish I could, but I would have to fire some-one, and—"

I waved a hand. "Out of the question. Don't fire some-one. I just want to help. What can I do? My attempts at styling didn't turn out so well."

"I think that was a problem with the clientele," my moth-er said. "Did I hear you say Allie's mother is interested in your services?"

"Yes, but she's the only one," I said. "I think I scared the rest of them off with the murder charges. Which is not ac-tually my fault!" I said louder, to the rest of the empty store, just in case. "I'm not good at much outside of shopping. I don't know, mom. I'm stuck here in this tiny little town, and I don't know what to do about it. I want to help you, but I'm afraid I'll only make things worse."

"Oh, no, honey. Business boomed the day after Grant's murder," my mother said. "God rest his soul—I'd never wish that on my worst enemy—but all of the regular gossips were here. It was like a haunted house tour visiting all the places Grant stepped before he died."

"That's morbid."

"Best day of sales in two years."

"Well, since we can't count on murder as a sales driving device," I said. "Let's think of something else."

"I didn't mean you had to solve all my problems, just that you should think about what you want to do while you're here. I hope you're here for a really long time. I want you to stay, and I want you to be happy. Take some time to think about what would make you happy."

I dug my toe into the carpet. "I read some self-help titles at the airport. It seems like I need to be an organic gardener,

a Zen Buddhist, and a minimalist with no material possessions in order to achieve happiness."

"I think you need to throw all those books away."

"Oh, I didn't buy the books," I assured her. "Much too
expensive. Those are just the titles."

My mother laughed, then opened her arms and pulled
me in for a brief hug. "I know you'll find what makes you
tick. Don't put all the pressure on yourself to save my store,
find a murderer, and get yourself all sorted out in a week.
These things take time. My only point was that you should
be thinking about it. Sooner or later, Grant's murderer will
be found, and you won't be able to distract yourself by playing cops and robbers any longer. By the way, I'll need the
truck this afternoon."

My mother's abrupt change of subject drove me back
to reality, but the rest of her thoughts wormed their way
into my brain and sat there, marinating, as I began the walk
home. My mother had offered to drop me at Gran's, but I
had my sturdy boots on and the sun was shining, so I decided to make the trek on foot.

Just as June had predicted, temperatures were creeping
up toward the mid-forties and the snow that had fallen this
morning was already beginning to melt. Maybe spring wasn't
so far off. With the change in seasons, I'd need to make some
updates to my life, as well.

I made it home and stood before the old Victorian
house, flexing my fingers and scrounging up the guts to go
inside. But I wasn't ready to be brave.

I chickened out at the last second and pointed my feet
toward Matt's instead. I tried to talk myself out of knocking

on his door before it was too late, but I couldn't. I heard the *rap, rap, rap* of my knuckles and felt the rush of relief as his familiar, smiling face appeared in the doorway.

"Hi," I said slowly. "I'm going to be honest. I'm not sure why I'm here."

"Didn't want to go home yet?"

I cocked my head to the side. "That's part of it. And now I feel horrible, like I'm using you as a distraction."

He laughed. "Use me as much as you like. I just had a ballgame on TV. Are you by chance here to steal some coffee, too?"

"No," I said, and then reconsidered. "But I wouldn't be opposed if you're offering."

He grinned again and gestured for me to follow him into the kitchen. "It's halftime," he said as an explanation when I glanced guiltily over at the television. "I'll let you know if we're missing anything."

"Thanks," I said, twining my fingers around one another. "Look, there's something I need to talk to you about that doesn't involve murder."

"Uh-oh, that doesn't sound good." Matt tapped the start button to the coffee machine and the crackle of newly brewed caffeine filled the room. "Are you breaking up with me? I feel like I've heard the start to this before—if you say *it's not me, it's you,* I will be forced to withhold your coffee."

"I know you're teasing me," I said with a flimsy smile. "Seeing how we're not dating and all, but that's actually sort of what I wanted to talk to you about."

"Aha."

I wasn't sure if it should be a relief that Matt looked un-surprised, or if that made things worse. Either way, I felt hor-rible. I felt like I was letting him down, even though there was hardly anything between us to let down. I'd only been in town a few days. How had things gotten so complicated this quickly?

"It's Coop, isn't it?" Matt ventured. "I heard you have a date with him tonight."

I hesitated, stunned. "Uh—what?"

"Small town, word travels like wildfire at the firehouse," he said with a joking smile. "No pun intended. It's fine, Jen-na. I'm not upset."

I stared hard into the faux-marble countertop of Matt's kitchen island. "I'm sorry, I don't know how things escalated so quickly. You weren't expecting anything from me, right? I didn't somehow agree to all that without knowing?"

He laughed. "You have nothing to worry about. We made a cake together, that's all. I used to make cakes with your Gran now and again when she needed extra hands preparing for a party. It's what neighbors do."

"Am I wrong in feeling like you don't want to be only neighbors?" I asked. "Is that all in my head?"

"I sure feel differently about you than I felt about your Gran," he said with a dry chuckle, "so if that's something to go off, then I guess the answer would be no—it's not all in your head. But I understand if you're not interested. I can't do much about the fact that my kitchen window looks into your yard, but I promise to leave you alone outside of normal neighborly interactions."

"No—*no*! It's not that at all," I said. "I don't want you to leave me alone. I'm sorry. Everything I'm saying is coming out wrong."

"Once again, you've nothing to worry about." Matt plopped a mug of coffee in front of me. It had a smiley face on one side, and he tapped at it gently with his finger. "Relax. I'm content with being *just neighbors,* believe it or not. You don't need to say more."

I nodded, feeling tears pool in my eyes. "I'm sorry," I sniffed. "You're just so nice."

"Can I give you a hug? I hate to see you like this."

I nodded again as he reached for me and pulled me against him. My head rested against his chest, a few stray trickles of tears dampened his shirt, and things felt right.

"It's okay." Matt stroked my hair, smelling of fresh coffee and spicy aftershave. He'd showered since I left this morning, and he smelled nice. "Just hang here for as long as you need."

"I don't know why I'm so emotional. I mean, I've been through a recent breakup, but—"

"Well, that explains a lot. Plus the fact that you moved across the country, were accused of murder, and had your house broken into. You're allowed to feel upset."

As he stroked my hair, I tried my hardest to stir up feelings of butterflies and shocks of adrenaline that resembled falling in love, but I couldn't get anything fluttering inside. I was content like this, as friends, and I hoped that would be enough.

"I suppose it has been a lot," I admitted, pulling back and wiping my eyes. "The murder and all that, plus the breakup, and more importantly, the stupid airline losing my bag with the latest necklace from Minnie Monroe in it!"

Matt moved around to his side of the counter. "For what it's worth, I don't think you need the necklace. You look great without it. Now, can we get you to stop crying? I hate to see you upset."

"I was worried about what you'd think—"

"Stop worrying," he interrupted. "You've been honest from the start." He raised his coffee mug in salute. "Friends?"

"I don't know," I said, letting a small smile peek out. "Can friends still come over in their pajamas and steal your coffee?"

"Anytime," he said. "If you're not ready to head home, how about you watch the game for a bit? I have two huge couches and a blanket that's magical."

"A magical blanket?"

"It's impossible not to nap underneath it," Matt said seriously, guiding me into the living room. "I dare you to try it."

I snuggled into one of Matt's two couches under the magical blanket. Matt sat on the other sipping his coffee—though a beer sat open and a bag of chips next to it from before I'd arrived—and kicked up his feet on the ottoman. The couch was squashy and lumpy and brown, and utterly perfect for warm winter naps under the glow of the afternoon sun.

Despite downing a cup of caffeine minutes before, I was out by the time halftime was over. I didn't wake until the game had concluded and someone was pounding on the door.

Chapter 15

One eyelid pulled open slowly, then the other, as voices danced around my skull. I couldn't remember the last time I'd been so deeply asleep that coming awake had felt like emerging from the depths of the Atlantic Ocean.

I shook my head, and still, the cobwebs remained. It sounded to me like Cooper and Matt were having another conversation on Matt's front steps. Maybe I was having déjà vu from this morning. Maybe this magical blanket had sent me back in time and I was getting a Groundhog-ish repeat of the day. Maybe...*crap*!

Maybe it was really happening.

I threw the magical blanket off my body and stumbled drunkenly into the hallway. I quickly shifted my sweater dress into position and ran a hand through my gnarly hair, but one glance in the reflection of the window told me I looked like a complete and utter mess.

I careened around the corner, stunning both men into silence. Cooper and Matt stared at me while I blinked sleep from my eyes. Behind them, the sky was tinged black with night.

"How long have I been asleep?" I asked, still trying to get my bearings. "I feel like I was hibernating for months."

"I told you, the blanket is magic," Matt said with a thin smile. "Guess it worked?"

169

"Guess so. I've never felt so refreshed in my life, and Cooper—where are you going?"

The chief had turned away at the mention of magical blankets and made his way down the front steps. If I wasn't wrong, there was a distinctly moody step to his gait. I gave Matt a frustrated expression.

"What did I say?" I asked. "I'm not dating him, either! Even less than you!"

Matt seemed pleased by this. "I believe he thinks otherwise."

"Oh, good grief," I said. "I have to go explain a few things to him. I'm sorry. Are you going to be okay here?"

"I'm fine," he said with a grin. Then he leaned in and surprised me with a quick kiss to the cheek. "You're always welcome here as a friend, Jenna. To use the magical blanket—or steal my coffee."

"Thank you," I said, clasping his hand in mine and squeezing it tight. "More than anything, I needed a friend this week. I would have hated to go home alone this afternoon, so thank you for being there for me."

"If you change your mind on what we talked about earlier," he said, with a raised shoulder, "let me know."

"I will," I said, smiling. "I promise."

As I threw on my jacket and boots, I broke into a jog from Matt's front steps and caught up with Cooper at the split between my front door and the driveway. "Hey," I called, skidding to a stop in front of the chief. "Where do you think you're going?"

I kept on skidding, however, and if it wasn't for Cooper's lightning fast response time, I'd have plowed right into a snowbank—again. As it was, he managed to catch my arm in time to pull me back, the movement snapping me right up against his chest.

I was breathing heavily, probably from the jog, and the unique scent of Cooper held me captive against him. The darkness, the smell of him, the proximity between our beating hearts—something held me there and loosed an entire net of butterflies in my stomach. Wings flapped firmly in every direction and electricity zinged all the way down to my toes. To my *great* dismay.

Why couldn't I feel this way about Matt? My warm, open, caring neighbor. Instead, I had to feel this way about the brooding, moody chief of police who seemed intent on catching me as I broke every rule in his little book. Those dark eyes, that dark, unruly flop of curls—I let out a guttural sigh. Things just weren't going my way here in Blueberry Lake.

"I'm sorry for interrupting you," Cooper said in a low, rumbling voice. "I didn't realize you were having sleepovers with Matt."

"What are you doing here?"

"I changed your lock. Your mother called when she saw my truck here and asked why you hadn't let me in."

"My mother is spying on me? And she called you?"

"I was worried," he said. "You didn't answer, but your mother said you should be home. She'd left you stranded without a car. So naturally, with there being a break-in this morning, I panicked."

"I'm sorry to have scared you," I said. "When I came home this afternoon from the thrift store, I didn't want to be alone, so I went to my neighbor's house. Now, it's freezing, so can we please go inside? I think we should talk."

"I'm not sure there's anything to talk about." Cooper gave me a tense smile. "Maybe I'll see you at the event tonight."

"Will you just listen for a minute?" I blurted. "Come inside so we can talk. If it makes you feel better, you can pretend it's to show me how to work my new door."

"I didn't get you a new door. I changed your lock."

"Whatever."

I felt the beginnings of a smile from him as I walked toward the house, stomping up the front stairs and letting myself inside without once thinking about the intruder who'd broken in this morning. One way to get over my fear of being alone in this big empty house was to get so worked up I forgot about the problem entirely.

I paused in the doorway and glanced back. Cooper hadn't moved. "Are you coming inside?"

The chief stood still with his hands in his pocket, no hat, and a hearty winter jacket. He looked like he belonged in this environment, his hair mussed lightly by the breeze and pricked with bright bits of drifting snow. He was downright gorgeous, and it wasn't fair.

Eventually, he shoved forward, climbing up the stairs and into the entryway. He left just enough space for me to close and lock the door behind him.

"Are you going to stand there and make me uncomfortable all evening, or would you like to kick off your shoes and stay for a minute? I'd offer you coffee, but I don't have any."

"So I heard," he said dryly. "You steal your neighbor's."

"That's right," I said, making my way toward the kitchen. I unearthed a few hot chocolate packets in the cupboard that weren't expired, and the teakettle Gran had used for the last seven decades. "Want some hot chocolate?"

He gave a muffled reply that I took to mean yes, and I pulled out two mugs from the cabinet. While I worked, he leaned against the counter looking like he didn't quite belong. He had no clue what to do with himself. The chief was so out of his element it was cute in a way.

"Let me show you how that door of yours works," he began, shifting his weight from one foot to the next. "It should be simple—"

"I know how to work a door," I said, giving him a wry smile. "I'm not that out of touch with the world. I just wanted to talk to you."

"Roping me in under false pretenses?"

I worried my light-hearted banter had gone right over his head because he sounded gruff and serious, but when I turned and found him watching me with the shadow of a grin, I knew he was teasing me right back. And that smile would be the death of me.

"Yes, exactly." I poured the hot water onto the chocolate powders, mixed in a tiny bit of milk and a whole lot of marshmallows. Handing one over to the chief earned me another look of incredulity. "What's this?"

"Hot chocolate and marshmallows," I said. "Try it. Your sweet tooth will thank me."

He took a sip. "Not horrible."

"Not horrible?" I frowned. "You must be the hardest man to please. These are *perfect*."

We lapsed into silence, the threat of normal, small-talk conversation hovering over us. I could tell that on one hand, Cooper didn't want to overstep his professional boundaries. On the other hand, I was almost certain he felt the same pull toward me that I felt toward him. And so we came to an impasse.

"The door—" he began.

"Sure," I said too quickly, interrupting him. "The door."

Cooper showed me how to unlock the back door. An utterly useless demonstration since it was like every other door in existence. He handed over the key.

"I feel about as stupid as I ever have," he said with a shy smile as I grabbed the key. "I probably didn't need to show you how to do that."

"I probably could've stopped you a few minutes back," I agreed. "You know, at the part where you said 'insert the key into the lock', but I didn't want to scare you off."

"Now why would you think I'm so easily scared away?" The chief leaned against the wall and sipped his hot chocolate. "Do I look that fragile?"

"You just about ran away after you found me at Matt's."

"That's different."

The back entrance was too small for a duo of full-grown adults, especially ones who didn't want to get too close to one another. The temperature felt like it had risen to a hundred degrees, and I fanned myself.

"How is that different?" I demanded. "I thought we discussed the fact that tonight isn't a date."

"It's not, but I was going to offer to give you a ride after seeing you didn't have a vehicle at your disposal," he said.

"But I am not the sort of guy who'll pick up another man's girlfriend."

"Matt and I aren't dating."

"It didn't feel like that to me," he said, raising a hand, "and I didn't want to step on any toes."

I narrowed my eyes at him. "I already told you that Matt and I are just friends. Do you not trust me?"

"I trust you just fine."

"So, you were going to just storm off to your big ol' cop car and let me walk to bingo?"

"I figured Matt could take you."

"Matt's—" I hesitated. "He's not going, is he?"

"Thought you would've talked about that," Cooper said, "or were you too busy *sleeping*?"

The way he said the last word felt heavy to me, as if he was insinuating other things had happened. I was getting sick and tired of arguing over nothing. I sighed. "Fine."

I let Cooper stew as I shuffled toward the kitchen. I topped off my hot chocolate with a ridiculous, snowy mound of marshmallows and slid onto a stool around the center island to sip my concoction in peace.

A few minutes later, I heard footsteps. I didn't bother to turn my head to look. A big part of me thought that Cooper would just keep marching right on out of this place without bothering to say goodbye.

"Fine?" he asked. "What's that supposed to mean?"

"Look, Cooper," I said. "Should I call you that? Or are you the chief today? I don't even know what to call you."

"I asked you to call me Cooper."

"Cooper," I said firmly, spinning on the stool to face him. I licked my lips and tasted sweet chocolate. It gave me confidence. "I went over to Matt's today to set the record straight."

"And—"

"Just listen," I said, waving a hand to cut him off. "I came into town a few days ago, and there's a whole slew of problems I've got to worry about besides men bickering."

"I wasn't bickering."

"You're bickering now," I said. "The thing is—I'm not ready for a relationship. I just got dumped publicly, and it still stings. I have to get on my own two feet before I even look at the opposite gender."

"You told this to Matt?"

"And I'm telling it to you," I said. "Matt is just a friend. You can trust me on that or not—whatever you want. I'm telling you the same thing I told him. There are no dates, there are no subtle messages hidden anywhere. I am not interested in anything but a friend. I'm being upfront so nobody's feelings get hurt."

Cooper studied me for a long moment, his eyes, deep and dark and penetrating, perused over me in great detail. It gave me the shivers.

He took a step closer, his eyes squinting as he studied my face, my hair, my lips. It dawned on me that we were much closer than we'd ever been and a part of me wondered if he was preparing to kiss me. His eyes flicked over my features once more.

"But that *hair*..." he said, breaking into a grin and reaching out to touch a strand of wild frizz. "What was I supposed to think you were doing over there?"

I swatted Cooper's shoulder. I couldn't help but laugh as I glanced at the reflection of my head in the microwave. I did have some crazy hair. "This is my sleep hair!"

"The magical blanket?" He grinned skeptically at me. "You can't seriously have expected me to believe that wasn't code for something."

"It wasn't! I told you not to look for hidden agendas. I'm saying things how I mean them. It's part of the new and improved Jenna," I said. "You know, I read the titles of a bunch of self-help books, and I think it's really benefiting me."

"Pity," he said with a quick shake of his head. "I liked the original Jenna just fine."

"Then it's a very good thing I didn't actually *buy* the books. I just read the titles," I said. "I'll forget everything I learned by Tuesday."

He laughed, and it was the first time Cooper had truly sounded carefree. His eyes shone, his teeth twinkled white, and his head was tilted back with a pleased expression. I liked what I saw in a way that was probably dangerous for my health. Especially since I'd just *ixnayed* the idea of a relationship with him.

"It's a very good thing then," he said. "Does that mean you'll let me give you a ride to bingo if I agree that it's not a date?"

I spun back to my hot chocolate and scooped out the last of the marshmallows. "In that case, I'd love a ride."

"Jenna, one more thing." Cooper blocked me from standing entirely as he stepped closer. His eyes roved over me, a slightly more somber note to them. "I hope you don't take this the wrong way, but in the spirit of being honest..."

"Yes?" I could barely contain the beat of my heart. It seemed rapid, wild, and I just wanted to lean forward and see if he'd seal the deal with a kiss.

Then his eyes flicked back up toward my head, and he gave a smug little grin. "You might wanna fix that hair... or people might think you and me are more than just friends."

Chapter 16

After storming away from the chief, I huffed it upstairs and changed clothes while he waited in the living room. I ran a few fingers through my tangled mane, decided that my efforts weren't accomplishing a whole lot, and switched to a messy bun.

I couldn't quite explain why I felt the need to slip into my new red dress with matching red heels—courtesy of my mother's store. I had also picked up a faux-fur coat that was two parts gorgeous and one part kickass. A swatch of red lipstick finished my look. In Los Angeles, I might be heading to a red-carpet premier of a client's film looking like this. In Blueberry Lake, I was going to bingo. Go figure.

I descended the stairs while digging in my clutch for the key that Cooper had just handed me. Apparently, my purse had eaten it.

"You know, I think I lost that key to the back door you gave me," I said. "Any chance you have an extra?"

When I got no response, I stopped walking and looked up. Cooper was standing there with a hand on his chest as if he were having a heart attack, and a stunned look on his face.

"Cat got your tongue?" I asked, but secretly, I was pleased with his reaction. I wondered if it was the heels or the lipstick, or some combination of them both. Maybe it was the one part kickass of the faux-fur coat that had him looking like a tornado had picked him up and dropped him somewhere that wasn't Kansas. "You ready to go?"

"You do know we're going to play bingo?" he asked once he regained his speech.

I frowned. "I know I'm forgetful, but I'm not *that* forgetful."

He cleared his throat. "You look—Jenna, you look amazing."

"Aw, in this old thing? Seriously. I got it second hand. Isn't it fabulous?"

"There's no way people are going to think we're not on a date when we pull up together."

I self-consciously patted my messy bun. "I thought I tied it back! Is my hair still all sleepy?"

"It's not the hair, it's the..." he hesitated again. "The everything. Nobody looks like that when they go to bingo."

"Well, I like it, so that's good enough for me."

"People are going to be staring."

"Yourself included?" I gave him a sly grin. "Because you're staring now."

Cooper blinked, turned away. "Sorry. Shall we get going? I feel like I should've brought you flowers or something with the way you're looking."

"Eh, good thing we're just friends." I caught him eyeing my feet. "Don't comment on the impracticality of my shoes. They're worth it."

"I was just going to offer you an arm to go down the stairs," he said. "If that doesn't upset the boundaries of your carefully placed friend-zone."

"I'd appreciate that." I accepted Cooper's outstretched arm after we inched out onto the front steps. Quickly closing and locking the door, I leaned on him as I pivoted back around. As we hiked down the steps, he cinched me a tiny bit closer.

"Doing okay?" he asked softly, his breath dancing over my ear. "Almost there."

I glanced at him in confusion. A quick look over my shoulder solved the mystery of his sudden closeness: Matt was visible in his kitchen window.

"Oh, you are just doing this to tick him off," I said, swatting at Cooper's arm. "I'd tell you to let go of me, but I'd break an ankle."

"He had you all afternoon," Cooper said. "It's my turn for the evening."

"What are you, sharing custody of me?"

"Isn't that what friends do?"

I made a face at him and dropped his arm the second we reached the car. I hadn't planned on arriving at bingo in a police cruiser, but then again, I hadn't planned on a lot of things happening as of late. He helped me into the car, and I pressed my hands to the heater as Cooper cranked it to high.

"I told you not to wear that," he said, glancing at my frozen hands. "You'll be cold."

"You seemed to like it just fine inside."

"Tell me about Becky."

"Excuse me?" I swiveled to face him, taken aback by the change in subject. "Becky *who*?"

"Right," he said, unconvinced. "What'd she do to you?"

"How do you know about Becky?"

"There you go," he said. "Keep talking. I asked around, and it sounds like you were pointing fingers at her for what happened at the bachelorette party."

"Are people tattling on me? This town is one big grade school recess. Nothing is private."

"Unlike Hollywood," he said sarcastically, "where the inner details of one's life aren't splashed across magazines for the entire world to watch unfold."

"Fine, you make a good point," I said, wincing with the open wound that was my own failed (public) relationship. "Still, this was a *private* party. And Becky was far from innocent. She purposefully tripped me while I was carrying a tray of drinks."

"You realize that sounds far-fetched."

"She had it out for me," I said. "She was watching me all evening, and even before."

"Before?"

I shut my mouth. I hadn't yet told Cooper about the creepy photo through the window thing that Becky had pulled off, and I figured he wouldn't take me withholding information well. Especially when an intruder had gotten into my house. One that might very well have been Becky.

"I won't make any judgements, nor will I be upset," he said, flicking a glance toward me as if reading my mind. "But I wish you would just be honest with me so I have all of the information."

After making him swear three times on his mother's life that he wouldn't be upset, I produced the photo May had found in Becky's jacket and handed it over. We'd just reached the bingo parking lot, so he waited until he'd pulled the cruiser into a spot before he took a good look at it.

His face hardened as he caught a glimpse of the figures in the image. "I can't believe you tried to hide—"

"Ah, ah, *ah*!" I tapped on the dashboard with my fingernails. "You're not allowed to be mad. Just digest the information and move on, Chief."

"Fine." Cooper cleared his throat and, looking furious, addressed me. "Why did you hide this?"

"I wasn't hiding this! I was going to tell you, but I didn't have the time."

"Because you were too busy making sure you placed me in the friend zone?"

"Cooper, don't make this personal."

"Police work in a small town is always personal," he said with surprising force. "There's a good chance that every person I arrest, I'll see again. Every person I warn, I will see again. Every person who I put behind bars—I'll probably see them again, too. I assure you I am very thorough and careful about my job. I care about the town and its residents. You're one of us, so I care about you. As a friend," he finished awkwardly.

It was the first time anyone had truly included me as one of the town's residents. My family had celebrated my return, and Matt had become a friend, and Allie was a hoot and a half, but there was still a sense of novelty with all that. The way Cooper looped me in as 'one of us' would be a moment I didn't forget anytime soon.

"Thank you," I mumbled. "That means a lot to me. I'm sorry I didn't tell you sooner."

"I'm not mad, Jenna, I just—" he sighed. "I'm worried."

"Don't worry about me—I'll be fine. I'm a tough cookie."

"I know you are, but this person is relentless, and even the toughest of cookies can crumble." He seemed to think his statement went too personal because he rushed on, rubbing his forehead with his thumb and forefinger to ease tension. "Let us revisit what we know."

"Sure," I said. "Grant Mark was murdered two days ago. You initially thought it was me, so you came barging into my place to welcome me to town."

"I don't remember it being exactly like that, but—"

"You barged in," I said. "But I forgive you because you care about me."

"Jenna—"

"You said it, and now you can't take it back," I said with a sly grin. "You care about me, and I know it."

"Look at you, being mature about it," he deadpanned. "So, we have a dead body and someone trying to frame you. We have this photo and an alleged tripping—"

"Becky *did* trip me."

"I am only basing my knowledge on facts. Which do not include tripping because it's your word against hers," he clarified. "We have someone breaking into your house to plant the other shoe. There were no prints lifted from the second shoe."

"The killer must watch NCIS, too. I wonder if they saw any episodes that I styled? Right—that's not relevant."

"We also know the murder weapon was a shoe you'd previously wielded as a defense weapon against the victim—"

"Hey, I was forced to do that. He was a creep."

"Eye witness accounts seem to agree with you," Cooper said. "As well as popular opinion of the victim."

"Which means that just about anyone who visited Something Old is a suspect," I said. "Because Allie bought the shoes, and someone took them from there."

"Except she wasn't at the store the whole time," Cooper said, his eyes landing on mine. "I found out Allie took a break that she didn't bother to tell anyone about."

"What do you mean?"

"I paid a little visit to a hotel this morning, and a front desk receptionist by the name of Brayden seemed to recall Allie hanging around the hotel lobby at the time of the murder. Seems he thinks she's got a thing for him."

"Come on, are you going to trust that guy?" I asked. "I saw him this morning. He has frosted tips."

Cooper looked startled. "And you imagine that the color of one's hair has a bearing on their ability to tell the truth?"

I crossed my arms. "Allie didn't do it."

"She lied about her alibi. She purchased the murder weapon hours before it was used. She has an odd fascination with you—and she had just witnessed Grant get handsy and make you uncomfortable. You don't think she was seeking some sort of vigilante justice? You must admit she has a wild imagination."

I thought back to all my interactions with Allie. Her interesting clothing choices, her voracious appetite at June's, her willingness to help my mother with whatever needed doing around the store. None of it added up to her murdering anyone.

But even as I told myself that, a slew of other instances crossed my mind. Allie's willingness to help me break into a murder victim's hotel room. Her obsession with a crime that didn't really have anything to do with her, other than the fact that she'd bought the shoes someone had used to kill Grant. Her very slight awe over the fact that I had come from a foreign land called Hollywood.

"I take it by your silence that you're not sure," Cooper said. "I think you need to be careful about letting her get too close. Is there any chance that photo came from Allie and not Becky, and it got mixed up in the jackets?"

"No," I said. "Allie wasn't at the party."

"I assume you're not going to tell me exactly how this photo came into your possession."

"Nope," I said. "But I don't think Allie's stalking me. Grant slightly ticking off a new friend of hers is hardly cause for murder."

"Unless there's something we haven't uncovered yet," he said. "There's always a reason—we'll find it."

"You're forgetting the fact that anyone could have taken that bag," I said. "The list of suspects is as long as my arm. The entire bridal party was there...including Becky, who was seen looking into bags."

"Did anyone see Becky actually take a bag? Or something out of a bag?"

"Well, no," I said. "But what about the letters?"

"Oh, you mean the tip I received this morning from two masked bandits who broke into Grant's room and dug through his possessions? Yes, there's that," he said dryly. "The letters have no signature. Without anything to compare them to, they're next to useless. No defining marks. Ordinary loose-leaf paper. We don't have the highest tech lab here to dig much further than that."

"What if we got something to compare them to?" I asked. "Is there anyone around here who could do a quick writing analysis?"

"I could," he said, "but nothing that would hold up in court."

"You could ballpark it though. At least enough to get a direction?"

"Yes. I'm not sure I like where your head's at, however."

"You will when this works," I said. "Give me ten minutes and a microphone at bingo."

"This will not end well."

"Relax, I'm not singing karaoke," I said. "*That* wouldn't end well, but this might just help us catch a murderer."

Chapter 17

"Ladies and gentlemen," I said, standing on stage at Blueberry Lake High's auditorium. "Thank you for letting me have your attention. Bingo will begin in a few short moments, but first, I have a fun surprise for everyone!"

To Cooper's dismay, I'd gotten an idea just big enough and just bold enough to *possibly* work. I'd convinced Cooper to get Stacy Simone—the head coordinator of bingo and a huge fangirl of the chief—to let me indulge the crowd in a special giveaway while the competitive bingo players found their seats and scoped out their boards.

Besides the potential to help catch a killer, my plan had the added bonus of bringing business and attention to my mother's shop. Because everything was so short notice, I had to be resourceful and use my God-given talents. I wasn't sure I'd been given all that many talents, but I sure as heck could style anyone who walked through the door of my mother's thrift shop for cheap, so therein lay the prize.

"My name is Jenna McGovern—I'm a new resident in town, though I've spent many wonderful summers here. My Gran ran the flower shop Green's, my mother lives over on Peach Street, and I'm a transplant from California." I paused to grin at the crowd. "I was a stylist to the stars out in Hollywood, and you may have seen my work in magazines, at award shows, and on television."

I took a quick scan of the crowd as the doors opened in the back, and the entire Duvet bridal party scooted in a hair on the tardy side. I caught sight of Lana and Eliza, along with their mother.

An unfamiliar face who I took to be the father-of-the-bride sat next to Brenda, his new wife. Mr. Duvet's first wife, Bridget, sat on the other end of the table and shot him dirty looks. The rest of the gang: Patty, Becky, and a few others, filled out the Duvet party.

Also present in the audience was the entire knitting club scooted up to one table. From it, Mrs. Beasley and June waved vigorously toward the stage. Sitting with the old ladies was Allie. Tonight she wore a scrunchie in her hair and a neon orange dress that was more latex than anything else.

My mother and Sid sat next to the two ladies who'd been looking at chunky sweaters in her shop, and near them sat May and Joe, who had linked up with the rest of the fire department. I was startled to find Matt in attendance as well, watching me with interest while May sat looking furious next to him. Matt must have told her about my visit this afternoon. *Whoops.*

By the time everyone had shuffled into their seats, I resumed my speech and smiled at the surprised grin on my mother's face as I announced the prize. "As a welcome to town gift, I want to offer one free styling session and a two-hundred-dollar store credit to Something Old. Redeemable this month only—the rest of the fine print can be found somewhere else."

"How do we enter the contest?" Mrs. Beasley called. "Can I give the coupon to someone else?"

"Um, sure," I said. "To enter, all you need to do is answer the following questions. Stacy has put paper and pens on all the tables. Fill out your name, email address, and then write a short paragraph telling me why you'd like to win the prize. I'll pick randomly at the end of the night."

Mrs. Beasley's hand raised again. "What if I don't have an email address?"

"I know where to find you," I said. "You can write your home address if you prefer."

"What if I live at my daughter's?" Mrs. Beasley asked. "Can I write the address to June's café? I spend more time there."

"Absolutely," I said. "Any other questions?"

"How long is a paragraph?" This came from my mother.

"Mom, why are you answering the questionnaire at all?" I asked. "I'm your *daughter*. You can make me style you for free."

"Maybe I want to give the prize to someone," she said, fluttering her eyes at Sid. "Just give me an answer."

"I don't know, a sentence."

"A sentence is not a paragraph," my mother said. "Is it a paragraph or a sentence?"

"How about a five-paragraph essay?" Allie raised her hand and shouted the question at the same time. "Hi, my name is Allie, and I have a question."

"Allie, I know you," I said, striving for patience. "And I heard the question. No essay needed. Just a quick line—"

"Is a line the same as a sentence?" My mother interrupted. "Because you've said line, sentence, and paragraph so far, and it's very confusing."

"I need your name and email address," I said finally. "That's all. Nothing more. Just write that down, fold it up—Mrs. Beasley, you can put whatever address you want—and we'll go from there. Any last questions?"

A few hands raised and I ignored them.

"Great," I said. "That'll be all—let bingo begin!"

I made my way down from the stage and ran smack dab into a grinning chief of police.

"Don't you just love town gatherings?" Cooper asked. "Blueberry Lake sure is something else."

"I feel like I'm on a movie set!" I said, exasperated. "Is it always this hard to wrangle people? How does the mayor do it? How do you do it?"

"Well—"

"Rhetorical," I said, pointing a finger at him. "Now, how about we grab a glass of punch and take a seat at an empty table with a view of the Duvet family?"

"There's no way I can convince you to just sit tight and play bingo nicely like everyone else on a Sunday night?" Cooper had grabbed two glasses of punch and a small stack of sugar cookies from somewhere. He handed a drink to me and took one look at my face. "I guess that's a no."

"Did you get one of those for me?" I noted he hadn't offered me a cookie. When he hesitated, I gave him a look. "You got four cookies for yourself?"

"I'll share if you play your cards right."

I found us a cozy little space tucked between an old gentleman who couldn't hear and an old lady who couldn't see. It gave us just the privacy boundaries we needed, as well as a good view of the Duvet family.

Unfortunately, it also gave my mother a good view of us. She waved vigorously from across the room, and when I ignored her, she stood up and waved harder. Eventually, I waved back.

"Good thing this isn't a real date, huh?" Cooper said. "Seeing how your mom seems to be chaperoning the event."

"This is not a laughing matter," I said. "I'm nearing thirty. She really needs to tone things down."

"She's just excited you're back."

"She's excited I'm here with *you*," I said, realizing I'd said too much. I'd piqued Cooper's interest, so I had to come up with something quick. "I just mean you have a steady job, and you're a *man*, so before you go strutting around like a peacock, just keep that in mind. The bar isn't set that high."

"Shame," he said with a wink. "I like a challenge."

That left me speechless, so it was a very good thing that Stacey Simone showed up at our table with a pile of entries from my spur of the moment giveaway.

"That was very generous of you, Jenna," Stacey said with a slight blush. "I hope you don't mind that I entered myself. My sister's getting married this summer, and I'd really appreciate some help picking out a dress. You know, on a budget."

"Anytime," I said, waving a hand. "I hope you are chosen as winner, but if not, swing by. I'll do it for free—you just buy the dress."

"Really?" She eyed me. "Will I look like...*that*?"

"Like this?" I burst into laughter as she studied me. "Honey, you'll look better. But yes, everything I'm wearing tonight is from my mother's store."

"Oh, my," she said with a gasp. "I'm going to announce that. Everyone is talking about your dress."

Stacey left in a flurry of mumblings to herself as Cooper leaned over to me. "I told you."

"Told me what?" I was already distracted thumbing through the stack of papers from the host. "Now's not the time to lord things over me, Coop."

"I told you that you looked beautiful."

I froze, a stack of papers in hand. Forcing myself to gently set them on the table, I continued on as if he hadn't said anything. "It's not Lucy or Kiana or Brenda," I said. "They write much too neatly."

As I filed the first of the notes to one side, I felt Cooper's eyes stuck on me.

"It doesn't make it *not* true if you ignore me," he said good-naturedly. "And you don't have to get upset. Can't a man tell a woman she's beautiful without it being a come-on?"

"I don't know—I've never thought about it. Why would you do that?"

"How the hell do I know?" he asked with a smile. "There's a first time for everything. Now, slide your bingo card closer to me. You just got B7."

And so went the next twenty minutes: Cooper marking both of our bingo cards while I thumbed through cards and quickly sorted the "possibles" and the "nopes" into two separate piles. The nope pile was thankfully much larger than the possible one. The handwriting was distinct on all the notes that'd been in Grant's bag, sort of fat, looping letters written in a precise hand. Some had a bit of wobble to them, as if the writer had been upset at the time of penning, or possibly they'd consumed a good portion of a wine bottle.

"Holy smokes," I said as one entry came up to be a near perfect match. "Cooper, look."

"I know!" he said, sounding excited. "*BINGO*!"

"No, Cooper—*what*?!"

Cooper reached over and grasped my hand, raising it high for the crowd to see. "Our newcomer has bingo!"

"No, no, I don't," I said, hiding under the curious attention from the rest of the room. "I think I made a mistake."

"I didn't," Coop said, and then began reading the numbers aloud.

When he finished, everyone cheered.

"Please come up and claim your prize!" Stacey announced. "Ladies and gentlemen, Miss Jenna McGovern! Now, ladies—take a look at her outfit. Everything she's wearing is from Bea's thrift shop. Aren't we all excited to find out the lucky winner to tonight's surprise giveaway?"

A distinctly female cheer rose up from the crowd. Meanwhile, Cooper had somehow stood and guided me toward the stage, giving me a pat on the back and a word of encouragement—along with a light shove—up the stairs while he waited behind.

I gave him a deadly stare as I stood straighter and forced a smile through Stacey's mock *oohs* and *ahhs* as she fawned over my red dress. It *was* a pretty fabulous red dress, I had to admit, which got me in the spirit of things until I spotted a huge problem. My new number one suspect had stood at her table and was headed toward the exit.

"Great, thanks," I said. "I'll announce the winner later. It's lovely reading all the responses, and thanks for this—*ah,* thing. What is the prize?"

"Meat!" Stacey said. "You've won a nice ham."

"A ham," I echoed, holding an oddly shaped piece of meat that I had no idea what to do with. "Right—thanks. Well, I'll just be headed back to my seat. Carry on bingo-ing!"

"Not so fast!" Stacey gripped my shoulders with her talon-like manicure. "Gentlemen, a little birdie tells me that Jenna is single! Jenna, can you confirm?"

I leaned reluctantly into the microphone and gave a smile that I hoped ended this interview. "I'm ah—single, but not mingling. Thanks, Stacey."

With that, I scurried down from the stage and fell into step with the waiting cop.

"You really know how to kill a party," Cooper said, and then hesitated. "Poor choice of words, sorry."

"Dark humor, I get it," I said, distracted as we wormed our way back to our seats. "A cop thing."

"Right. With how much you refuse to leave this situation alone, you'll have a badge soon, too," he said. "Why are you in such a frenzy? Take a seat. Have a cookie—I'll share."

My phone began pinging nonstop with messages, so I looked down and found a plethora of texts, mostly from people in the room:

Allie: Your shoes are great. Your boobs look awesome.

Sid: Does this single and not mingling mean you're taken?

Sid: Look at you and Cooper! Does this mean you're a couple?

Sid: Cutexfrjekawltr

Sid: Whoops. I mean cute;;;;

Sid: CUTE!!!!

Sid: A real partnership is just that—team work! Look how well you and Coop are working together!

Sid: I knew you'd just love living here.

"Why's your stepfather texting you about me?" Cooper asked, shifting uncomfortably.

"Why are you peeking over my shoulder?" I shielded my phone from him. "It's my mother, obviously. When she married Sid, she learned how to text. It's still a novelty."

"Allie—"

"Don't comment on her texts," I said "Come on, my suspect is on the run. Think we can slip out unnoticed?"

"Seeing as you're holding a gigantic ham and are currently the center of attention, I'm going to say no."

I glanced around the room, and sure enough, surreptitious glances followed my every movement. I swore that when I breathed, the entire room followed suit.

"I'm going anyway," I said. "Will you watch my ham?"

"Not a chance," he said. "Leave the meat behind—I have a better idea."

I set the ham on the table and ignored the conversation that broke out between the man who couldn't hear and the woman who couldn't see. It was like a bad rendition of *Who's on First*.

Cooper's plan was to loop his arm around my waist and guide me out of the auditorium with his hand on my lower back. I considered elbowing him to keep his space, but I refrained for two reasons. One, if this was some sort of undercover police work, I didn't want to spoil things. Two, he felt nice against me.

When we exited into an empty hallway, Cooper's hand dropped at once and he took a step away.

"I'm going to try not to take offense about how quickly you moved away from me," I said, nodding toward the gap between us. "Do I smell?"

"Yes," he said, and then quickly added. "Good. You smell *very* good, I mean. Trust me, if you want to stay friends, it's better if I stay away from you."

I felt my cheeks flame red. "What was that all about then?"

"People will think we left for some private time," he said simply. "Your mom will make sure nobody follows us."

"I don't want people thinking I'm making out with you!"

"Gee, you know how to build up a man's confidence."

"It's not *you* that I have a problem with," I admitted. "It's the making out bit. Plus..."

"You broke up with Matt this afternoon," Cooper said knowingly. "I see. You don't want him to get the wrong idea."

I scowled. "Stay out of my love life. I didn't break up with anyone. There was nothing to break."

"I thought you didn't *have* a love life to stay out of."

"I don't! Just—look at this," I said, grouchy. "I'll clear the air about us making out later, even though the damage will already be done."

My phone pinged seven more times, confirming the damage was currently worsening. Gossip spread through this town like a wildfire, burning anything less than interesting in its path. I silenced my phone and refused to think about Matt. Hopefully he hadn't fallen prey to the gossip fires of Blueberry Lake, and if he had, I'd set the record straight tomorrow.

"Look," I said, pulling out the note I'd clasped into the pocket of my faux-fur jacket. I gave it to Cooper. "Now compare *that* to these photos."

I pulled out my phone and flicked through the photos of the notes I'd taken, ignoring the bar of texts pinging across the top.

"I'm assuming you'd like me to ignore the fact that you shouldn't have these photos at all," Cooper said lightly, glancing between the phone and the sheet of paper in his hand. "Or the fact that none of this would be admissible in court."

"Come on," I said. "The handwriting is a match. And we know that Patty dated Grant at one point. Doesn't it make you want to question her at the very least?"

"I'll admit, I'm intrigued."

"From the sounds of the letters—they started out sweet and then turned sour. Lovers quarrel gone wrong?"

"There were five letters in total," Cooper said, squinting as he searched his memories for them. "The first three must have been from when they were romantic with one another. They're—"

"—very descriptive," I finished. "The fourth letter sounds melancholy, and in the fifth, she threatens to kill him. Let me talk to her first before you do. She'll be more willing to open up to me."

"Did you just hear yourself?" Cooper stared at me in amazement. "She threatened to kill someone, and you'd like to talk to her *alone*?"

"Yep."

"That's insane."

"Maybe, but it's not like you can't stand right around the corner with your handy-dandy gun and listen."

"Handy-dandy gun," Cooper echoed faintly.

"Or whatever," I said. "Come on, we have to find her."

"I am not agreeing to this unless you promise you'll stay within hearing and firing distance," he said. "End of story."

"Don't *shoot* anyone!"

"I'm not planning on it, but I'm not letting another murder happen on my watch, either."

"Fair," I said, and stuck out a hand for us to shake on it. "Now, I have an idea."

Chapter 18

"Aha, *there* you are," I said, kicking open a subtlety placed back door that led to the alley. "Found you."

Patty looked up at me and grinned. "You don't smoke, do you?"

"No, but I did win a ham. I had to get away from the mobs of people out to congratulate me."

She gave a snort of laughter. "Long way from home, aren't you?"

I knew instinctively that she meant Hollywood, and it was true I'd considered Los Angeles my home for a long, long time. But that was beginning to shift, I realized. Home was a more liquid concept to me now, seeing as I had virtually nothing left to tie me to the West Coast. If anything, my only ties were here now.

"I don't know," I said, loud enough for Cooper to hear. He'd tucked himself just behind the door to the alley. I'd left it open a crack as I'd slipped out, though it was virtually impossible for Patty to tell in this darkness. "I'm starting to like it around these parts. Never thought I'd say that."

"Your gran's house has that effect on people," Patty agreed. "Are you thinking of sticking around longer term?"

"I'm beginning to think it might not be so bad. The people around here are nice. Mostly," I said, sobering as I prepared to grill Patty on her love letters to the deceased. I had genuinely begun to like her. If I had it my way, she would not be the murderer—but then again, I didn't really have a choice.

"You're not out here to chit-chat," Patty said, reading my face correctly. "What's bothering you?"

"These," I said, raising my phone and turning it to show Patty the photos of the notes. "It's your handwriting, isn't it?"

She studied the writing passively for a moment, neither surprised nor alarmed, and then shrugged. "The way you're talking, it doesn't sound like I have a choice but to admit it."

"Did you kill him?" I asked.

"Do you really think I'd risk my life for that weasel?" She puffed on her cigarette. "I know you think you're just doing your job, but use your head, pretty girl. I wouldn't have killed him with a shoe."

"How would you have done it?" I asked, playing along. "If not by high heel."

She gave a course laugh. "I'm not playing that game, sweetheart. I didn't do it, and I wouldn't have done it. I know it looks bad what with the notes and all, but it wasn't me."

"Do you have an alibi for the time of murder?" I asked. "Maybe you were with the rest of the bridal party?"

"Nope," she said. "No alibi. I went shopping at your mother's store with the rest of the party the day of Grant's death. We bought a lot of stuff and then a few of us ran home to drop things off. We had the shower the next day, and I didn't feel like spending any extra time with the group. I like my solo time, my private space, you know what I mean?"

I did know what she meant, so I nodded before continuing. "Come on, Patty. If you didn't do it, you're not being helpful. You admitted to writing threatening notes to the victim and have no alibi for the time of murder."

"Are my fingerprints on the crime scene? Did anyone see me there?" She shrugged. "Nope. Because I wasn't there, and I didn't do anything wrong."

"Except threaten to kill your ex-boyfriend."

"Except that," she said. "But I didn't *mean* it. I was just steamed. We'd broken up recently."

"Had you been together a long time?"

She snorted. "No. About a week. I only met him through the bridal party a few weeks back. We had some chemistry, so we explored that if you know what I mean."

"Sounds like a whirlwind if all this took place over the course of seven days."

"I wrote him a letter each day we were together," Patty said. "That puts us at...what? Five days? Yeah, I was upset when he called things off, but only because I felt like he'd used me. Not because I *loved* him."

"Your notes were pretty romantic."

"Yeah, well. I was feeling him in the moment. Only a week later did I realize he was a jerk, and I'd just been infatuated with the person I thought he was."

"Did you break up with him?"

"No, he dumped me. Said I was too clingy. Probably the notes were a bit much, but I thought they were cute."

"Except for the one with the death threat."

"Yeah." She wrinkled her nose. "Not so cute. But I was angry, and I'd had a whole bottle of wine to myself that night. I never meant to actually *give* him that note. I was just venting."

"How'd he get it then?" I asked. "If you weren't actually trying to threaten him?"

"Girl, you just got broken up with in a public way," Patty said. "I'm sure a few unpleasant thoughts ran through your head about your ex. That's all this was—I was writing down my feelings instead of eating them. My therapist says it's good for me to get all the poisonous thoughts out and then burn the notes. I burnt a shitload of notes."

"Why didn't that one end up in the burn pile?"

"I told you, I have no clue. I probably just hadn't gotten to it yet. Or maybe someone found it and planted it on him."

"Let me try to understand," I said. "You think someone snuck into your house and took a letter from you to Grant, then broke into your ex's backpack and slipped it there?"

"Nobody had to break into anywhere," she said. "I kept the notes in my purse or the pocket of my jacket, depending on the day. I would write them when I was out and about and felt the urge. My therapist says to live in the moment, and if I was feeling upset, I should stop what I'm doing and write about it. I was sitting at Panera eating a half-sandwich with my soup bread bowl when I wrote that last note."

Panera didn't exactly seem like murder-plotting territory to me. I also wondered if it might be worth a visit back to Grant's hotel room for additional questioning of Brayden along with the pulling of security tapes. Could the murderer have snatched the note from Patty's purse—possibly during the bachelorette party?—and then snuck into Grant's room after his death and placed it there?

"I gave Grant the rest of the notes," Patty said thoughtfully. "I would slip them into his backpack instead of handing them over because that felt more romantic. Those letters were really eloquent, don't you think?"

"Sure," I agreed. If I ignored the lipstick blotches on the page and the overly descriptive acts of romance. "You're a poet, Patty."

It was a bit of a stretch, but then again, maybe the murderer had gotten lucky. Maybe he or she had found Patty's threatening note—either in her purse or jacket pocket—at one of the bridal party events. The culprit could have taken the incriminating note and planted it in Grant's backpack to cast suspicion on Patty.

"Did you tell anyone about the notes?" I asked. "Is it possible someone knew your tendency to vent on paper?"

"Yeah, I told a whole slew of people. Whoever would listen really," Patty said. "You might have guessed, but I have a hard time keeping my trap shut. I'd find it incredibly difficult to provide a list of everyone who knew I wrote a threatening letter to Grant."

"Great, that really narrows down the list."

"Look, I'm sorry. I know you're on the hook for his murder, and I know you didn't do it." Patty watched me carefully. "But I swear to you, I didn't do it either. I mean, dig around and ask about me if you want—I'm an open book. You won't find anything."

"I know," I said, my shoulders curling in as I collapsed against the brick wall. I rested my head back. "I never thought you did it, but I had to ask."

"Of course," she said. "You'd be doing a bad job if you didn't."

"Any thoughts on who might've done it?" I asked. "By the way, why didn't you tell me all of this at the party when I was asking?"

"I told it all to someone there," she said with a frown. "It wasn't you?"

I shook my head.

"The night gets a bit fuzzy," she said. "Those Lanas were horrifying. I wasn't meaning to keep secrets. I also wasn't aware I was being investigated—while also under the influence of The Lana signature beverage. But anyway, back to your other question..."

She paused to tap her chin in thought. The night air whipped cool around us, and the soft sound of a faulty microphone and shouted bingo numbers filtered out to us.

"You know, I might look into Will," she said finally. "I think he could've done it."

"You mean Lana and Eliza's father?" I asked. "What incentive would he have to kill Grant Mark?"

"Eliza *really* disliked Grant," Patty said with a huff of breath. "Like really, seriously disliked him. She tried to date him once and things went way south. She told anyone who would listen what a horrible guy he was."

"And you think her father might have heard and gotten ticked?"

She shrugged. "He's got a bit of a temper. And he'd do anything for his girls."

"And getting rid of Grant could've been a two-for-one," I mused. "Daddy Duvet would have finished off the man who made his daughter uncomfortable on a date, *and* the man who is ruining his other daughter's wedding."

"Yep," Patty said. "Exactly. I'm not sure how the shoe plays into things since Daddy Duvet isn't a high heel wearing sort of guy, but I suppose he's smart enough to frame someone."

"How would he have gotten the shoes in the first place?" I asked. "He wasn't there during the shopping trip, was he? Someone must have grabbed the bag from behind the counter for him. An accomplice?"

Patty bobbed her shoulders up and down. "I've given you my theories, the rest is up to you, detective."

"Thanks for your help," I said. "Enjoy your, ah, smoke."

She nodded, holding a deep lungful of smoke as I slipped back inside and found Cooper waiting for me with a smirk on his face.

"Hey there, detective," he said pleasantly. "You're pretty damn good at making friends with the enemy."

"She's not the enemy," I said. "She didn't do it."

"You don't think William Duvet did it, do you?" Cooper picked up his pace to match my hurried stride. Somehow, he still made it look easy. "It seems a bit arbitrary to me to murder a man because his girls had a complaint."

"Do you have a daughter?"

"Negative."

"Then I'm not sure you can judge what a father would or wouldn't do for his daughter," I said. "Grant was a creep, and the Duvet girls tend to get what they want. If they wanted Grant gone badly enough..."

"You think Grant might have messed with the wrong family."

"A guy like that pushing it too far? Yeah, I'm not surprised."

"Jenna." Cooper stopped walking and waited until I did the same. "I want you to stop looking into things. This is getting dangerous."

"That just means I'm getting close to the answers," I said. "I can't stop when the murderer is within my grasp."

"That's exactly the reason you need to stop." He took two steps closer, leaving a just-barely-comfortable amount of space between us. "Let me handle things from here."

"Because you're some big macho man?" I joked. "Yeah right."

"Because I'm a cop, and you're an untrained civilian who's been poking her nose where it doesn't belong."

"Gee, don't pull your punches there, chief."

"I'll always be honest with you, Jenna—you have my word," he said. "And I've let this go on for long enough."

"As if I haven't been helpful!"

"I didn't say that," he said. "But I'm putting an end to it now. I don't want the murderer coming after you because you're getting too close."

"I don't particularly like when people tell me what to do, chief."

"Jenna, this is for your safety."

"I understand," I said stiffly. "Thanks for your concern."

"Don't overreact. I'm trying to protect you."

"I don't want your protection," I said. "I mean—I appreciate what you do for the town, but I just want your friendship. You telling me what to do isn't how this works."

"Fine, will you please lay off the case?"

"I'll think about it, but I'm not making any promises." I softened somewhat at the pinched look of concern on his face. "Look, I'm sure you have a lot of work to do, and so do I—starting with awarding the winner of the giveaway. Why don't I grab a ride home from my mother and Sid so you can get started on your stuff?"

"Jenna, please don't do this."

"No hard feelings! I'm just—"

"There you are!" Stacey Simone rushed out in a flurry of manicured fingernails. "Did you pick the winner?"

"Ah—sure," I said. "Is it time to announce them now?"

"Everyone's waiting for you in there! Where'd you disappear to?"

I let her shuffle me away while shooting an apologetic look over my shoulder at Cooper. I felt a little bad for the way things had ended between us, but it was nothing I couldn't fix after a good night's sleep and a breath of fresh air. I'd make things right tomorrow.

"Ladies and gentlemen, she's back!" Stacey waved her hands like Vanna White. "Though gentlemen, I must make one correction. It appears that our Jenna McGovern is not as *single* as we thought!"

"Correction," I said, leaning forward to the microphone. "I'm still single. No mingling happening here."

But my mother was already leading a wild cheer that probably drowned me out. I watched as Matt stood and left the fireman's table. My gaze shifted to May who sent me a disappointed glare in return. Even Joe looked less than happy. When I glanced to the other side of the room, Cooper was nowhere to be seen.

Wonderful. In the span of five minutes, I'd ticked off everyone in town who'd been somewhat of a friend. *Fabulous work, Jenna.*

Someone brought the stack of forms to the front of the room, distracting me for the moment. I closed my eyes and randomly drew one, smiling at the name before me. "Stacey Simone," I said. "You're the winner! And I'll draw a second prize winner to take my ham since I can't cook to save my life."

"How generous!" Stacey cooed.

There was a huge inhalation of breath while I called out the name. "Mack Groveland, you win the ham!"

The woman who couldn't see tapped the man who couldn't hear at my original table. "Mack, you won!"

"What?" he said. "How do you know? You can't see anything."

"I don't know what you won, but I heard your name!"

"What game?"

"Maybe you could take care of distributing the prizes," I said, handing the mic back to Stacey. "Thanks for letting me take over for a minute."

My mother made a beeline toward me as I descended from the stage, but thankfully, I knew a handy dandy exit that led to a back alleyway and managed to dodge her questioning looks. I snuck outside and found the alley empty. Patty must have called it a night after her cigarette because I hadn't seen her return to the gymnasium.

I wasn't all that far from home (then again, nothing in Blueberry Lake is all that far from home!) seeing as the town itself is about three-square miles. Farmland, lakes, and trails sprawl a good way around the city center for those interested in such things. Gran's house, however, was situated right off the main drag in the cozy residential section nestled next to the shops.

Still, walking in high heels after a snow storm posed a problem.

I seriously didn't want to ride home with my mother, and it appeared Cooper and Matt had both left already. May might take pity on me and have Joe drop me off, but I sensed she'd give me a piece of her mind along the way, and I wasn't in the mood for that.

"Howdy! Need a ride?" Allie asked, appearing behind me in the alley. She'd burst onto the scene through the same rear door that I'd taken, and I wondered if she'd known it was there, or if she'd followed me.

"No," I said, "it's fine. I need the fresh air."

"Sure, but you won't be able to walk tomorrow if you try to make the trek home in those shoes."

"Allie, were you following me?"

Her cheeks turned pink. "No, what made you think that?"

"The fact that we're alone in a deserted alley?"

"I know my way in and out of every building in this town. I wanted to avoid the crowd."

"Allie, I have to ask... why didn't you tell me the truth about where you were when Grant was murdered?"

"What are you talking about?"

"Your alibi."

"Alibi?" She scrunched up her face. "You never *asked* for my alibi. I mean, I was working at the shop, and you knew that."

"Right, but I heard otherwise today. That you took a break around the time Grant ended up dead and didn't tell anyone about it."

"Who told you that?"

I frowned. "It's true?"

"I don't know why you're making a big deal out of this when you never asked where I was in the first place."

"I'm just trying to make sense of the situation."

"Yeah, I took a break," Allie hedged. "But I didn't kill Grant, if that's what you're thinking."

"Why'd you follow me tonight?"

Her jaw opened. "I would never hurt you, Jenna. You are my friend. Or at least, I thought you were."

"I thought so too."

"It wasn't a lie. I don't have to recount my every move for you."

"You purchased the murder weapon, and it mysteriously disappeared," I said. "You can understand how that looks incriminating?"

"I barely knew Grant! Why would I kill him?"

"Maybe you saw him being a creep and decided to act," I said. "Vigilante justice? You admitted that you have a wild imagination."

"You know what? I don't have to take this," she said, her lip quivering. "I was out here to offer you a ride because I saw Cooper leave. You upset a lot of people tonight—except for me. I'm the only one who was willing to give you the chance. But now you've finished the job. I hope you're happy."

"I believe you, okay?" I said grudgingly. "I'm sorry, I probably didn't phrase this all very nicely. But I'm on edge, and it took me by surprise. Regardless, the cops will have more tough questions for you."

"Fine," she said with a shrug. "Let the cops talk to me. I can deal with them. I just didn't think I'd have to defend myself to a friend."

"Where did you go on your break?" I asked. "Why won't you tell me?"

She studied me for a long moment. "Give me your shoes."

"What?"

"You wear a size eight? I'm a little bigger shoe size than you, but with these boots it'll be fine."

"What are you talking about?"

"I'm assuming you don't want a ride home with me if I'm a potential murder suspect," Allie said easily. "And everyone else is leaving. It's Frankie's night off, so you're not getting a cab anywhere in town because he'll be at the bar."

"I'm not taking your boots."

"You'll freeze and lose all your toes and break an ankle if you try to walk home in those ridiculous heels," Allie said. "It's not as fun to only have seven toenails to paint because you lost three to frostbite."

I considered briefly what seven toenails would look like as opposed to ten and winced. "Why are you doing this for me?"

"Because we're friends," she said softly. "Come on, I'm going to head out."

"I'm not taking your shoes."

"Do it for me then," she said with a cheeky smile. "Because I want to wear your shoes for a night. They're very gorgeous, and if you hadn't bought them, I would have."

"Aren't they perfect?" I showed them off and returned her smile. "Allie, I believe you. I just wish you'd tell me the truth. Where were you at the time of Grant's murder?"

"I can't," she said. "And I know you trust me, but this is the way things will have to be for now. Shoes now, or the deal's off. Do it for me."

I knew she was manipulating me, but we sat down on the edge of the stairs and traded shoes. Allie spent a good deal of time studying the way my red heels looked on her feet and preened under my approving gaze.

"I think I got the better end of this deal," she said, standing and wobbling once before steadying herself. "I'll take the boots back tomorrow—I have another pair at home."

"Friends?" I asked her.

"Friends," she said, and gave me a hug.

Then she disappeared, and I began the lonely walk home.

Except I wasn't destined to be alone for long.

Chapter 19

I trudged along having a full-on pity party for myself. Snowbanks were piled on either side of me, the wind whipped at any exposed skin, and as it turned out—the oh-so-trendy jacket I'd picked up from my mother's shop did a horrible job of keeping out the biting breeze. I was beginning to understand that in wintry weather, looks weren't everything when it came to clothes. A depressing realization.

The thought brought on even more melancholy visions. I'd be stuffed into a fat old jacket soon enough with a furry hat the size of a pumpkin. My feet would be shoved into things that gave me the whole Big Foot vibe and my legs would be hidden completely by some drab, dull fabric that blended in with everyone else's attire.

Snowflakes drifted and swirled, some of them landing on my eyelashes and icing over so it was difficult to blink. My walk home was less than a mile, and on a pleasant night, it would've been an absolute joy.

I passed the main drag with a few lingering lights twinkling in windows. June's café gleamed merrily with fairy lights, though the sign out front deemed it long past closing time. My mother's shop, Mrs. Beasley's knitting store, and the local market all sat quiet and snuggled in for sleep.

Only the Blue Tavern sat open, where Frankie the cabbie could be heard regaling the other poor souls with his rendition of 80's power ballads. For a moment, I debated ducking inside to warm up. I could give my mother a call and send for Sid to pick me up. He'd be quiet and apologetic. I liked Sid for that very reason.

But sheer stubbornness kept me going. I wasn't going to forfeit my independence just because of a little cold. If Gran, an ancient specimen of a human being, had managed to live through these winters up until the day she died, I could do it too. I was a strapping (in theory) young woman with energy (re: caffeine) to plow through. Plus, if I burned calories trudging through snow, I could have a second hot chocolate today and still fit into my clothes...if my suitcases were ever returned.

With newfound resolve, I turned onto the slightly darker street that led into the residential section of Blueberry Lake. I'd made it thirteen steps exactly when I saw the headlights swing onto the road. My mother happened to think thirteen was her lucky number, but it certainly wasn't mine.

As I spun to face the headlights, I threw an arm up over my eyes to shield the glare, waving with my other arm to alert the driver of my presence. Too late, I realized the car hadn't *missed* seeing me in the dark...they were aiming for me. I yelped as the car leaped onto the sidewalk and plowed straight for me, hurtling past the snowbanks with a disgusting scrape of its bottom against snow, ice, cement—something screechy.

I froze for several long, painful moments before instinct and adrenaline kicked in. With mere seconds to spare, I took a flying leap toward the snowbank and landed on a hard-packed pile of the stuff while the car's front rammed against the icy slope just inches from my face. I could smell the burnt rubber.

I continued to roll, down and away, even as the car cranked itself back onto the road in reverse. For a split second it paused, and I wondered if the person or persons inside were having a debate about whether to come after me.

"Please go, *please*," I muttered, scrambling further away from the road.

Beyond the snowplowed banks was a stretch of grasses, currently covered in snow, that cozied up against a line of trees that quickly turned into a light forest. It was the same bunch of trees that butted up to the back of my property. I didn't exactly fancy disappearing into a dark wood at night, but I'd prefer that to ending up squished against the road with tire prints running down my back.

I was a fairly easy-to-please person, I thought. I only asked that people didn't run me over or chase me into a dark forest at night. And for people to not accuse me of a murder I didn't commit. That's all I asked, and yet, it seemed I asked too much.

Hesitating, my cheek against the cool snow, I stayed tucked into the shadows. After what felt like an eternity, the sound of tires screeching signaled the car's decision to leave the scene, and I collapsed in relief as a spray of snow flitted down on top of me.

As I lay still, trembling and chilled, my heart pumping a million miles an hour, it was all I could do not to give up entirely. A part of me wanted to close my eyes and just rest, just stay here, waiting for somebody to arrive and tell me everything had been a joke. Unfortunately, I couldn't let myself do any such thing because I was wearing ugly boots, and I refused to be found dead of frostbite while wearing ugly shoes.

As I listened to the thump of my heart, I did my best to hold back the last vestiges of panic as a list started forming in my head of the day's awful events.

Someone had broken into my house this morning.

Someone had tried to run me down this evening.

Either I was doing something wrong...

Or I was doing something very, very right.

When the sound of a car engine rumbled beyond the snowbank, my body tensed, and I burrowed deeper into the snow. *They'd come back to finish me off!*

It was only after a familiar voice pricked through the snow that I scrambled to my feet and blinked my eyes against a second, more friendly set of headlights.

"Matt?" I called. "*Matt*, is that you?"

"Jenna?!" My neighbor's tall, familiar figure plunged through the snowbank with absolutely no regard for his clothes.

"Stop," I called. "Wait there! You'll ruin your shoes, and those are such beautiful shoes."

"Oh, Jenna," he said, letting out a guttural laugh that sounded like a sigh. "I'm glad to see you're okay."

"I'm *not* okay—I'm upset," I said crossly, "but your shoes seriously won't be okay if you go any further. Let me come to you."

Matt didn't listen to a word I said, stomping his beautiful shoes straight through the snow until he reached me. He opened his arms, tentatively at first, but when I leaned against him, he wrapped me in a tight embrace.

"Everyone was so worried about you! Why'd you bug out right after the show?"

"It felt like everyone was upset with me. You walked out mid-bingo, Cooper disappeared, May looked annoyed..."

"Cooper got a call from the station. He stepped into the hallway to take it, and by the time he returned, you'd gone. He practically sent out a town-wide search party for you and the only reason he didn't was because your mother might've had a heart attack if she thought you were missing."

"And you?"

"Yeah," he said with a small grin. "I was a little frustrated at the thought of you getting together so quickly with Coop, so I stalked out. But Cooper called and asked for my help in looking for you."

"He did?"

"He was really worried. You weren't answering your phone, and he couldn't find you at the bingo hall."

"I'm sorry," I said. "I hadn't realized my phone was on silent. And I thought everyone had left already."

"It's only Cooper and I who were looking for you," he said. "I thought you might've tried to make the walk home, so I came this way. Cooper followed a different route."

"Thank you," I said, resting against his chest. For the first time in all this, I shivered. "Man, it's cold out here."

"Come on, you're soaked through. We need to get you home."

"Oh, you mean the house that was broken into earlier this evening?" I said dryly. "Real joy. I'd stay with my mother, but *ugh*—I'd really prefer not to."

"I do have the magic blanket," Matt said. "You can take the bed, and I'll take the couch if you want to come over."

"No, it's fine," I said. "I'm a big girl. It's just annoying people are so determined to run me over and frame me for murder when I didn't do anything but move home."

"Is that why you're in the middle of a snowy field?" Matt stepped back, holding me at arm's length from his body. "I thought you were trying a stupid shortcut through the woods and got lost."

I shook my head. My teeth had begun chattering, and I was finding it more and more difficult to talk. Waving an arm, I dragged Matt up the embankment and onto the sidewalk where I pointed out the tire tracks and explained the events that had driven me off the road.

"I have to call Coop," he said, his face drawn. "This is serious, Jenna—are you sure whoever was driving didn't just skid and lose control?"

"Does it look like they skidded?" I pointed out the tire tracks. There was no ice underneath, and the marks showed a steady curve of the wheel. "No, they jumped the curb, then pulled around to wait after I dodged over the snowbank. I think they must have seen you coming. That's what made them take off."

"You say 'them'—did you see how many people were in the car?"

I winced. "No, I didn't see much of anything. The color of the car was dark, and the plate had blue writing."

"So, it had a Minnesota license plate," he said. "Like every car in town. Was it black? Blue? Deep purple?"

"I don't know," I said. "I glanced right at it, and it was like staring into a spotlight. I saw stars and I jumped. I don't know if it was maroon, blue, black, navy, what have you. I don't know if one person was driving or if there was a car full of people."

"Get in," he demanded, gesturing toward his vehicle. "I'm taking you home."

I decided not to argue since there was a good chance I wouldn't be able to work my limbs properly enough to walk home anyway. I was trembling, shaking, wet, terrified, furious—a bit of everything, and I decided that for once tonight, I'd take the easy road and get a lift home from my handsome neighbor.

When Matt got in the car, his face was grim. "Coop's on his way. In the meantime, you're coming with me."

"Um—"

"Please don't argue. You can use my shower and sleep in the bed—I'll take the couch. Don't tell me you actually want to stay home alone tonight?"

"I'll be fine," I said. "I'm a grown woman."

"I have hot chocolate," he wheedled. "Just pop over with me and shower while I prepare it. Your teeth are chattering. Plus, you'll have to talk to Cooper anyway when he arrives, and I told him to meet at my place."

"I can't believe you guys are on speaking terms after everything."

"I told you, I respect the guy and the way he does his job," Matt said evenly. "That doesn't mean we don't indulge in a little friendly competition."

"Friendly competition." I snorted. "Right."

"But when things really matter," he said, his face turning sober, "we work together. We're all in this together, after all. Blueberry Lake ain't that big."

"So I've noticed."

"What do you say about the hot chocolate?"

"Do you have marshmallows?"

"Let's just say I don't do instant hot chocolate—I do gourmet," he said. "June's recipe."

"Fine," I said with an exaggerated sigh. "Twist my arm."

Chapter 20

I shuffled straight into Matt's shower, pleasantly surprised to find his bathroom actually quite clean—not just bachelor pad clean. He would make one lucky lady very happy someday, I thought, noting his neat selection of spare toothbrushes, flosses, soaps and shampoos. He had a real thing for hygiene that a girl could appreciate, unlike some of the men I'd dated in the past.

Standing under the hot stream of water easily became my favorite part of the evening. I let it cascade over my shoulders, drip through my hair, splash against my face. I stood there until the warm water ran out, and then I stepped from the shower and relaxed in the makeshift steam room. I purposefully hadn't turned on the fan, so the entire bathroom had become a sauna. I was sweating by the time I wrapped a towel around my hair and applied lotion to my wind-chapped skin.

My skin was so dry and broken that the lotion brought tears to my eyes as it stung, and only once I'd let it soak in completely, did I start to feel normal again. I shuffled into a BLFD (Blueberry Lake Fire Department) T-shirt—borrowed from Matt. It smelled deliciously like fresh laundry, as did the sweatpants he'd loaned me. I looked like I'd put two pillowcases over my legs, but I didn't care. I'd never been more comfortable.

As I opened the bathroom door, a rush of steam cascaded out, making me feel like a genie as I appeared in the hallway. I was aware as I moved that I smelled distinctly like Matt—his shampoo, his soap, his lotion. It was odd. I couldn't decide if I liked the feeling, or if it weirded me out.

I walked delicately into the kitchen, my bare feet trudging along and finding the carpeted floor surprisingly soft against my feet. It'd been vacuumed recently, and once again, I was taken by Matt's sparse but dedicated housekeeping skills. With a bit of a woman's touch around here, this place could really shine.

"That was the best shower of my life," I said, as I rounded the corner to the kitchen where I could hear the clattering of pans and smell the thick, creamy hot chocolate. "I don't know what it was, but—oh, *hello*."

Cooper and Matt stood shoulder to shoulder across the island in the kitchen. It was clear they'd been talking in low voices, and I'd interrupted with my appearance. Two mugs had turned into three on the counter, and as we all waited in suspended silence, a slow *glub* of chocolate bubbled on the stove behind the men.

Matt leapt to attention and grabbed a spoon. "That'll be done then," he said, stirring. "Take a seat, Jenna."

I did as he said, feeling watched, as if I were standing naked in front of a live audience, while Cooper scanned me from head to toe. I could tell he was trying to hide all expression from his eyes, but there was a glint of something raw and possessive in his gaze when it landed on the firefighter T-shirt and the sweatpants that were so obviously not mine.

"I have an extra sweatshirt in the car if you need," Cooper said eventually. "You might be cold in a T-shirt."

"Um, I'm fine," I said. "I don't plan on staying here long. Also, my house is next door. We were just waiting for you, and Matt promised me hot chocolate, so..."

"Right," Cooper said. A look passed between them that made Cooper all growly as he turned to face me. "Tell me exactly what happened tonight. Every step of the way after you left the stage."

"Okay," I said. "Well, when I saw you'd left—"

"I didn't leave," Cooper said. "I stepped into the hallway to take a call from the station, and you scrambled out of the place before I could find you."

"Sorry," I said. "I thought you were upset with me."

"I was, but I never would have left you alone without a ride," he said looking mystified. "You think I'd do that?"

"I didn't really think, to be clear," I said. "I was stressed. It was a very stressful event."

"Weren't you wearing shoes before?" Cooper asked.

"Shoes?" I shook my head. "You'll have to be more specific."

"I distinctly remember you had on those red, ah..." he trailed off at the look on Matt's face. "I noticed a pair of ladies' boots in the doorway. When did you change?"

"Long story," I said with a sigh. "Let me get some hot chocolate, and then we'll talk."

Matt pulled out the marshmallows and dumped some in a bowl. We each helped ourselves in a tense silence. Once I'd filled my mug to the brim and took a few long, indulgent sips, I crossed my legs onto the stool and launched into my version of the evening's events.

I covered my brief interaction with Allie, her lack of alibi as well as my firm belief that she wasn't a murderer. The rest of the story made for quick work as I described my jaunt back through town with as much detail as I could remember, although admittedly, it was not much.

"You don't remember the color of the vehicle—except that it was darkish," Cooper said, raising an eyebrow. "You have no clue who was in the car or how many people. Nor can you tell me the make, model, or even type of car."

"It was a regular old car," I said assuredly. "Not like, a van or something."

Matt and Cooper exchanged a manly sort of look that I couldn't decipher.

"*What*? I'm not into cars," I said. "I bet neither of you could tell me which perfume I was wearing tonight or the shade of my lipstick."

Cooper cleared his throat and Matt took a giant sip of hot chocolate. The latter scalded himself on it and tumbled into a coughing fit.

"And more importantly," I added with satisfaction. "It was dark outside, and I was blinded by the light. I think that's a song, but it's also the truth."

"Who's on your active list of suspects?" Matt said. "There's Patty and Allie for starters."

"Becky," I added quickly. "And I suppose William Duvet, but that's only if we believe Patty. And I would mark Allie off the list."

"We're not marking anyone off the list who doesn't have an absolutely airtight alibi," Cooper said. "And Jenna, I don't think it's a good idea for you to stay at your house tonight."

"I've already voiced my agreement," Matt said quickly. "And I've offered Jenna my bed."

A stony silence filled the room.

"I'd take the couch," Matt said dryly.

I rolled my eyes. "I'm fine. I can take care of myself."

"Someone tried to run you over tonight, Jenna. Earlier today, that same person probably dropped the companion to the murder weapon inside your house," Cooper said, his eyes narrowed. "I think they've sent you enough warning signs. If it'd make you more comfortable, I can drop you off at your mom's place on the way back to town."

"I can drop her off," Matt said. "Either way works for me."

"Nope. I didn't move home to stay with my mother," I said. "Not happening. Would either of you stay with your mothers if you were in my place?"

Matt and Cooper exchanged another uneasy look.

"Fine, stay home alone," Cooper said, throwing his hands up in the air.

"I think that's a horrible idea," Matt said. "I don't think she should stay home alone."

"She's going to make her own choices," Cooper said, moving to the sink and depositing his mug there. "I was just trying to help her out as the local friendly police chief."

He flicked on the water and rinsed the mug out—another display of impressive cleanliness. I liked Sid well enough, but I don't think he knows my mother even has a dishwasher.

And my ex-boyfriend certainly couldn't do much with the dishes except press *Start*.

"Stop it," I grumbled. "I get the picture. And I appreciate the help, but I can take care of myself."

Cooper wiped his hands on the rag and faced Matt. "I can do a drive-by once an hour, and maybe you can peek out your window if you feel like it every now and again."

Matt looked upset. "You can't leave her alone in there."

"Well, I certainly can't force myself into her house, nor can I kidnap her," Cooper said with a grim smile. "What choice do I have?"

"Fine! *Fine*. You're right. I don't really want to go home alone," I said. "I'll sleep on Matt's couch. Is that what you wanted me to say?"

Cooper broke into a broad grin. "Was that so hard?"

Matt looked over my head to Cooper. "I need to take lessons from you."

Cooper shrugged. "You grow up with sisters and you learn there's no changing a woman's mind. It's always gotta be their idea—isn't that right, Jenna?"

I squinted my eyes at Cooper and battled back a flare of frustration. "I'd like a word with you, mister. Alone, please."

Cooper followed me as I turned and stalked down the hallway that lead from the kitchen to the front door. He watched as I shoved my bare feet into boots and my arms into the fur coat, which Matt had kindly placed on a hanger in the closet.

"Bare feet in your boots?" Cooper asked. "What about socks?"

I glared at him. He shut up.

"This won't take long," I said, and yanked the door open.

Cooper followed suit, shrugging into a jacket and shoes, before accompanying me onto the front steps. He closed the door behind him before leaning against it and studying the expression on my face. "Is this where you tell me off for being a controlling jerk?"

I frowned. "Well, it's a lot less fun if you do it for me."

"Jenna, I might have come off like a jerk, but I swear I was only trying to help you out. I wouldn't dream of telling you what to do."

"This is the worst telling off ever," I said. "I was getting all steamed up, and now you're being all nice and logical. How unsatisfying."

"Funny, you have a way of getting me all steamed up, too."

There was a pull in my gut to step closer to him, so I did. The lights glittering up and down the front path sent an interestingly shaped glow around Cooper's face, making him look more mysterious and alluring than ever.

"I'm going to take off," Cooper said, finally breaking the precarious silence. "I'm glad you're not staying alone tonight, even if it means you're having another sleepover with *him*."

"This is the first sleepover," I corrected. "The other was a nap-over. And it's only out of necessity. I'm not exactly happy to be vacating my home."

"Good." Cooper's eyes fixed on my face where my recently-dried hair was blowing about in the wind and obscuring my vision. Seemingly on impulse, he reached out and brushed some of it into place. "You really shouldn't be outside with wet hair in weather like this."

"It's not—"

"Jenna, I need to be clear with you," Cooper blurted, his eyes widening slightly as if he'd surprised himself with the confession. He pulled himself to his full height and moved closer to me. "If you don't mind."

The last time we'd been standing this close, I'd had on my gorgeous red heels which had propped me up a few inches. Standing on the front steps in Allie's boots had me looking up at Cooper, falling into his dark, wise eyes that gleamed with a hint of something more.

"Um, okay."

"I know we didn't have a date tonight, but that didn't stop me from having a nice time," he said gruffly. "And I'd like to kiss you, Jenna McGovern," he whispered, and his breath filtered over my cheek. "Unless you prefer I don't."

I stood frozen there, knowing my answer should be no, but every instinct in my body screamed otherwise. My hand came to rest on his chest, and I sighed in relief as he closed the distance between us. His lips were soft, tender despite his sometimes-grouchy exterior. One of his hands came up to rest against my cheek, warm against the cool winds that circled us.

It was short-lived and sweet, no French-ness about that kiss, I thought, as he pulled back. Which left me with a frown.

"Did I do something wrong?" I asked. "Didn't you like that?"

His eyebrows raised in complete shock. "What?"

My fingers raised and pressed against my lips. "It was just really short."

"Jenna, it was wonderful." Cooper's voice was low and soft. "But you've made it painfully obvious that you're not ready for a relationship."

"Ah."

"While I'm not starting anything, I also don't want to leave you with any doubt about how I feel about you." He stepped closer again, his words sending shivers down my spine as they trickled over my ear. "Just because I'm patient and take things slow, doesn't mean I'm not interested in you."

"Oh, *ah*—okay then."

"And I am positive..." His hand came up, wound through the back of my hair and pulled it tight. "Absolutely certain that the wait will be worth it."

Darned if the man didn't know how to make me go weak at the knees. "Cooper, I—"

But just then, the expression on Cooper's face told me something was wrong. Immediately, all my insecurities rushed back. Did I have bad breath? (Impossible, seeing as I tasted like hot chocolate—which was *always* a good taste.) Maybe he was put off by my lack of makeup. Or the fact that I'd worn boots without socks. Or maybe he hadn't liked the kiss, and he was just too polite to say so.

"We're not alone," Cooper murmured, his hand resting possessively on my shoulder.

I glanced up, found a car sitting in my driveway—a black one, or maybe dark blue?—and a small figure waiting on my front steps. Her hand was raised to knock on Gran's old door, and it was impossible to tell what direction she was facing from this distance and in this darkness, but if I had to guess, she'd spotted us. The front porch was casting a spotlight sort of glow around us, making our figures easy to see from a distance.

When I recognized the figure, I gasped. "Becky!"

"Well," Cooper said with a sigh. "I suppose it's back to work."

"For what it's worth, I had a nice time tonight, too," I said. "Death threats aside."

He grinned. "I just hope that when you feel ready for a relationship, you'll remember tonight."

I opened my mouth and floundered for a response, but I was too late. Cooper was already opening the door to Matt's house and waiting for me to head inside first. However, I turned my attention to Becky instead, as she climbed down my front steps and made her way across the well-trodden path between Gran's house and Matt's.

"It's fine," I said to Cooper. "You can go inside."

"I'm not leaving you alone out here," he murmured softly.

"Jenna?" Becky called, leaning forward when she got close enough and squinting. "Is that you?"

"Becky, what are you doing here?"

"We need to talk," she said carefully. "It's about Grant."

Chapter 21

Cooper briefly explained the situation to Matt, who graciously opened his house to yet another guest in the very late hours of the evening. With every second, the clock ticked closer to midnight, to a new day. I wondered if this new day would be filled with more threats and close calls. One of these times, it wouldn't be a close call—and that thought made me queasy.

The four of us shed our remaining outdoor gear and moved to the living room. Matt and Becky took the two free-standing loungers, while Cooper and I sat together on one couch. We allowed a gracious foot of space between us.

There was a slight change in atmosphere between Cooper and me, and I hoped it wasn't obvious to the others in the room. In retrospect, Becky had probably arrived at the right time because her presence had forced us to focus on more pressing issues than one lousy kiss: Grant's murder, and my life. Specifically, keeping me alive.

"What brings you here, Becky?" Cooper asked. "Or to Jenna's, I should say."

"I-I have a confession to make," she said, and the room stilled. Becky sensed the trepidation from the three of us and waved her hands nervously. "No—it's not what you think. I had nothing to do with Grant's murder. In fact, I loved him."

"You loved Grant?" I blurted out. I knew Cooper was the trained professional when it came to questioning people, but I had a vested interest in these matters and found it impossible to hold back. "Patty said you'd only gone out with Grant a few times."

"Patty," she said with a guttural exhale. "Yeah, I guess she would say that."

"What do you mean?" Cooper was back in action. "Please give us a step by step account of your involvement with Grant Mark."

"Fine," she said, twisting a napkin between her fingers. Her eyes were rimmed red, and her hands were shaking. She was a mess. But a mess because she was a killer, or a mess because of something else, it was difficult to say. "There's not much to tell, but here it goes: I dated Grant, and we were in love. He wanted us to keep things under wraps for a bit, and—and at first I thought he just wasn't ready to tell anyone."

"But that wasn't the case?" Cooper's voice adjusted to one of compassion, and I was impressed by his ability to handle different interviewees. Becky was warming before him like a marshmallow over a fire. Golden and gooey and malleable in his hands.

"No," she said firmly. "At least, I figured that out tonight. He was just keeping things quiet because he wasn't as serious about me as I was about him."

"I thought you'd only gone on a few dates," I said. "Is that not accurate?"

"Not exactly," she hedged, and then let out a sob. She paused to blow her nose. "I mean, I guess we only went out on a few public dates, and the rest of the time we just hung out at his house."

"How serious did you think things were?" I asked. "Were you thinking along the lines of exclusive dating or moving in with one another?"

"He proposed!" she cried. "He proposed to me. I thought we were going to be the next big wedding in Butternut Bay. I thought we'd give the Duvet wedding a run for its money."

"Were you engaged at the time of Grant's death?" Cooper's question sent Becky into a wail of sobs. "I'm sorry, but I need to ask these things if we're to find his murderer."

"I know, I know. That's why I've come here tonight—to set the record straight. I was filled with all sorts of jealousy and frustration and anger about someone stealing Grant from me," Becky said with a hearty sniff, "but as I realize now, that wasn't the case. He was never mine to have; he was just feeding me lines."

"What's the timeline on this?" Cooper asked. "When did you get engaged?"

"I don't think you can really call it that—he..." she gave an embarrassed sort of splutter and then a sheepish smile. "He didn't have a ring. I know, I'm a sucker. I believed him."

"It's not your fault," I said instinctively. "If you let yourself fall in love, you're vulnerable. There are no two ways about it."

"Maybe," she said, sounding as if she were reassuring herself more than anyone else. "But I didn't handle our breakup well. I sort of, well, I became the crazy ex-girlfriend."

"How so?" Cooper prodded.

Becky sighed and fixed her gaze on me. "I'm sorry, Jenna. I followed you around the first few days you came to town.

Not obsessively or anything, but on the day of Grant's death, I was walking over to June's to grab a coffee before meeting the bridal party at your mother's shop."

I nodded, thinking that matched with Allie's timeline. The bridal party had arrived not long after I'd left, but before Grant's murder. "You saw Grant talking to me through the window?"

"The two of you looked very cozy," she admitted. "I even snapped a picture to use as evidence, but then I realized how horrible and creepy that was of me. I had a polaroid camera to use for the party, and I meant to destroy the photo, but I don't actually know where it went."

"Interesting," I said noncommittally. "And what about this morning?"

"What about this morning?"

"You showed up at my house," I said. "You broke in, and..."

"Hold on!" She raised a hand. "I didn't break in anywhere."

"You tripped me last night at the party," I said. "Admit it."

"I'm sorry," she said. "I did. It was pure jealousy. I was so upset and convinced that Grant broke things off with me to go out with you."

"Well, he didn't," I said, "and you cost my cousin a nice payday. I think she deserves an apology."

"Of course," Becky said with a sigh. "I'll take care of May tomorrow. But I swear, other than the photo and the tripping, I didn't do anything."

"What convinced you to come to Jenna's tonight?" Cooper asked, the skepticism still evident in his voice. "Why confess now?"

"Because Patty told me everything," Becky said. "When she came back from talking to you in the alley, she went on a moan about Grant, and I realized that he hadn't left me for Jenna at all—he'd left me for *Patty*."

"Timeline," Cooper insisted. "When was this happening?"

"I started dating Grant two months ago, but it wasn't until a few weeks back that things really started heating up. We had these two amazing weeks where we spent almost every day together," she said, "and then I sensed he was getting sick of me. I almost broke up with him, but then he offered up the engagement talk and waxed poetry about getting married. I was overjoyed!"

"But it was a line," I said. "To keep you around."

"Yes," she said stiffly. "Grant doesn't like to be dumped. He does the dumping. He kept me around for two more days, then one night he just left a note on the windshield of my car. My *car*! All it said was: *Sorry, this isn't working. Grant.*"

I scowled. "That's awful. I'm sorry, Becky."

"At first, I was so surprised I just holed up in my apartment for a week thinking he'd come back to me. I mean, if it was love, he should have, right?" She seemed to still be trying to convince herself. "By the time I got my head on straight—er, sort of straight—I drove over to his house to demand an explanation. But he wasn't alone."

"Did you see who he was with?"

"A female," she said. "I peeked through his front windows and saw all of her shoes and jackets and everything. I didn't stick around to watch. I drove away and tried to forget it, but the thought simmered there. I think now that must have been his week with Patty."

"But when you saw him in my mother's shop, you thought it must have been me in there," I said. "Because of the way he was leaning in close and whatnot."

"Yes," she said sheepishly. "It hadn't even crossed my mind that he'd pick up another woman and let her go within two weeks after breaking up with me. I know, I'm naive and stupid. And I'm truly sorry for any heartache I've caused you."

"It's fine, Becky—I forgive you. It's really not your fault. We all tend to get a bit crazy when we have broken hearts," I said with a sympathetic smile. "I know. I've been there—recently."

Cooper's hand reached out and landed on my thigh where he gave the slightest of squeezes. As if realizing it wasn't appropriate to do so, he slipped his hand away just as quickly. Not quick enough, however, to prevent both Matt and Becky from seeing it.

My face turned as red as the soles of my Christian Louboutin heels.

Nobody dared say a thing.

"Anyway," I said, clearing my throat. "I really appreciate you coming here to set the record straight, Becky. Grant didn't seem to inspire a lot of warm and fuzzy feelings in most people, which is probably why it's been difficult to pin down who wanted him dead the most."

"I swear I didn't kill him. I loved him, and I might have been upset, but I never would have done anything physical," she pleaded. "And once I realized he'd been messing with me, and he'd probably said the same thing to a hundred different women, I stopped caring so much. I just—I'm tired. I want to move on. I needed to get this off my chest, but I swear I have confessed to everything. I didn't kill Grant."

"I know, we believe you—" I started, but I was interrupted by Cooper's next question.

"Where'd you go tonight after bingo?" he asked. "Your exact route, please."

Becky frowned. "I get the feeling you don't believe anything I'm saying."

"I believe what you're saying just fine," Cooper said. "I just want to be sure you're not leaving anything out."

Her lips tightened into a thin line. "I assure you I'm not, Chief Dear."

"Then you won't mind giving me an in-depth description of where you went after bingo."

Becky looked annoyed, but it didn't hold her up for more than a few seconds. "I went home, okay? I was upset because of what Patty had told me, so I went home to lick my wounds. Then I came here."

"Late on a Sunday night, you went home, settled in for—*oh*, an hour or so?—and then decided to come back out on a snowy evening just to get a few things off your chest?"

"You don't have to believe me," Becky snapped. "But it's the truth. I'm sorry I came here—I didn't do anything wrong, and I was just trying to help."

"I believe you," I said again. "Cooper, what are you doing?"

His eyes blazed, and I knew. He was still furious that someone had tried to flatten me like roadkill, and while the thought of his protectiveness was touching, I got the feeling he was trying to force a square peg into a snowflake-sized hole. Becky hadn't tried to kill me—I just knew it.

"I believe you," Cooper said finally, looking at Becky. "But I had to be sure."

Becky's face paled. "Oh, my gosh. They came after you, didn't they?"

Her question was directed to me, and I gave a little shrug. I wasn't one for being the center of attention, hence the reason I styled *others* for the spotlight. "It's not that big of a deal."

"Yes, it is," Becky said. "And I suppose if you want proof, you could swing by and check out my driveway—there are fresh tire tracks there from my car to show I went home after bingo. I know it's not a hundred percent dependable, but it's something. I wouldn't have had time to be two places at once."

"Where do you live?" Cooper asked, pulling out his phone and opening a notes app. As Becky gave him her address, he frowned. "She couldn't have gone home and come after Jenna. There wouldn't have been enough time. Becky, what time did you leave the bingo hall, and can anyone else verify?"

"Sure. The entire bridal party was there until nine thirty," she said. "Ask any one of them. I suppose Patty left a little early, but she was upset."

Cooper glanced at Matt, and I could see the two of them wondering if she'd been upset enough to take to the roads with a rage.

"What color car does Patty have?" Matt asked in his first foray into the conversation. "Did you notice?"

Becky scrunched up her face. "I think it's like this purple-maroon sort of color, but I can't be sure."

"Could be described as 'dark,'" Matt mumbled. "Especially on the stretch of the road where it happened."

"What happened?" Becky asked, looking between the two men. "Do you think it was Patty?"

"I don't know," Cooper said, "but I have my work cut out for me. Thanks for coming, Becky. Is there anything else you can think of that you'd like to share?"

She bit her nails. After a minute, she shook her head. "I don't think so. That's all I've come to say. That, and I'm sorry."

I stood and crossed the room to Becky, squatting awkwardly next to her chair and giving her a hug. "It's okay."

Becky's thin fingers grasped me back. "I don't know why you're hugging me, but I appreciate it."

"I'm a hugger," I said. "And I know what it feels like to be dumped when you don't expect it."

As we parted, Becky gave me a grateful smile. We might never be the best of friends, but at least we'd moved past enemies and into an odd sort of truce.

Matt walked her to the front door after we said goodbyes and waited until she'd gotten into her car and pulled away from my house. Then he returned to the living room and stood at a distance while Cooper and I remained on the same couch.

The whole aura suddenly shifted to one of discomfort, so I stood and crossed my arms over my chest. "That was interesting, huh?"

Nobody was fooled by my faux-nonchalance, nor did they pretend to be. Cooper merely glanced down at his phone. "I'm going to head over to Becky's to check for the tire tracks. I warned her to park on the street—I'll be able to tell about what time the tracks were made based on snowfall levels."

"I don't think she did it," I said. "Why would she come here to confess?"

"I can think of plenty of reasons she'd come here to confess, even if she had done it," Cooper said. "But I agree that it probably wasn't her. I'll still be following through to be safe."

I shrugged. "Fine by me. What about Patty leaving early?"

"I have a feeling," Matt wondered, "that you might find her if you check the Blue Tavern."

Cooper gave a nod. "She's a regular there, and she enjoys her—*ah*, adult beverages. Especially in times of stress. I'll swing by there to verify her alibi after Becky's." He sighed, then shook his head. "I'll spend the rest of the night cross checking vehicle registrations for 'dark' cars with the names of the bingo attendees. Thankfully, Stacey had a sign-in sheet, so I have a full roster of attendees."

"I'm sorry," I said, my face pinching in frustration. "I really wish I paid more attention in the moment. I know a *dark car* isn't much to go off, but—"

"Don't be ridiculous," Matt said. "What were you supposed to do when a car was crashing onto the sidewalk? You did the right thing taking care of yourself first, and we'll figure out the rest of it."

Cooper cleared his throat at Matt's mention of the word 'we', and the room fell into stony silence again.

"What can I do?" I asked. "Speaking of *we*. I'm part of this, too. Remember?"

"Get some rest," Matt said, at the same time Cooper said, "Sleep."

I frowned. "That's not very exciting."

"I'll be doing a drive by on the hour until about four, and then I'll have Rick take over," Cooper said. "I'll be back at it in the morning."

"And I'm supposed to just hole up here and wait?" I asked. "I don't think so."

"Just for tonight," Cooper said. "Give me a few hours to sort through what we have, and I'll be back first thing in the morning."

"You'll be useless if you don't sleep," Matt said. "Plus, we're out of urgent leads to follow. It'll be a quiet night. Rest."

As if on cue, a yawn cracked through my brave exterior and rendered all my tough talk useless. I rolled my eyes at the involuntary motion and finally shrugged. "Fine. But tomorrow, I'm back in the loop. You'll give me something to do that's helpful, or I'll go insane."

"Fine," Cooper agreed.

Matt moved first. "I'll get the bed ready with some clean sheets."

"I'll take the couch," I said. "Really—I feel more comfortable here."

"If someone comes in the house," Cooper said, "it's better if Matt's on the main floor."

I narrowed my eyes at him. "I can defend myself. I want to sleep on the couch."

Cooper gave a guttural sigh, explaining without words that he thought I was being difficult. "Wait here."

As if I could go anywhere. I had a night-long prison sentence right here in Matt's living room. At least there was hot chocolate and coffee and super warm showers and magical blankets. Things could definitely have been worse.

Cooper returned and handed me a canister. "Pepper spray," he explained. "Keep it near your head just in case. I don't think anyone would dare break into Matt's house, but you can't be too safe. And, just in case, I've jotted down my cell number so you can call me in case of emergency."

I glanced at the ugly black can of pepper spray and frowned. "I'd really prefer a pink one."

"Okay, princess," Cooper said. "We'll get you a pink one tomorrow. For now, this one will work. I'm going to take off, so I'll see you both in the morning. Matt—thank you for your help."

Matt gave a nod that wasn't entirely friendly, but it was respectful enough. The two men walked toward the front of the house, and I followed them from a safe distance. As Cooper shrugged on his jacket and stepped outside, his dark, piercing gaze met mine. He raked his eyes over me like hot coals, and I shivered.

"Goodnight," Cooper said quietly, and then he was gone.

Once he'd left, Matt silently turned on a heel and returned to the living area. He shuffled through some blankets, plunked a few soft-looking pillows on the couch, and eventually stepped back to survey his handiwork.

"How does that look?" he asked. "Anything else you need?"

"Matt, I'm sorry."

He looked up, feigning nonchalance. "Sorry for what?"

"I have a feeling you know something happened between me and Cooper tonight," I said. "I swear I didn't mean for it to happen, and I told him the same thing that I told you. I'm not ready for a relationship."

Matt scrunched up his face with a melancholy grin. "Lucky guy."

"Excuse me?"

Matt gave a grin that lit up his face, despite the frustrated shake of his head. "He got in a kiss before you shooed him away, didn't he?"

I didn't expect to laugh, but I did. I burst into a fit of giggles that happened to be contagious because Matt began laughing too. I eventually padded across the room as the chuckling died down and rested my head against his chest as I gave him a hug.

"I hope you know that I appreciate you," I said. "And all you've done for me."

"I know." He squeezed me tight, then rested his cheek against my forehead. "I just—I like being around you, Jenna. I hope that even if you choose...even if you end up dating Cooper, we can still be friends."

"Of course!" I backed away, surprised. "Always."

He gave me a thin smile, then planted the lightest of kisses on my forehead. "Get some sleep. I'll be upstairs if you need anything."

I climbed under the covers as Matt began shutting down the house. He flicked off the lights and checked the door locks, and everything felt so safe and secure here in Matt's little house that I was drifting to sleep by the time I heard his footsteps climbing upstairs to his bedroom.

As my mind entered sleepy la-la-land, I wondered if I was doing things all wrong again. Matt was clearly interested in me—he was such a nice, stable guy in a nice, stable home in a nice, stable neighborhood. He was nice, nice, *nice*, and handsome.

I didn't have a track record for dating nice guys...and look where that had gotten me. Maybe it was time for a change. Maybe I should try looking at the nice guy for once, I mused, as my mind flicked over to Cooper.

While Cooper was nice in a way, he was more of a wild card. He was a challenge, he drove me bonkers, he got under my skin. I equally wanted to push him away and pull him closer. But in my experience, fires that burned bright, flamed out quickly.

Maybe, I thought with a sigh, *I'd be better off keeping both as friends*.

Even in sleep, an uneasiness washed over me. I doubted that would be possible. Realistically, I'd have to make a choice sooner or later. But for now, I wouldn't think about that. I'd focus on finding Grant's murderer first because somehow that felt like the easier problem to solve.

Chapter 22

Morning sunlight dripped through the windows and plinked onto my face, gently washing me awake from my cozy little burrow on Matt's couch. The magical blanket had once again provided me with a deep, restful sleep, and I was beginning to believe in its special powers. I debated asking Matt if it was for sale.

The smell of percolating coffee wormed its way through to the living area and perked up the rest of my senses. I sprawled, yawning as happily as if I'd been on vacation. I curled the blanket around my shoulders and padded barefoot into the kitchen. "What's the price tag on this magical thing?"

I stopped talking at once because Matt was on the phone. I hadn't heard him speaking from the other room, and at first, I thought it'd been me being totally oblivious, but upon closer inspection, I realized he'd been purposefully murmuring quietly into the speaker so as not to be heard.

"—I'm sorry, I can't be there this morning. I need someone to cover for me," he said. "I have a, uh, family emergency."

I frowned, then retreated from the kitchen before Matt noticed me standing there. I dug around for my phone. Once I found it, I located my mother's number and dialed.

"Good morning, darling," she hummed. "Do I hear the sounds of a happy girl? How was your date last night?"

"Mother, it wasn't a date."

"I don't know who you think you're fooling. Poor Matt."

"I just called to see if I could use the truck today."

"Do you have another date?

"No. And I'm planning to stay single for a while."

There was silence both from my mother and from the kitchen. There was no way Matt *hadn't* overheard me talking to my mom. His call must be over.

"The truck, sure," Bea said finally. "It's just—I thought there was something between the two of you."

"Yes, and it's called friendship," I said. "Can you bring the truck by?"

"I'll be there in a minute and will drop it off on my way to work. You will be coming into the store today, won't you? We really need to get to work on some improvements, or I won't have a store left to improve. The burst in spending from Grant's Murder Day will only hold me over for so long."

"You say that like it's a holiday," I said grimly. "I'll swing by the store to drop you off, but I can't stay long. I have a few things to take care of, and then I swear I'll devote myself to you and the store for as long as you need."

"Okie dokie, darling, that sounds good. Say, I wonder how Matt's taking the news that you went on a date with Cooper."

"It's, ah, fine," I said. "I am actually at his house right now."

"Cooper's?"

"Matt's," I said. "We're also friends."

"Hmm," my mother said. "Interesting."

"I'll see you in twenty minutes," I told her. "I have to run home and shower first."

She gasped. "Why didn't you shower before going over?"

"Long story," I said. "See you soon."

"Should I go to Matt's house or yours?" Bea asked point-edly. "This whole situation is *very* confusing."

"Mom, they're twenty feet apart. Either one is fine."

She harrumphed and hung up.

Matt appeared around the corner. "Making plans?"

"I'm sorry," I said, grimacing. "I heard you turning down something that sounded like work this morning, and I didn't want to be the reason you missed anything important. I'm going to head to the store with my mom for a bit. I'll be safe there—it's public. It's a Monday morning, and it feels like a fresh start." I spread my arms wide and grinned. "Hopefully no murder attempts this week."

His smile didn't touch his eyes. "Coffee?"

"Oh, yes, please," I said. "It smells heavenly."

"I was planning to stay here with you this morning," Matt said as he poured me a mug full. "Cooper swung by once already to check on you, but you were still out. We're both invested in making sure you don't find trouble by lunch."

"Don't worry, I'll have a chaperone at the shop," I said. "My mom will watch me like a hawk, and I'm sure Cooper will swing around too in his handy-dandy lookout vehicle."

"I'm sure he will," Matt said dryly. "Well, in that case—I suppose you'll want to head home to change. Mind if I walk you over and sit with you until your mom comes? Coop would kill me if I let you out of my sight and into that house alone. At least until we catch whoever's after you."

"Sure," I said. "So long as you bring the coffee."

The next half hour was uneventful. Matt and I walked back to my place, and while I showered and changed, he played on his phone in the living room. Or that's what I thought was happening until I came downstairs and found he'd whipped up a quick breakfast with supplies he must have brought over from his own house because I certainly didn't have eggs in my refrigerator.

"I thought you might object if I told you what I was up to," Matt said, grinning over my stove. "So, I slipped some supplies into a bag and figured I'd whip us up something to eat. I won't last five minutes at work if I don't eat breakfast."

We were just sitting down to eat when a car pulled up out front. I figured it would be my mother, so I stood and wiped my hands on the sides of my plain black dress—one of my recent hauls from the thrift shop—and scooted to the front door. Before I could reach it, there was a brief knock and then the door swung open to reveal Cooper.

"My, this looks cozy," he drawled, glancing over my shoulder at the kitchen. "Got enough for one more?"

"Um," I hesitated. "How did you know we were here?"

"Matt texted me to let me know the change in plans."

"Ah, good. Glad y'all are coordinating intel on my whereabouts," I said. "What brings you here?"

"Thought I'd give you both an update and check on the happy couple this morning," Cooper said. "There were tire tracks in Becky's driveway last night like she said, and she had an alibi during the break-in yesterday. Patty was at the bar and had an alibi during the break-in as well, so I am somewhat back to the drawing board. It'll be a long day of checking out dark vehicles."

As if on cue, Matt scooped the rest of the eggs onto a plate and slid it to the far end of the table. Cooper and I took it as a sign that we were to eat while the food was hot.

I pretended that eating breakfast with both men wasn't awkward at all. It was difficult. There is a reason I'm not an actor, and it's because I suck at acting. So, after an unbearably quiet breakfast, I finally wiped my hands and stood, grateful to hear tires crunching out front.

"Well, I'm off to the shop, so I'll see you two later," I said. "Lock the door on your way out, please."

With that, I fled the house and scurried into the warm safety of my mother's truck.

"Is that Cooper's cruiser?" my mother asked. "If you were entertaining him, I can come back later."

"Nah, he's got entertainment," I said. "He's hanging out with Matt. How about we head to the store? The faster the better."

My mother cleared her throat and gripped the steering wheel with white knuckles. "People will talk, you know. A pretty thing like you acquiring a plethora of male friends and not taking a romantic interest in any of them..."

"Drive, please," I said through gritted teeth. "I love you, mom, but stay out of my romantic life."

"Fine," she said. "I just hope you find someone who makes you as happy as Sid makes me. Marriage is really the very best thing I've ever done."

"Mmm," I murmured. "For me, shoes seem to do the trick just fine."

I COULDN'T DROP MY mother off fast enough. I would've let the wheels of the truck keep on rolling if it had been up to me, but my mother insisted I pop my head into the store for a few minutes.

I hadn't *actually* intended to go to the store. I had a few things I wanted to check up on with regards to the case, but it hadn't seemed like a bright idea to tell Matt about it. He would have told Cooper, and they would have nixed the idea without asking my opinion first. And I didn't intend on waiting around for the next attack.

"Good morning, sunshine," Allie chirped happily as I dropped the boots I'd borrowed from her on the counter. She pretended as if last night hadn't happened at all. "Oh, thanks for returning the boots so quickly. I'll get your shoes back soon, I promise."

"Sure," I said, unsurprised to glance down and find my red high heels firmly planted on Allie's feet. They were mismatched horribly with some odd looking green patterned pants and a matching sweater. But her scrunchie was the exact same shade as the shoes, and according to the Instagram influencers, scrunchies were coming back in style, so I supposed that was something. "Whenever you remember them would be great."

"Yeah, thanks," she said, and grinned wider. "Are you sticking around today? I could use some help organizing the sweaters, and maybe you could tell me how you get your nails to look so nicely polished. It looks like I hit my fingers with a hammer."

Sure enough, Allie had tried to match her nails to my shoes, and her fingers looked to be a bloody mess with red polish streaks. I winced. "The only cure for that is a lot—and I mean a lot—of nail polish remover," I advised. "I'll show you some other time—I have some business to take care of this morning first."

"Are you going hunting for more murder clues?" Allie whispered. "I heard something about a break-in yesterday at your place. Is that true?"

"Maybe," I said. "Say, what color is your mother's car?"

"Um, green," she said. "Lime green. One of those weird boxy sorts of cars. Why?"

"No reason," I said. "I was just looking for someone from bingo yesterday. I found a stray mitten and was looking for its owner. Dark-colored car is all I saw."

"Might be Mr. Duvet," Allie said easily. "He has a dark car—he left around the same time as me from bingo, but I think his wife might have stayed back with the bridal party. He was alone getting in the car."

"Mr. Duvet—Lana's dad?"

"That's the one. Is it a man's mitten?"

"Mitten?" I already had forgotten my cover story. "Oh, yes. A man's. In fact, I'm going to run it over to him right now, and then I'll be back to help with the nail polish."

"Oh, great," she said. "I'll get started taking this mess off. I think I've been scaring away customers."

I bid her a distracted goodbye as I hurried away from the register and shouted a 'be back soon' to my mother. She was with a customer and therefore couldn't respond, which was just perfect. For all I knew, Matt or Cooper might have gotten in touch with her and explained that I needed a chaperone—which would be detrimental to my plans.

As I drove toward the Duvet house, an address Allie had quickly rattled off when asked, I dialed Cooper and put him on speaker. "Come on, answer," I muttered, but he obviously didn't hear me. I got his voicemail.

I quickly left a message for the chief and then dialed Matt to the same result. Apparently, both were busy at work. It would take Cooper all day to get through his list of cars and event attendees, so I figured I might as well take a quick peek in the Duvet garage, and if I found a dark car that was the approximate shape and size, I could point Cooper in the right direction and spare everyone a lot of time and effort.

And if Allie had been wrong and there was no dark car—well, no big deal. It was a five-minute detour for me, and I needed the break from people anyway.

William and Brenda Duvet had moved into a much more modest house than the one he'd shared with the former Mrs. Duvet. Now, Will and Brenda lived in an average, newly-built, suburban-style house that had a cookie cutter feel, save for the slight clutter of pots strewn across the front lawn. Most of them were still under several feet of snow, giving the yard a somewhat lumpy appearance that was a stark contrast to the rest of the straight lines and sheer white exterior of the house. I came to a stop and parked across the street.

As luck would have it, the garage door was open.

Wide open.

It was a two-car garage, and one space was empty. There were fresh tracks in the snow, which told me someone had just left. The other space was taken up by a white SUV.

With a sigh, I realized my attempts to speed the investigation along had gone nowhere fast. The car *definitely* hadn't been white. While the Duvets might own a second car that fit the description, there was no saying when Mr. or Mrs. Duvet would return with it. It'd be a waste of time to sit around and wait, so I figured I'd head back to the store and try again later.

I was just putting the car in drive when the rev of an engine startled me to attention. I glanced up in time to see a car—a *dark* car—careen around the corner and fly up the Duvet's driveway and into the garage.

My heart pounded as the driver of the vehicle threw it into park. I didn't need Encyclopedia Brown to confirm that this might be the vehicle that'd come close to running me down the previous evening. I took a few deep breaths, waited for the garage door to close, and forced my tight knuckles from the steering wheel.

Once the garage door had closed, I dialed Cooper and Matt one more time each, but again, I got no answer from either. While hanging up from a second attempt to reach Cooper, the Duvet's garage door inched up again. The same black car backed out of the driveway and headed off in the opposite direction. Mr. Duvet was in the driver's seat.

"Interesting," I muttered, wondering why he'd needed to stop home for all of five seconds. "Very peculiar."

A sudden urge caused me to kick open the door and climb out of my mother's truck. Before I could fully register what was happening, I'd climbed the front steps to the Duvet house and knocked on the door. I needed to ask Mrs. Duvet a few quick questions to see if I could find out if her husband had an alibi for the time of Grant's murder.

"Hello, Jenna," Brenda said, pulling the door open with a smile. "What a lovely surprise. Come inside. What can I do for you?"

"Wow," I said, startled. "I'm surprised you remembered my name. That's pretty good for only meeting me once."

"Yes, well, you've become somewhat famous around the Duvet house these days," Brenda said with a tight smile. "I've heard your name tossed around a few times."

My smile must have frozen on my face. "Right, disaster queen. I'm sorry about the bachelorette party."

"Oh, I got a good laugh over the spillage. I'm not exactly a family favorite with Lana and Eliza and Bridget, so believe me, I understand how you feel as an outsider." The new Mrs. Duvet gestured for me to come further inside. "I just made some cookies. Would you like one?"

"I never say no to a cookie," I said as we wound our way to a small living room with a view of a neat, square garden that was currently under mounds of white, but would be a pretty little view in the spring. "Thanks."

Before heading into the kitchen, she paused in the doorway and leaned against it. "I feel like I'm being rude again, but we didn't have an appointment, did we? Am I forgetting something?"

"No, not at all. I just have a few quick questions to ask you."

"Oh?"

"It's probably nothing," I said. "But I'm sort of helping the police a bit with the Grant Mark murder, and I'm in charge of gathering alibis. I don't suppose you could give me one for your husband on the day of Grant's murder?"

She frowned. "That was... Friday?"

I nodded.

"I imagine he was at work, but you'd have to ask his secretary. He left at eight thirty in the morning as usual and arrived home around six thirty. I didn't think anything of it." She stepped closer into the room. "Do the police suspect him of something?"

"Like I said, I'm just the help," I lied. "I don't know all that much except they're trying to get the alibis of everyone who might have known Grant."

"Ah, ok," she said. "Though I don't think my husband knew Grant all that well, but I imagine the police are just being thorough."

"Yes, exactly." I hesitated, then blurted out my next question. "Did your husband drive to bingo last night?"

Her hands folded across her chest, her lips pursing in thought. "Yes, why?"

"Just wondering. Were you with him?"

"At the event, yes."

"In the car, I mean, after the event."

"No—we took separate cars. He had to come straight from the office. It's a busy season, so he works some weekends."

"Where was your husband this morning?"

"This morning? Nowhere. He worked from home for an early morning meeting and just left to go to the office."

"Ah. Were you home all morning?"

"No, as a matter of fact, I just walked in the door," she said. "I was at the grocery store. Let me quickly grab those cookies for you while they're hot."

I frowned, realizing that the person who I'd seen pulling into the driveway wasn't Mr. Duvet as I'd thought. It was *Brenda* squealing into the garage in her husband's car—or the car they shared. My shoulders stiffened.

Something was wrong.

Brenda had offered me hot cookies—cookies fresh from the oven—yet there was no scent of recently baked *anything*. No melting chocolate chips, no gooey dough, no sugary scent of melting butter and goodness drifting in the air. My nose was never wrong.

And the cookies, I realized, were the least harmful of Brenda's lies.

I scrambled for my pepper spray as the pieces clicked into place, then remembered my purse was sitting in the passenger's seat of the truck. It had been *Brenda* who'd tried to run me over last night, and *Brenda* who'd picked up the bag of shoes from behind the register—she must have been at my mother's shop that day with the bridal party, only nobody had thought to mention her presence. There was still a tiny chance I was wrong about all of this, but I doubted it. Everything felt right.

Or rather, wrong. Very, very wrong.

The best I could do for a weapon was a small perfume bottle and a can of shimmer powder in my pocket. While excellent for accenting cheekbones and casting a light, floral scent around my body, neither of those items felt exactly like a weapon of choice. I stood and made my way toward the hallway, trying to discreetly thumb through my recent contacts to ring Cooper.

"That's not a cookie," I said at the sight of a gun in Brenda's hand. "What's wrong? Put that thing down."

"I know you're figuring things out as I speak," she said. "You might have come to find my husband, but I can't have you leaving."

"How did you know Grant?" I still clasped the perfume bottle in one hand and the powder in the other, and my fingers rested on my phone. I dared not move to complete a call just yet, for fear she'd take the phone away. She seemed too focused on the gun to have noticed the phone. "I don't understand what your motive was to kill Grant."

"There wasn't one," she said, her hands shaking as she held the gun on me. "I didn't want to kill him. At least, I didn't intend to—not that he didn't deserve what he had coming to him."

"He might have been a creep, but that doesn't give you the right to kill him," I said. "What did he do to you?"

"Nothing to me, but to Eliza and Lana. He was ruining Lana's wedding, and she complained about it nonstop." Brenda gave a huge eye roll. "And the whole town knows that the *marvelous* Bridget Duvet gives her girls whatever they want. How am I supposed to compete with that?"

"What does Grant have to do with Duvet family issues?"

Brenda took a step further into the room, the gun wobbling dangerously as she kept it trained on me. "I thought if I could just meet up with Grant and give him a talking to, get him to step down from the wedding, maybe the girls would actually *like* me."

"This is about getting the Duvet girls to like you?"

"I'm their stepmother! I've loved and cared for them for years, and I get nothing in return. Lana didn't give me a single role in her wedding. Everything that my husband and I do for the girls is always: 'Oh, thank you, *Daddy*!' But what about me? Am I not part of the family now, too? I married their father!"

"I'm sure it takes time," I said. "We all know you're not a killer, Brenda. If it was an accident, we can get you help. We'll work with the police and everything will be okay. How did you get the shoes?"

"The shoes were a complete coincidence," Brenda said. "I bought a cute picture frame at your mother's shop, and it was in the same size bag as the shoes. I grabbed the shoes on accident, and I didn't realize it until I got home. I was actually on my way *back* to your mother's store when I met up with Grant."

"And you had the shoes in the bag."

"Yes. A shame," she said, "because I really liked that picture frame."

"What happened when you ran into Grant?"

"I had asked Grant to meet in private. When we reached the rendezvous point, it turned out he thought I was interested in him." Brenda shuddered. "When I turned down his romantic gestures, he started saying nasty things about the girls, and I just got so angry!"

I could see the fury in Brenda's eyes. It was clear she was sliding toward unhinged.

"I took out the shoe because it was the only thing I had in my hand," she said. "Then I swiped at him. I thought if I could just scare him enough, he might back out of the wedding. I'd only meant to threaten him, not kill him—but..."

"But you didn't stop in time," I said quietly. "And the heel landed in Grant's throat."

Brenda's eyes hardened. "After that, it became easier to cover things up rather than confess. I knew about the notes Patty wrote to Grant because she talks when she drinks too much, and nobody notices me anyway. It was a simple matter to take those notes from her purse and plant them in Grant's hotel room. I just rented a room at the Blueberry Hotel and waited around until that bozo at the front desk left the master key unattended."

"And the shoe in my house," I said. "That was you, too. And last night's attempt to run over me."

"I knew you would put things together. Your suspicion of Becky, combined with her obvious distrust of you, was a nice distraction for a while, but I knew in time that would fade." Brenda took another step closer. "I wish I didn't have to do this."

"Brenda, you're not a killer."

"I am now!" She hissed. "And I'll kill again if it means I won't be caught."

"Don't do anything you'll regret. Right now, you can claim Grant's murder was an accident. But if you kill me with that gun, it's no accident."

"Drop your phone and kick it over to me."

I did as she asked. But while I moved, I was finally able to hit the dial button on Cooper's number. Flipping the phone upside down, I kicked it across the room after stalling for as long as possible.

"Brenda, you already killed one man," I repeated, loudly enough for Cooper to hear if he answered the phone. "Don't make it two bodies."

"You already said that," Brenda said, and then froze at the sound of a voice. A male voice, tinny and distant. Her face paled as we both glanced down at the phone on the floor. "What did you do?"

Cooper had picked up!

Brenda bent to retrieve the phone, and her concentration lapsed for the briefest of seconds. As soon as the gun's barrel left the kill zone on my chest, I quickly uncapped the bottle of perfume and leapt sideways, away from the gun. I charged toward Brenda, tossing the sweet-smelling liquid straight at her eyes.

The gun in her hands swiveled wildly as I hit my mark. Brenda screeched, a hand clawing at her face to clear the burn. I lunged out of the way, and a shot rang out a second later. My head throbbed, and my hearing felt dull and sluggish. The bullet had taken a chunk out of the wall.

I launched a second attack as I rose to my feet and rushed at Brenda. I needed to get the gun from her hand. When I was close enough, I tossed the loose shimmer powder at Brenda's face. I knew from experience it stung like the devil when it got in the eyes.

Brenda's cry of frustration told me I'd hit my mark for a second time. The powder hit her skin, mixing with the dripping perfume to create a cakey slop, and as she raised a hand to wipe her eyes free, I dove at her waist.

We clattered to the floor, arms and limbs intertwined and tangling. Brenda's shooting hand crashed into the wooden floorboards of the hallway as we tussled out of the living room and rolled, and rolled, and rolled. The gun skidded away, just out of reach as I pinned her down.

"You won't make it a second dead body," I gasped. "I'm not going out that easily."

"Neither am I," Brenda growled. She landed a well-placed kick that sent me sprawling. She scrambled to her feet, but instead of going for the gun across the room, she held a shoe in her hand. *My* shoe. "Then again, Hollywood, maybe it's best you go out the way you came in."

"Don't you *dare* ruin another perfectly good pair of shoes!" I snarled, scrambling away from her. My elbow hurt, and I could taste blood, but I ignored it all as Brenda charged.

She swiped at me with the heel, but I dodged it and wrapped around her knees. She screamed, toppling over as I forced the shoe out of her hand. In my haste to disarm her, she got a solid punch in straight to my nose, and I felt blood spurt down my face as I recoiled.

At that moment, the door burst open and two male bodies appeared, Cooper first, Matt just behind him. I sat heavily on Brenda's chest, struggling as she writhed underneath me.

"A little help?" I gasped. "I forgot the pepper spray in the car."

Cooper rushed to my side and had Brenda restrained—lying on her face with her hands cuffed behind her back—in under a minute. Matt took up the slack, hurrying to my aid and helping me limp away from Brenda's scathing commentary.

"Um, Jenna—question." Cooper glanced at me, satisfied that Matt had done his once over and declared me physically sound, save for a bloody nose and some bruises. "Why is there glitter everywhere?"

"It's not *glitter*," I said through a nose stuffed with gauze. "It's shimmer powder. Get your weapons straight, chief."

Chapter 23

"It's the purple princess," Matt said with a broad grin as I stepped into his house the next morning. "How are you feeling?"

"Would you hate me if I begged you for a cup of coffee?" I raised a hand to my aching nose. "I didn't have time to make it to the store yesterday."

Matt laughed. "Would you hate me if I had a friendly breakfast for two ready and waiting? I figured you'd be over."

"I'm that easy to predict, huh?"

"Call me optimistic," he said, smiling cheerfully. "Come on in—you look... colorful."

Yesterday's tussle had granted me two pretty purple eyes. I had spent a good chunk of time after my shower this morning studying the exact patterns of blues and deep purples that made up my black eyes for research purposes. If I ever found my way back into Hollywood, I would be able to replicate bruises like nobody's business. I'd have to update my resume.

After my tussle with Brenda, yesterday had passed quickly. I'd mostly been content to hide out at home, relishing in the safety of my own house, seeing as the murderer loose in Blueberry Lake was no more.

I'd been forced to go to the hospital for a more thorough exam, but Matt's assessments had been correct—I'd walked away with nothing save for an intimidating black eye, a few bruises and scratches, and the lifelong knowledge that I'd taken down a gun-wielding killer with nothing more than perfume and shimmer powder.

After, I'd given Cooper my formal statement. It hadn't taken long because Brenda had decided to sing like a bird in her efforts to try and convince everyone and their stepmother that Grant's murder had been in self-defense. She mostly ignored the whole bit about attempting to kill me, too.

The town seemed shocked by the development, Mr. Duvet most of all. He hadn't taken the news well. His daughters, on the other hand, quickly discovered a somewhat delicious side effect of finding out their stepmother was a killer. Immediately, they became the center of town sympathy—and the Duvet girls *reveled* in it, wearing black dresses out and about, bursting sporadically into tears as if in mourning.

I'd let everyone else carry on with the gossip while I'd hunkered down alone with my magazines. One blissful night's sleep later and some puffy skin, and I was feeling as good as new. Good enough to crawl back to Matt's kitchen and properly beg him for coffee.

As we sat down to breakfast, I caught a whiff of fresh maple syrup, and I saw the French toast fresh off the griddle. We ate in near silence simply because everything tasted that good. When we finished, I pushed my plate back and rested my hands on my stomach.

"That's a cure for everything," I said. "Thank you, Matt. You didn't have to do that."

"Neighborly duties," he said with a wink. "More coffee?"

"Please."

As he refilled my cup, I reflected on the easy space between us. There was no pressure to impress, no awkward silences, and even our lapses in conversation were comfortable.

"Matt," I began.

"Don't," he said, then quickly corrected himself. "I mean, don't try to explain. I know what you're feeling."

"You do?"

"I like this," he said with an easy shrug. "I enjoy being around you. I mean that, Jenna."

The knock on the front door startled me from responding. I glanced at Matt. "Who knows I'm here?"

"I'll give you one guess."

I winced. "Sorry."

Matt waved me off. "Coop texted to say he'd swing by. Said he needed to bring you down to the station to answer a few last questions."

I glanced down at myself, grateful I'd showered and dressed in normal clothes this morning. By the time I stood up, Cooper had let himself into Matt's house and appeared surprisingly chipper in his nice-looking jeans and quarter-zip sweater. He smiled at me, and I grinned back.

"Mind if I steal you for a bit?" Cooper asked. "I have a few red-tape things that need to be taken care of. I'll buy you a muffin from June's if you need a bribe."

"I'm stuffed to the gills," I said. "But I'd take another coffee."

Cooper's eyes flicked past my shoulder, down the hall to where the remnants of breakfast lingered on the kitchen table. "Of course," he said easily. "I'm glad to see you've ignored all advice about sensible shoes. May I?"

I ignored his sarcasm and looped my hand around his. I was wearing heels—the very same heels Brenda had used against me. I wasn't going to let her terrify me into wearing ballet flats for the rest of my life. It was a bright, almost-spring day, and I had felt like looking good when I woke up this morning. (Aside from the whole black eye issue.)

I bid goodbye to Matt, hopped in the car with Coop, and we made our way toward the station. I was barely paying attention, focused instead on the rapidly depleting snow mounds as I wondered if it was time to start bringing Gran's house back to life.

I'd really need to sort my job situation out soon so I could afford the repairs needed. I had some savings left, but nothing substantial for the long run, and it would drain quickly once repairs started.

But the thought of renovating my grandmother's cottage-style flowerbeds and stuffed-full herb gardens was exciting. The berry bushes—blueberry, raspberry, blackberry, and more—would be turning green soon enough, and the apple tree in the back yard would spout its gorgeously pungent flowers. Best of all, the lilacs would be peeping out within months. Today felt like a fresh start full of blooming and greenery and life.

As we drove, I thought back to Allie's mother requesting a styling appointment, and Stacey Simone's excitement at winning a prize package to Something Old. Maybe I could find a way to bring enough business to my mother's store that I could afford to go full time with her. It might not be my forever career, but it would be a wonderful start.

"What are you thinking about?" Cooper asked out of the blue. "You look concerned."

"Concentrated." I glanced over at him and gave a cautious smile. "I think I'm feeling happy. Really happy."

He smiled, reached over and squeezed my hand. We drove the rest of the way like that, and I was so distracted by the feel of his fingers on mine that I barely noticed we hadn't pulled into the station's parking lot like he'd said, but somewhere else entirely.

"But this is—" I hesitated. "What are we doing at my mother's shop?"

"I needed to grab a quick statement from Allie, too," he said, climbing from the car. "Do you mind?"

"Allie?" I frowned, following suit. "But she didn't do anything. I mean, her nail polish skills are horrendous, but you can't arrest her for that."

My joke fell flat as Cooper navigated the walkway to Something Old and pushed through the door without waiting for me. Disgruntled, I hurried behind him. I threw the door open, mid-retort. "Hey, mister, what do you think—"

"*Surprise!*"

All at once, oodles of faces appeared before me. Men and women burst from hiding places across my mother's shop. Heads poked out from behind racks and limbs waved from between hangers. Most of them familiar, though there were a slew of folks I didn't recognize.

"Welcome home, darling," my mother said, standing happily at the front of the pack. "To you *and* your bags."

"What is this?" I glanced around the room spotting everyone I cared about. Mrs. Beasley, Cooper, and Allie. A woman standing next to Allie who was probably her mother. May and Joe, wrapped in an adorable embrace. Stacey Simone and a herd from the bingo crowd. My mother and Sid, of course, and the entire Duvet bridal party. And finally, June Bixby and her grandson.

"Matt?" My mouth parted as I spotted him. "How'd you beat me here?"

"Cooper did some creative driving to buy me time," Matt said with a grin. "Welcome home, Jenna."

June smiled and hugged her grandson. There was a cake on the table that featured a pair of high heels and some sort of edible glitter, along with balloons and confetti, and in the middle of it all...

"My bags!" I darted across the room and draped myself over my luggage. Someone had perched each one next to the cake on the table. I hugged each bag to my chest and maybe kissed one of them on the zipper. "How did you get them?"

"Allie went to the airport in person," Cooper said, grinning at me. "That's why we didn't question her about her alibi. She was hunting down your bags—that's why she couldn't tell you her alibi at bingo the other night. It would have ruined the surprise."

"Oh, Allie," I said, and pulled myself to my feet. "I'm so sorry I doubted you. Thank you for everything."

"No problem," she said, stepping forward and engulfing me in a hug. "Maybe I can keep these red heels as a little thank-you for getting the bags back."

"They're yours," I said, giving her a loud smack on the cheek and leaving behind a bright red lip-stain.

"And the cake, is that from you?" I turned to hug June. "It looks incredible."

"No, but I'll take that hug anyway," June said, beckoning toward me. She pulled me into an embrace that felt almost as if I were hugging Gran. "Welcome home, darling. Your grandmother would be so pleased you're here."

I shared hugs around the room, earning an invite to the Duvet wedding and acquiring seven styling clients (thanks to Allie's proud boasting of her new red shoes).

May elbowed her way to the front of the crowd and pulled me into her own embrace, clucking her tongue. "You have been busy, lady. We're glad you're home."

"I'm glad to be home," I said. "Please don't be mad at me."

"Oh, honey, I'm not mad at you," she said. "I was only mad the other night because I didn't win the free styling package—it had nothing to do with Matt. That was a *steal*. I need two hundred bucks of free maternity clothes and someone to style them on me."

"Happy early baby shower," I said. "That'll be my gift to you."

She squealed in happiness. "Oh, and by the way," she said, before the other guests could elbow me out of the way. "That cake? *Matt à la Mode*."

The party was a roaring success, and it was three hours later before guests started trickling out. The cake was demolished and half of my mother's store had been emptied of inventory.

"Look at that, Jenna," my mother said, sidling up to me as she absently wiped crumbs from the table. "I guess Jenna's

Welcome Home Day out-performs Grant's Murder Day in terms of sales. This is the highest grossing day ever, and I hadn't even intended to sell a thing! We just wanted to celebrate you being home."

"Thanks, mom." I gave her an affectionate squeeze. "I must admit, it is starting to feel like home."

"I'm so glad to hear that, honey."

"Although, I *do* have a favor to ask you," I said, facing her with a determined look in my eye. "Drop the bet. Matt and Cooper are my friends."

"I know, darling. It's dropped. May and I feel bad enough already," Bea said. "I'll let you find your other half on your own time. *If* that's what you want."

"Thanks, mom. I appreciate it."

"Though you will need to take a plus one to the Duvet wedding," she wheedled. "Any idea who you might be taking?"

"Allie!" I called above the lingering crowd. "Wanna be my date to the Duvet wedding?"

Allie stuck a foot out in response. "Only if I can wear these shoes."

"Deal." I turned to my mother, who was doing a noble job of masking her disappointment. "Love you, mom. I'm glad to be home."

Cooper found his way over to me next. He'd spent most of the party hanging quietly around the outskirts. Frankly, I was surprised he'd stuck around at all.

"You're a woman in high demand," he said softly. "I just wanted to say it's good to have you home, Jenna."

"It's good to be home," I said. "Are you headed out? I'll walk you to the car."

As we stepped outside, he shoved his hands in his pockets. "I'm sorry we got off on the wrong foot—what with Grant's murder and all."

"I think we transitioned to the right foot," I said cautiously. "Don't you?"

"Just about," he said, and then leaned forward and pressed the lightest of kisses against my lips. "There we go, that's better. Don't you think?"

"Cooper, I—"

"I'm sorry, I couldn't resist," he said. "I'll leave you alone now to figure things out."

He turned away and slid into his car without looking back. I felt a pang of something in my chest. Fresh beginnings, new relationships, exciting opportunities. On an impulse, I strolled over the car and knocked on the window. When Cooper rolled it down, I gave him a smile.

"Don't leave me *too much* alone, okay?" I said with a grin. "You owe me a muffin."

He returned the smile, a look of relief flooding his face. "See you around, Jenna."

"Bye, chief."

I watched Cooper drive away, then slid back into my mother's store to help with cleanup. As I did, I got to thinking how a few misplaced luggage bags, a hunt for a murderer, and some fabulous new friends had me feeling like I belonged.

Somehow, I sensed June might be right about more than just the weather. Spring was indeed around the corner, but more than that, I suspected I'd found my new home in this funny little town called Blueberry Lake.

THE END

Author's Note

Thank you for reading! I hope you enjoyed meeting Jenna McGovern and the folks of Blueberry Lake. The second book in the series is available to be ordered on Amazon. Click HERE[1] to see the synopsis!

Thank you for reading!

Gina

Now for a thank you...

To all my readers, especially those of you who have stuck with me from the beginning.

By now, I'm sure you all know how important reviews are for Indie authors, so if you have a moment and enjoyed the story, please consider leaving an honest review on Amazon or Goodreads. I know you are all very busy people and writing a review takes time out of your day—but just know that I appreciate every single one I receive. Reviews help make promotions possible, help with visibility on large retailers and most importantly, help other potential readers decide if they would like to try the book.

I wouldn't be here without all of you, so once again—*thank you*.

---

1. https://www.amazon.com/gp/product/B0813PBQVR/
   ref=dbs_a_def_rwt_bibl_vppi_i2

List of Gina's Books!²

Gina LaManna is the USA TODAY bestselling author of the Magic & Mixology series, the Lacey Luzzi Mafia Mysteries, The Little Things romantic suspense series, and the Misty Newman books.

List of Gina LaManna's other books:

Women's Fiction:

Pretty Guilty Women

Murder in Style:

Secrets and Stilettos

Lipstick and Lies

The Hex Files:

Wicked Never Sleeps

Wicked Long Nights

Wicked State of Mind

Wicked Moon Rising

Wicked All The Way

Lola Pink Mystery Series:

Shades of Pink

Shades of Stars

Shades of Sunshine

Magic & Mixology Mysteries:

Hex on the Beach

Witchy Sour

Jinx & Tonic

Long Isle Iced Tea

Amuletto Kiss

Spelldriver

MAGIC, Inc. Mysteries:

---

2. http://www.amazon.com/Gina-LaManna/e/
BOORPQDNPG/?tag=ginlamaut-20

The Undercover Witch
Spellbooks & Spies (short story)
Reading Order for Lacey Luzzi:
Lacey Luzzi: Scooped
Lacey Luzzi: Sprinkled
Lacey Luzzi: Sparkled
Lacey Luzzi: Salted
Lacey Luzzi: Sauced
Lacey Luzzi: S'mored
Lacey Luzzi: Spooked
Lacey Luzzi: Seasoned
Lacey Luzzi: Spiced
Lacey Luzzi: Suckered
Lacey Luzzi: Sprouted
Lacey Luzzi: Shaved
The Little Things Mystery Series:
One Little Wish
Two Little Lies
Misty Newman:
Teased to Death
Short Story in Killer Beach Reads
Chick Lit:
Girl Tripping
Gina also writes books for kids under the Pen Name Libby LaManna:
Mini Pie the Spy!